IN THIS
QUIET EARTH

Recent Titles by Nicola Thorne

RETURN TO WUTHERING HEIGHTS *
RULES OF ENGAGEMENT *
THE HAUNTED LANDSCAPE *

The People of This Parish Series

Volume One: THE PEOPLE OF THIS PARISH
Volume Two: THE RECTOR'S DAUGHTER
Volume Three: IN THIS QUIET EARTH *

* *available from Severn House*

IN THIS
QUIET EARTH

Nicola Thorne

SEVERN
SH
HOUSE

This first world edition published in Great Britain 1998 by
SEVERN HOUSE PUBLISHERS LTD of
9–15 High Street, Sutton, Surrey SM1 1DF.
First published in the U.S.A. 1998 by
SEVERN HOUSE PUBLISHERS INC of
595 Madison Avenue, New York, N.Y. 10022.

British Library Cataloguing in Publication Data

Thorne, Nicola
    In this quiet earth
    1.   Title

    823.9'14 [F]

    ISBN 0 7278 5301 5

Typeset by Hewer Text Composition Services Ltd,
Edinburgh, Scotland.
Printed and bound in Great Britain by
MPG Books Ltd, Bodmin, Cornwall.

'The People of this Parish' series

The story so far:
In 1880 young Sir Guy Woodville brings his new Dutch bride
Margaret to his ancient Dorset family home, Pelham's Oak. With
Margaret comes a much needed dowry to restore the fortunes of
the impoverished but noble Woodville family. The marriage is
one of convenience for Guy, if not for the rather plain bride
who is very much in love with her handsome husband.

Guy has a rebellious high-spirited younger sister, Eliza, who
spurns her family's attempts to marry her well. She elopes with
Ryder Yetman, the son of a local builder, causing great scandal
in the sleepy market town of Wenham, over which the Woodvilles
have presided for centuries as lords of the manor. Volume One,
The People of this Parish, follows the fortunes of the Woodvilles
and the Yetmans as they intermarry and breed, their joys and
sorrows, triumphs and disasters.

Margaret and Guy have three children: pious George, who
falls in love with the rector's daughter, Sophie Lamb, and elopes
with her to Papua, New Guinea where he quickly dies of fever.
The only daughter, Emily, dies young, and the heir is Carson,
a charming rebel with an eye for the ladies or, preferably, the
buxom country girls, and who would rather be a farmer than
a baronet with a large estate.

Eliza, meanwhile, has been ecstatically married to Ryder,
who becomes a prosperous builder, and they too have three
children. Ryder, however, is killed in an accident and Eliza
marries Lucius, the brother of Margaret, her sister-in-law,
who is a cold, mean-minded man and refuses to help his

stepson Laurence when he is facing bankruptcy. This leads
Laurence to commit suicide, leaving an embittered widow and
a young family.

Book Two, *The Rector's Daughter*, is mostly concerned with the
fortunes of Sophie Woodville when she returns as a widow to
her birthplace, accompanied by her two young children. She is
not welcomed by George's parents, who feel she is responsible
for his untimely death; but her parents too disapproved of the
marriage. Sophie endures many vicissitudes before being happily
married to her father's curate, even though when he proposes he
knows she is pregnant with the child of another man.

Also in this book Carson, after his mother's death, is prevailed
upon to propose to a wealthy but plain and withdrawn young
girl, Connie, in order to save Pelham's Oak and the Woodvilles
from financial ruin. But he does not love her and when his father
remarries, to a supposedly rich woman, Agnes, Connie leaves
Wenham to travel the world with her wealthy guardian. Book
Two ends on the eve of the First World War.

The latest volume, *In This Quiet Earth*, takes up the story of war
hero Carson, having now inherited the title from his late father,
returning at the end of hostilities to find the Woodville estate
once more in financial difficulties, due largely to the excesses
of Agnes, his stepmother.

Soon after Carson's return the rejected Connie, now transformed from an ugly duckling into a swan, once more enters
his life . . .

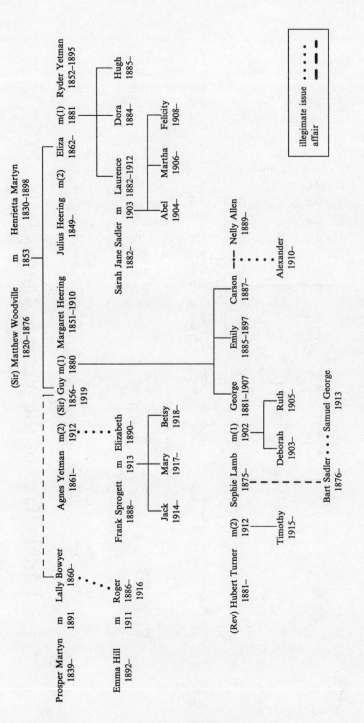

Family Tree of the Woodville Family 1820–1919

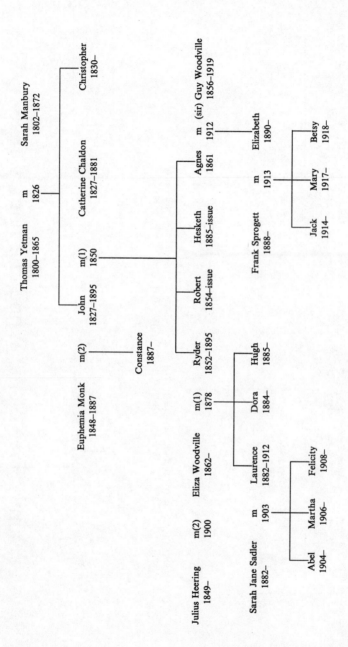

Family Tree of the Yetman Family 1800–1919

Part I

The Survivor

Prologue

May 1919

"We commend to Almighty God the soul of our servant, Guy."
With a broad, sweeping gesture the Rector made a sign of the
Cross over the bier standing in front of the altar, flanked by four
tall candles, and then stepped back to allow the pall bearers to
shoulder the coffin. In the background the organist struck up a
stirring voluntary and the funeral procession of Sir Guy Woodville,
thirteenth baronet, who had died in his sleep at the age of sixty-three,
moved towards the open doors of Wenham Parish Church.

It seemed that all the town had gathered to pay homage to
a man who, while he may not have been universally loved, was
respected as its first citizen, the latest in a line of Woodvilles
who had dominated the remote area of North Dorset since the
seventeenth century.

And that line would hopefully be continued by his son, Carson,
who, together with his stepmother, Agnes, headed the line of
family, friends and dignitaries that followed the coffin to the
Woodville vault in the churchyard overlooking the River Wen
from which the town got its name.

As the procession came to rest in front of the family vault
Carson moved forward, waiting for his stepmother to join
him before both followed the coffin into the Woodville vault.
There, while the Rector intoned the prayers for the dead, Carson
watched impassively as his father's coffin was securely laid on
a slab over those of his little sister Emily and his mother, who
had predeceased him.

His stepmother wept silently as the brief ceremony ended, but Carson remained stiff, apparently emotionless. He had seen too many men die in the last four years to be moved even by the death of someone as close to him as his father. He doubted if anything would ever really move him again. To him it seemed sometimes as though all those previous nuances of feeling – love, kindness, compassion – had been drained away forever.

He was now a cold, somewhat aloof, passionless man.

The Rector, the Reverend Hubert Turner, finished his prayers. For a few moments silence reigned in the darkened vault. Carson looked around at the coffins of the generations of Woodvilles, now no more. One day he would join them. The wonder was that he hadn't already or, rather, be under some unmarked grave, or part of the mud of the Somme, or the earth of Flanders' fields.

Agnes, dressed in deep mourning, head bowed, preceded Carson and the Rector into the daylight. They both stood for a moment gazing at the crowd as the Rector turned and closed the door to the vault. The heavy iron bar swung to.

There was absolute silence everywhere save for the cry of the birds sweeping low as they went in search of food for their young, or the distant bleat of new-born lambs in the fields. Silence was something Carson found very hard to get used to. In his ears there was always the distant roar of heavy guns, the sharp staccato of machine gunfire or the whine of enemy aeroplanes swooping low to attack.

Dressed in uniform he was an imposing figure, over six feet tall, well-built with a striking head of closely cropped ash-blond hair, slightly grizzled at the temples. He was thirty-two but he looked much older. The lines on his face, the tough rather forbidding expression in his eyes, the resolute set of his mouth, could make him pass for forty. On the sleeves of his khaki uniform were the crown and pip, insignia of lieutenant-colonel. Above his left breast pocket the ribbons of many campaign medals included those of the Military Cross and bar.

4

In This Quiet Earth

Yes, in many ways Sir Carson Woodville, Bt M.C. and bar, had had a good war.

But now he had to face the peace and, like many other survivors of the most savage and brutal wars in history, he would find it was not easy.

5

Chapter One

The war had changed all their lives. Nineteen-fourteen seemed to mark the end of the old order, the old way of life. Looking round the room now, and comparing the crowd there to the throng that had gathered in the year 1880 to celebrate the marriage of Guy Woodville to Margaret Heering, it did indeed seem like another lifetime. Then she, Eliza, Guy's sister, had been a headstrong girl of eighteen. Now she was a woman of fifty-seven, twice married, a grandmother.

And the man they had buried today had then been a young man of twenty-four, his bride a few years older. He had joyfully scooped her up in his arms and carried her over the threshold into the vast hall, newly redecorated with her money, as was the rest of the house, to greet the bridal pair.

The drawing room of the Woodville family home, Pelham's Oak, a few miles from Wenham, in which they were now gathered, had glittered then with fresh paint and gold leaf, and was thronged with people many of whom, forty years later, were dead. Their father was dead, but their mother, Henrietta, had been there, happy to see Guy married and the family fortunes restored with the help of Margaret's wealth, but fretful at the same time about the future and her status in the house. She had reason to be as she and her daughter-in-law never got on.

Eliza recalled that she and her mother had had a row because Eliza was anxious to shed her wedding finery and get into ordinary clothes and, rather like her daughter Dora – another tomboy – was doing now, get away from all the jollification to exercise her horse.

7

At Guy's wedding there had been a marquee in the garden for the servants and the lower orders, who had driven over from Wenham in their horse-drawn carts or tramped across the fields to return the same way, very much the worse for wear. Today there was no marquee on the lawn because the war had evened things out. Class was not quite as it had been, and those same lower orders, or their progeny, dressed in their best, kept the same company as Guy's family and friends indoors, though a little apart, standing in groups aside from the rest. Ted, the old Woodville groom, was there in a black serge suit, starched white collar and black tie with his wife Beth, who had been Eliza's servant and beloved companion for many years. But their daughter Elizabeth was not there, maybe because she had not been asked.

So many family secrets had accrued over the years that it was sometimes difficult to remember them, or who knew what. Memory became vague and sometimes faded altogether; but Eliza thought she remembered most of the secrets because they were all linked with Pelham's Oak and with the town of Wenham which could be seen a few miles distant perched on a hill with the church tower of St Mark, where they had laid Guy to rest, prominent for miles around.

Yes it *was* another lifetime, Eliza thought, turning to gaze out on the land she knew so well and loved so much, every inch of which she had walked or ridden over on horseback. When she was eighteen it was her beloved horse, Lady, who had taken her to the cottage, just discernible in the distance, where she had fallen in love with her first husband, Ryder. If only Ryder were here now, she thought, sighing, and there was a gentle touch on her arm and a voice said:

"Penny for them, Mother?"

"I was thinking of my youth," Eliza answered taking her daughter Dora's hand. "The day that your Uncle Guy brought his bride back here after their marriage. I was remembering the scene in this room on that very day, and the people who were alive then and are now no more." A lump came into her throat and she paused. "But it seems a lifetime away."

"It is, Mother, nearly forty years." Dora gave her mother's hand a sympathetic squeeze.

"But life didn't seem to change very much in those days. We had the same way of doing things. We even seemed to wear the same kind of clothes. Our attitudes were the same. But now everything has changed. The war has changed all our lives, and both Ryder and Guy are dead."

Dora instinctively threw her arms round her mother's shoulders and drew her head down on her breast, both oblivious to the company in the room.

"Are you alright, Aunt Eliza? Would you like to lie down?"

Eliza shook her head and breaking away from her daughter, attempted to smile at Carson who was gazing at her with concern.

"Just memories, dear Carson. Memories of your father and my husband, Ryder. Memories associated with this house. Sad days like this bring such memories back." Eliza raised a hand, her fingers delicately touching the row of medal ribbons above Carson's breast pocket. "Your father was very proud of you."

"He longed to see you before he died. Yet you failed him," a voice interjected accusingly as, unseen by the little group huddled together by the window, Agnes had quietly joined them and stood listening to the conversation. Startled, they looked up to see Agnes gazing at them. The false tears that had flowed so readily during the funeral had quickly dried to be replaced by the expression Eliza knew well: firm, determined, calculating, judgmental. A hard woman who, she thought, had driven Guy into an early grave.

"It would have been nice if you could have made the effort to see him, Carson," Agnes continued in the manner of a schoolmarm addressing a recalcitrant pupil. Dressed in black she looked formidable, though still fashionable, heavily encrusted with jewellery. Agnes could turn even funereal black into *haute couture*. To Agnes appearance was very important,

9

and she always took care to look her best. She was not tall, inclining now to plumpness. Her beauty was still visible but fading. The blue eyes flecked with grey, once considered so limpid and beautiful, had the quality of steel. Although Guy had continued to be besotted by her until the end, she had developed early the traits of intransigence and shrewishness until she had become somewhat frightening, a termagant whose word had to be instantly and unquestioningly obeyed. She terrified most people but not Carson who continued to stare at her unflinchingly.

"I made every effort, Aunt Agnes," he said politely.

"I find that hard to believe."

"Why should Carson lie to you?" Dora stared at her aunt with ill-concealed hostility.

"Ask Carson." Agnes tossed her head and gazed defiantly back at him.

"I have no reason to lie to you, Aunt. All I can say is that it was impossible for me to reach England in time. Had you emphasised how near death Father was I might have been able to persuade my commanding officer to release me."

"None of us really knew how ill your father was," Eliza said in a low voice, wishing to forestall a family brawl in public. Nervously she looked round, but no one was paying them any attention. Other members of the family were circulating among the guests, but out of the corner of her eye she observed Arthur, the Woodville family butler who was making his stately way across the drawing room floor towards them.

"Sir Carson, if I may have a word?" The butler hovered discreetly at Carson's side and then murmured something into his ear. Carson nodded, looked at his stepmother, cousin and aunt, excused himself and then followed the butler through the crowd, which parted for him, and out of the door of the drawing room. In the hall a rather stout man dressed in a dark suit stood earnestly inspecting the family portraits on the wall.

"Mr Temple," Carson strode towards him, hand extended, "I didn't expect to see you so soon. We only today buried my father."

Mr Temple's expression was apologetic.

"I am sorry, Sir Carson. Had I known it was the *very* day of the funeral itself I should, of course, have postponed my visit. But I imagined you might be in a hurry to return to your regiment and I have to discuss very important matters with you pertaining to your late father's will. Incidentally . . ." he paused and inclined his head towards Carson. "My deepest condolences to you and your family on your sad loss."

"Thank you," Carson bowed politely in reply.

Preceded by Arthur, Carson and the solicitor crossed the hall towards a door which Arthur opened, standing back to let them pass into a small room which was known as the study though it was a long time since anyone had studied there. It was a small, impersonal room with a leather topped desk, behind which there was a hard chair, two deep leather armchairs and a bookcase. It faced north and, despite the mildness of the spring day, it was rather cold.

Arthur remained, hovering by the open door.

"Would Mr Temple like refreshment, Sir Carson?"

Carson looked at his guest.

"Well . . . a cup of tea would be very nice."

"Or something stronger?"

"Well . . ." his guest indicated by a change of expression that that might be even nicer.

"I think whisky, Arthur." Carson looked up at the butler. "I don't know if Mr Temple has lunched, but a sandwich might be nice too."

Arthur bowed and, leaving the men to their deliberations, withdrew, quietly shutting the door behind him.

Carson pointed to one of the leather armchairs facing the window. He himself leaned against the desk, arms akimbo, feet on the floor.

"I can't get used to being called 'Sir Carson'," he said with a note of amusement in his voice. "Whenever I hear it I think it refers to someone else."

"It is indeed an awesome responsibility," Mr Temple agreed

looking up briefly from the unwieldy stack of papers he was drawing from his briefcase. He was a youngish man with a moon face, slightly flushed, gold-rimmed glasses and the preoccupied air of someone with rather too much to do, whose mind was always on the task ahead of him. Streaks of blond hair fell untidily across his shiny brow, and his pale blue eyes blinked rapidly. He was a relatively junior member of the firm that had looked after the Woodville family's affairs for generations, and his duties lay heavily upon him. Towards Carson he was at once deferential yet familiar, as though in acknowledgment of the fact that they were of an age.

He was also clumsy. A batch of loose papers fell on the floor and, as he bent to pick them up, Carson leaped off the desk to help him.

"Here, you'd better put these on the desk," he said, gathering up a sheaf which he looked at with some anxiety. "Are these *all* pertaining to my father's will?"

"In a sense." Mr Temple coughed nervously.

"But they look like bills."

"They are bills." Mr Temple transferred the rest of the contents of his briefcase to the desk and sat on the hard chair behind it. "And they do, I'm afraid, pertain to the estate of your late father."

He began to sort through them, to put them in some kind of order, when there was a knock on the door and Arthur entered followed by a footman bearing a tray on which there was a bottle of whisky, two glasses and a plate of sandwiches.

"On the desk if you please," Carson cleared space on the side and then shook his head as Arthur attempted to unstopper the bottle and pour the whisky into a tumbler. "I'll see to that thank you, Arthur. See that we're not disturbed, will you?"

Arthur bowed and, preceded by the footman, withdrew.

By this time Mr Temple had restored some order to the masses of loose papers putting them all into neat piles. In front of him a large parchment document, undoubtedly the will, occupied pride of place.

"You see the reason for this haste," Mr Temple nervously cleared his throat again, "is that the late Sir Guy left a mountain of debts and here," he indicated the imposing document before him, "is his will."

As if a solemn moment had approached Mr Temple adjusted his spectacles and grasped the will firmly in both hands, elevating it a little above the desk and staring at it fixedly. Reacting to the solemnity Carson sat in the chair facing the desk, resting his hands on its arms, his expression grave and thoughtful.

"This is really a very short document," Mr Temple said glancing at the date. "It was made by your father, doubtlessly anticipating his death, in the last twelve months. Your father, in fact, had very little to leave. The estate is entailed through the male line, although in certain circumstances it may be broken up or sold. So the house and all the land and dwellings, including the London house, go to you, as doubtless you expected. Unfortunately, Sir Carson, there is very little else to inherit. Your father was practically impoverished at his death. He did, however, leave some items of jewellery that belonged to his mother to his sister, Eliza. He left some very small bequests to other people. Fifty pounds each to the butler Arthur and the bailiff, Ivor Wendor, and," he paused and looked across at Carson, "the sum of one hundred pounds and a diamond and sapphire ring that belonged to his mother, to Elizabeth Yewell, lately of Riversmead and now, I believe, going under the name of Mrs Frank Sprogett resident in Blandford, and the mother of two children."

"Elizabeth *Yewell*?" There was a note of incredulity in Carson's voice as he leaned forward, gripping the arms of his chair.

"Yes, Elizabeth Yewell." The solicitor glanced again at the document. "Now Mrs Sprogett." He looked curiously up at Carson. "Was she of any special significance to your father?"

"She is the daughter of two former servants of my family, Ted and Beth Yewell. Ted used to be a stable lad here and Beth was brought from Cumbria by my Aunt Eliza and Uncle Ryder."

13

"Well," Mr Temple drummed his fingers on the table, "maybe this was some way of saying 'thank you' to them?"

"Well, it's a very curious way of saying thank you. I simply don't understand it. My father knew Ted well, but hardly his wife and daughter."

"Maybe your Aunt Eliza can help?" Clearly the lawyer was anxious to get on. "But the point I am making, Sir Carson is that there is very little cash left in the bank, scarcely enough to take care of the legacies, never mind death duties. All we have," he clamped a hand firmly on one of the piles of paper, "are a mass of debts."

"But *how*?" Rising from his chair Carson poured the solicitor a drink, passed it to him and offered him a sandwich.

Mr Temple was hungry as well as thirsty and eagerly seized both to refresh him from his labours. For a while there was silence while he drank and munched, staring ruminatively at the will as though trying to plumb its depths. Carson remained standing by the desk, now a glass in his hand, looking thoughtfully at the reams of paper that littered it.

"It seems that your stepmother was a very extravagant lady. Many of these are two or three years old." Mr Temple spoke between mouthfuls indicating with a flourish of his sandwich the largest pile. "On learning of your father's death, some who have been owed money the longest have issued writs."

"And my stepmother is not mentioned in the will?"

"In the preamble Sir Guy says she is well provided for. I must say there is no doubt of that. There are bills for jewels purchased in Bond Street, clothes bought at various expensive London stores. The milliner's bill alone is *enormous*. There are bills from the furrier, a shoemaker in Jermyn Street, haberdashers, decorators . . ."

"*Decorators*?" Carson exclaimed throwing up his hands. "But this house looks as though it's falling to pieces."

"It seems they were engaged on the *London* house. This seems to have been completely redecorated, restored and, possibly, refurnished in the past two or three years. It would seem that

your stepmother spent a considerable time there. There are also
bills for purveyors of fine foods and wine, so evidently she did
a lot of entertaining. I may say that all these bills were made
out in your father's name and sent to Pelham's Oak."

"But my father was a very sick man. He has had a bad heart
for years and was practically bedridden."

The solicitor shrugged his shoulders, and gave Carson a
knowing look. "What can I say?"

"Have another sandwich," Carson said passing him the
plate and adding a couple of fingers of whisky to his near-
empty glass.

Carson scooped one of the piles of bills towards him and
began examining them one by one. Finally with an exclamation
of disgust he pushed them away and, going to the window, stood
for a few moments staring out, as his aunt Eliza had an hour
or two before, at the familiar scene before him, every bit of
which he too knew as intimately as she did. In the distance her
daughter, his cousin Dora, the tomboy, had shed her funeral
garb and was putting a horse through his paces over a series
of makeshift jumps in the field.

Before him stretched meadow after meadow interspersed with
copses, streams, farm dwellings, plump healthy cattle contentedly
grazing on the green pastures.

His land. But for how much longer? Carson turned again to
see Mr Temple watching him with what could have been an
expression of pity in his eyes, as if he knew what was going
through his client's mind.

"Have you private means, Sir Carson?" the solicitor enquired.
"I mean I have no idea how you are situated financially. I know
you have had a *very* distinguished war record . . ."

"Apart from my army pay and a few items of clothing I haven't
a bean." Carson made the gesture of one ruefully emptying his
pockets. "For the last four years I have been fighting so I dare
say much of my pay has accrued in the bank, but it would not
amount to more than a few hundred pounds. This woman,"
his tone of voice was contemptuous as he looked once again

at the bills on the desk, "appears to have got through many *thousands*."

"Then maybe *she* has private means?"

"I always thought she had. That she was a widow of great wealth." Carson looked around him at the shabby, poorly furnished room. "I always understood as well that some of her wealth was to be used to restore this house, but as far as I can see nothing has been done to it for years. The whole place seems to be falling apart."

"And have you spoken to your stepmother about this?"

Carson shook his head.

"Lady Woodville and I are not on the best of terms. Apart from making arrangements for the funeral we tended to keep to our quarters. There was a great deal for me to do in a short time. Comforting my Aunt Eliza, for instance, who was devoted to my father."

"I can understand that." The solicitor's tone was kindly. "Nevertheless, Sir Carson, I think you and Lady Woodville should have a very long talk to see if you can save your inheritance from going under the hammer in order to pay your father's debts. Although the estate is entailed I believe that there is provision for it to be sold if the upkeep proves impossible."

When Carson returned to the drawing room most of the guests and a few family members had departed. A worried looking Eliza remained, talking to the rector's wife, Sophie Turner, while Prosper and Lally Martyn looked on. Small groups of guests lingered, interspersed with servants in the process of clearing up. Agnes was nowhere to be seen.

A sudden silence fell upon the room as Carson appeared and went immediately over to the family group. Then, among those left, desultory conversation resumed.

"I'm terribly sorry," Carson said.

"But what kept you?" Eliza sounded concerned. "Is something wrong? Is Agnes ill?"

"Agnes?" Carson shook his head. "I haven't seen her."

"She said she was not feeling well and went to her room."

"I have been closeted all afternoon with the solicitor," Carson's expression was grim, "concerning the contents of my father's will and other matters which I cannot go into now. We'll have a family conference in a day or two. First of all I have to speak to my stepmother." Carson looked restlessly around him. Then his eyes alighted on his great-aunt by marriage, Lally Martyn, a former dancer, still a beautiful, beguiling woman, though in her late fifties. Since her marriage to Carson's Great-Uncle Prosper, she had figured significantly in the Woodville family fortunes.

"Has Emma gone?" he asked.

"Emma took Alexander home," Lally replied. "He was very tired, poor lamb. I did wonder whether we should bring him."

Carson grunted. Lally's beautiful, widowed daughter-in-law had been avoiding him. Every time he tried to catch her eye in church she had looked away. When he took her hand in the reception line, she had hurriedly removed it and passed on.

At that moment some more guests decided it was time to go and came up to take leave of Carson and the family. They were local people from Wenham, some tenants of the Woodvilles: farmers, shopkeepers, the bank manager. They were dressed in their best and their expressions were sombre. Carson had a kind word for them all, and then they talked to Eliza and there was much tutting and shaking of heads, as though Sir Guy's passing had been a sudden event, when everyone had been expecting it for years. The whole group then, including family, moved towards the door, but Carson stopped for a moment by the window and his aunt paused with him.

"She's a fine horsewoman," Carson indicated his cousin still practising her jumps in the field.

Eliza nodded.

"What will Dora do now that the war is over? Will she stay nursing?"

Eliza shook her head. "No, she can't wait to get away. I think she'll come home and take up her life here."

"No men in Dora's life?" Carson looked quizzically at his aunt who shook her head.

"I think there may have been someone, but he was killed."

She looked anxiously up at Carson, and then at the backs of the guests and remaining family members disappearing through the door.

"What made Mr Temple detain you for so long? Is everything all right?"

"Father left *nothing* but a mountain of debts," Carson hissed at her. "Debts run up by Agnes. Thousands of pounds. You see why I must talk to her first. Also," he looked closely at his aunt, "he left a bequest and a piece of jewellery to Elizabeth. Elizabeth Sprogett, you know who I mean?"

"Of course I know who you mean."

"Does it make sense to you, Aunt?"

"It makes sense," Eliza looked hurriedly at the door where the family lingered waiting for them. "But I can't tell you now. I'll explain it to you one day. Let's go and get Dora."

That night and the day following, Agnes stayed in her room. She sent a message through her maid that she was unwell, did not wish to be disturbed, and her meals were sent up to her. Carson felt that she knew about the lawyer's revelations and was avoiding him. The following morning he was awake early, breakfasted alone and then summoned the bailiff Ivor Wendor saying that he wanted to do an inventory of the estate. Ivor had been with the Woodville family for many years, knew every inch of the place and loved it.

"The last time anything was done here, Sir Carson," Ivor said looking up towards the roof and scratching his head, "was when Mrs Turner, Mrs Woodville as she then was, came to look after your father after your mother died. Although little was done about repairs Mrs Woodville kept the house in tip-top shape." Ivor paused and sighed. "It was as if the poor lady

18

hoped she would be able to live forever in the house that, had her husband not died, would have been hers. She had a real fondness for the place, Sir Carson." A blush stole up Ivor's grizzled cheeks rather as though he felt he might have spoken out of turn. "That is *not* to say . . . what I mean is . . . you are the heir now, Sir Carson. The rightful owner of Pelham's Oak. I didn't mean any disrespect . . ." He paused awkwardly, as if thoroughly confused.

"My dear man," Carson gave a laugh and threw an arm round the shoulders of his good servant and old friend, in whose company he used to carouse in the taverns when he was younger. In those days there was no exaggerated respect shown to the surviving son of the house who was known as a tearaway with a reputation for hard drinking and chasing the women. In those days it was simply Carson, one of the lads, no 'Sir' or 'Mr' about it.

Carson's elder brother George had died abroad when Carson was twenty and nothing much changed in the way Carson was regarded by the locals until the war came and he enlisted in the Dorsets and was sent immediately overseas. He returned a few times in the course of the war, twice with superficial injuries that needed hospitalisation first and then periods of rest. But gradually his old boon companions, those who remained behind and had not gone to the war, usually older men like Ivor, realised that a change had come over their rabble-rousing companion. He had become quieter, less boisterous, almost contemplative. They understood that this was because he had at the time seen too much of death and destruction to be able to let go. They hoped, however, that after the war, should he survive, he would be returned to his old self. But they had reckoned without the death of his father and his elevation to the baronetcy that had been in his family for three centuries.

For some time Carson and Ivor continued their walk round the estate looking at the house from all angles while Ivor made extensive notes, pausing every now and then to chew his pencil or shake his head.

"In fact the whole place has not had the attentions of a builder since my father married my mother nearly forty years ago," Carson said, once their inspection was completed. They were leaning over one of the fences surrounding the paddock.

Ivor nodded. "And even then they left the roof. The roof definitely needs doing, Sir Carson. We have leaks in the servants' quarters, and the structural damage the rain will do will make the work even more expensive and prolonged when it does take place."

"It's going to cost thousands of pounds." Carson shook his head wearily.

"And then some more." Ivor snapped his book shut and stuck his pencil in the top pocket of his jacket. "After the reroofing the entire outside needs repainting and repointing, the stone repaired where it has been worn by the weather. As for indoors . . ."

Carson held up a hand as if to block his ears. "Please don't start about indoors," he begged. "I've had enough bad news for one day. I think I'll take a ride and try and clear my head."

The two men walked towards the house, and before they parted at the junction of the path to the stables, Carson faced Ivor and put his hands on his shoulders.

"Thank you, Ivor, for all you've done, looking after the place while I was gone. My father has left you a very small sum of money to mark his gratitude . . ."

"Oh . . ." Ivor blushed again and lowered his head in embarrassment. "That weren't necessary."

"It's not very much. A mere fifty pounds. However I hope to restore the house and our fortunes and I want you to stay on and also, Ivor, to do as you used to do and call me Carson. I like it that way. I prefer it."

Ivor looked at him and ruminatively scratched his cheek. "Don't know how as I can do that now, sir. Things have changed."

"I'd like it. I really would."

But, still embarrassed, Ivor abruptly turned and stalked back towards the house leaving Carson to wonder if his attempt to democratise the situation had been the right thing.

Didn't country folk, after all, prefer the old ways, and weren't they, perhaps in many ways the best? He would not refer to the question of the name again, but accept his new status as gracefully as he could.

Carson saddled his horse himself, an old favourite called Pulver, who was a direct descendant of his Aunt Eliza's horse, Lady. Most of the horses divided between Riversmead and Pelham's Oak were related by blood.

Pulver welcomed his master with a whinny and trotted along the bridle path that led through the fields to a copse by the stream running along the bottom.

While Pulver drank thirstily Carson sat gazing up at the house which, from a distance, looked rather splendid, its blemishes invisible in the sunlight.

Strictly speaking the correct name of the ancient home of the Woodvilles was Pelham's Court, named after Pelham Woodville who had started the house in the reign of Charles I in front of a great oak tree. Legend was that this too had been a refuge of Charles II before his final escape to France after his defeat by the Cromwellian Army. Pelham's son, Charles Woodville, was ennobled by the grateful monarch after the Restoration and gradually the house became known as Pelham's Oak in his honour.

Originally it had been constructed of Dorset brick, but in the eighteenth century one of the descendants of Pelham and Charles had wanted to flaunt his wealth by owning a much larger mansion, rebuilt in the Palladian style and faced with Chilmark stone.

Over the centuries the Woodvilles had undergone mixed fortunes. Some made money, others had difficulty holding on to it, but with Carson's grandfather, Matthew, the rot had really set in. He had been a sickly, scholarly man with no interest in, or aptitude for business.

Much land had been sold off and the house had gone into

21

Nicola Thorne

steady decline until Matthew's son Guy, no better equipped than his father at managing money, had married Margaret Heering, an heiress from Holland. It was her fortune that had been spent on restoring the house to its former splendour as one of the finest in the county.

Thank heaven for that, Carson thought, as Pulver finished his drink, and after circling the copse he turned the horse back up the hill towards the house again. Had it not been for his mother the house would by now have been a ruin. But her family had soon reined in her money after observing her husband's tendencies towards dissipation and extravagance. After Margaret's death it appeared that what was left of her fortune did not belong to her husband or children, but reverted to the Heering family.

Once again, destitution threatened and Carson was about to marry a woman of fortune, whom he did not love, when Aunt Agnes, who had mysteriously left this country twenty years before, appeared on the scene and dazzled his father enough for him to wish to marry her. Thankfully Carson thus felt absolved from his obligation to marry for money, and his father married Agnes. Less than two years later Europe was engulfed by war and, in comparison, all these family matters seemed rather trivial.

But not so now. Carson rode up to the house with a heavy heart. Many burdens pressed down on him. Not only was he grieving his father, but he was facing a problem of enormous debts, the possible loss of his home, an ongoing struggle with his stepmother and the uncertainty of his place in the affections of a woman who continued to mesmerise him: Emma Martyn, widow of his adoptive cousin Roger, who had been killed in the war.

But when he had first loved Emma she was married, a rather feckless, yet incredibly beautiful, young woman of twenty-one. All at once the war, that had loomed so large, seemed, now that it was over, to recede. Reality was the present, and what could happen in the future.

At the top of the hill Carson stopped his horse and listened.

22

The silence, the stillness, was profound. Pulver was listening too, sniffing the air with that peculiarly heightened sense that all animals seem to have.

Yet despite the splendour of a May morning in England, in peace-time, a chill ran through Carson. He imagined that in this quiet earth he could hear the rumblings of subterranean thunder as though the echoes of conflict would surface all over again, destroying not only his inheritance, his home and his family, but everything he held dear.

Chapter Two

There was no love lost between stepson and stepmother. Almost from the beginning Agnes and Carson had never got on. Carson had transferred himself to a cottage on his Uncle Prosper's estate to be out of the way of Agnes who, even before her marriage to his father, had swept into the house like a tornado, unsettling the staff by her brusque and imperious manner, impetuously throwing out some of their best antiques on the grounds that they were old fashioned, and ordering refurbishments which were never carried out when she subsequently transferred her interest to the London house.

Not long after the marriage his father had a heart attack and slowly sank into invalidism, worn out by worry about the war, the fate of his son and members of his family, the future of his house and estate, and the absence of his wife who preferred to spend most of her time in London while the bills for her extravagance came flooding back, to be hurriedly stuffed by him in a drawer.

Carson had never been intimidated by his stepmother who was also a distant relation by marriage. Her brother, Ryder, had been Aunt Eliza's first husband. He had been killed in an accident when Carson was about eight, but he still retained affectionate memories of him.

No one seemed to retain happy memories of the youthful Agnes. She had been a troubled, troublesome and difficult young woman and Carson was a small child when she had disappeared, no one seemed to know why, to resurface twenty years later as a lady of consequence. Agnes was thus a woman of

25

---

some mystery and she seemed to revel in this role. On the third day after his father's funeral Carson had been informed that she would see him, precisely at eleven o'clock in the morning, in the drawing room.

As usual he had gone riding first thing, and he'd been aware of her looking at him from the window of her bedroom. She'd watched him for a long time, but he gave no sign that he was aware of her somewhat malevolent presence looking down. When he returned for breakfast Arthur gave him the message that Lady Woodville wished to see him.

As for Carson, he very much wished to see her. He still had on his riding clothes and Agnes gazed at him disapprovingly.

"I do object to riding clothes worn indoors, Carson," her eyes travelled to his feet, "particularly *boots*."

"I'm sorry, Aunt," Carson said without the least trace of contrition, "but this is my house and I shall do as I like in it."

"Oh really?" Agnes had been drinking coffee and now, pouring another cup, passed it to him. Carson noticed that suddenly she appeared agitated and her hand shook.

"You surely know it is my house, Aunt Agnes. It is passed from eldest son to eldest son or, in my case, the surviving son. George of course would have inherited had he not died, or had he had a son it would all have been his. However," he took the cup from her and, looking round to find himself a seat, sat down. Balancing his cup carefully in his hands he crossed his legs with every appearance of a man at ease with himself. "However, Aunt Agnes, I am hoping to return to the army and remain there at least for the next few years so I am happy for you to continue to live here for the time being, provided," he drank from his cup, put it on the table at his elbow and took a leisurely look round the room, "that you do something about restoring it."

"*Restoring* it?" Agnes exclaimed. "Restoring this wreck of a place? Are you mad?" She too swallowed her coffee and replaced the cup on a tray.

"My dear Carson I intend to spend not a moment longer here than is necessary. As soon as the formalities about your father's death are completed I shall be returning to London, and staying there." Her tone was at its most haughty and imperious, its most authoritative and unbending. "Big as this house is there is not room for both of us, and I dare say you will be returning to it from time to time."

Carson rose and, turning to the window, remained for a few moments gazing out of it, his hands clasped behind his back. He then addressed her, his back still to her.

"My understanding, Aunt Agnes, is that when you married my father you undertook to cover the cost of repairs to this house. Even then, two years before the war, they would have cost thousands of pounds." He swung round and gazed at her. "I went over the estate the other day with Ivor and our estimate is that, due to neglect, the cost, including a new roof, has risen to many thousands of pounds."

Slowly Agnes rose to her feet and faced him. She looked pale but she had discarded her widow's weeds for a light, summery dress in fashionable crêpe-de-chine and her fair hair was arranged in an Edwardian roll that was by now rather old fashioned, but which suited Agnes and which, together with her high-heeled shoes, gave her much needed added inches.

"Then if that is what you understood, Carson, you were either deceived or you deceived yourself. I never undertook any such thing. I have never particularly liked this house nor the town of Wenham, considering it too small and parochial for my tastes. Frankly, I feel stifled here and your father knew it perfectly well when he married me." She leaned forward and stabbed an accusing finger at him. "Maybe it is on *your* conscience Carson that, instead of marrying poor Connie Yetman, who loved both you *and* the wretched house, and who had ample means to repair it, you jilted her, ruined her life and deprived yourself and your father of, if I understand the situation correctly, much needed funds with which to restore your patrimony.

"I believe Miss Fairchild *bribed* Sir Guy into persuading you to offer marriage to my poor half-sister in order to get hold of her fortune. *I* never gave any undertaking of any sort I can assure you. I had far too much sense than to offer Guy what money I had to throw away on a white elephant like this. You should have been more careful, the pair of you, father and son, not so greedy and, believe me, in view of what has happened the two of you deserve what you got. The only person who did *not* deserve what *she* got was Connie whose life was ruined by your treatment of her. The only consolation that I can see for that sadly deceived girl is that Miss Fairchild left her so well off it has cushioned her life against predators such as you and your father. She will never have to marry for money, and I hope to God that the poor dear has the good sense to see off any more fortune hunters who may come her way."

"I find your words very unjust, Aunt Agnes," Carson said bitterly. "I was sincerely attached to Connie, but I was too young to marry—"

"*Don't* try and deceive me my dear young man," Agnes said witheringly. "I got the whole story from Guy on our honeymoon. The poor fool had not the sense to see that I had no intention of throwing what money I had away on him or his house."

"So that, of course, you married my father for love." Carson's tone was sarcastic. "We all know that. There was no question in your mind of acquiring a title or respectability, was there, Aunt Agnes?" and before she had a chance to answer he went on: "As soon as you were 'Lady Woodville' which, my informants told me, was all you ever wished, you virtually left my poor, sick father to his own devices while you rushed up to London where you spent a fortune on certain items that you did not pay for, for all your *alleged* wealth. I wonder how much of it there really was?" From an inner pocket Carson now drew a sheaf of bills and hurled them on a low table placed between them. "These, Lady Woodville, were sent to my father for settlement while he was a very sick man already worried to death about his health, the war, mourning the deaths of so many members of the family and his friends, to say nothing of his loneliness at the absence of someone who, for all her faults, he undoubtedly loved. How he could forgive *you* I will never know, for I never can."

Silence fell between the two antagonists while Agues stared at the bills lying untouched on the table and Carson, hands in his pockets, teetered backwards and forwards on his heels, gazing at her. "Look at them, Aunt," he commanded.

"I know what they are." Primly joining her hands Agnes turned fastidiously aside as if the sight affronted her, as well it might. "Do you think for a minute I would have run up these bills without your father's knowledge and consent? Do even you, so eager to condemn me, think I would have had the house redecorated had he not wished it? Does any self-respecting woman buy *herself* jewels? No she does not. Your father urged me to enjoy myself, knowing that he was not well enough to join me. He was a generous man." Momentarily she paused and, real or false Carson had no means of knowing, tears came into her eyes. "He was a generous man to a fault. *I* did not know he had not the means. I did not realise – though I should have – that marrying for money was a Woodville trait." She angrily brushed the tears away and her voice took on a hard note. "I did not realise that your father hadn't a penny to call his own, though I should have. For a so-called woman of the world I must seem to have been naive. After all I knew he was on the verge of selling the house before I appeared on the scene, and then the strange engagement of yourself and Connie was talked of by everyone. A couple more unsuited it was hard to imagine: a shy, timid little virgin, plain as a pikestaff and the local stud who had never done an honest day's work in his life—" She stopped suddenly holding up her hands, as though to shield herself, as Carson advanced towards her his fist raised threateningly. In the nick of time he took himself in hand and stopped, knowing he could not have answered for the consequences. He began to sweat freely at the thought of what might have happened if he had struck his stepmother: cashierment from the army would surely have followed, his medals stripped from him, perhaps a prison sentence had she suffered serious harm. Disgrace, dishonour, ruin, the end of all his dreams. What an irony it would have been to have survived the war only to have forfeited his freedom in this way.

He felt himself beginning to shake violently, and sat heavily down, wiping his freely perspiring brow with a handkerchief. Agnes too seemed glad to resume her seat, probably equally terrified of the consequences of what might have happened to her looks, if not her life, had her stepson lost control.

"I think I had better leave," Carson said after a moment while he recovered, his voice unsteady. "As you say, this house cannot contain us both. I will have to decide what to do." He got unsteadily to his feet and gazed down at her. "Plans are already forming in my mind, but I will have to discuss them with Aunt Eliza. All I know is that, whatever has happened in the past, things have got to change." He pointed to the table between them. "These bills have got to be settled as writs have been issued and the creditors are being kept at bay. I cannot help thinking, Aunt, that they are your responsibility and not my father's."

"Then let the estate pay." Agnes gave an airy, dismissive wave of her hand. "Surely there is money there to take care of them? And, talking of the estate, Carson, what of your father's will? Should I not be in on it? Do not I, his widow, have a share? I am presuming that is what kept you so long with the solicitor the other day. I heard he had called. Unfortunately I had my migraine coming on so felt unable to cope with more worry."

"You more likely probably guessed about these bills, Aunt Agnes," Carson said angrily. "You're no fool. As for the will . . ." he felt inside his inner pocket once again and produced the parchment document which he handed to her. "You may read it, for it is not very long. My father said he had provided for you . . ."

"Huh!" Agnes snorted and, shaking open the will, leaned back in her chair to peruse it. "Guy never provided a thing for me in his life except for some jewellery left to him by his

mother and . . ." she stopped and, with an exclamation, brought
the document closer to her face. Carson guessed that, but for
her vanity, she should be wearing reading spectacles. "What is
this . . . ah, I see."

"Elizabeth Yewell is a strange bequest is it not, Aunt?" Carson
was watching her reaction keenly.

Agnes merely shrugged, closed the document and put it back
on the table. "It is of no consequence," she said offhandedly.
"So much for my folly in marrying into the Woodville family.
He chooses to leave money and jewellery to servants." She rose
and squared her shoulders as if she herself were trying bravely
to face an uncertain future.

Momentarily Carson felt a stab of pity for her. Much as he
disliked his aunt there was something vaguely heroic about her.
In a way she was an adventuress, as he had been an adventurer.
They seemed to understand each other. The war and its aftermath
– particularly its aftermath – had changed them both, brought
them down to earth. What did he really know about his father's
widow, her way of life, her circumstances or the extent of her
fortune, if any?

"I shall leave here today to stay with Aunt Eliza," he said.
"We can communicate through solicitors. But before you go
rushing back to London, Aunt, I must tell you that it is my
intention to put the London house on the market as soon as
possible and," he allowed himself a sardonic smile, "as you
have spent too much of my father's non-existent money doing
it up, it should now fetch a very good price."

Carson had very little to pack. He still had the instincts of
a soldier and travelled light. In fact Carson had very few
possessions. Unlike most of his brother officers he did not even
own a car. Carson had always been very close to the land and
remained at heart a country boy. He had never been attracted
by the sophistication of the city, and held himself aloof from
the bright lights of London or Paris.

Yet, despite his attachment to his roots, the past four years had brought about a considerable change in him. He had learnt to kill, to ambush and to maim. He had learnt to harden his heart against the sights of suffering and pain, the cries of anguish, the screams of the dying; to leave a man when he knew that nothing could be done. Once or twice he had administered a lethal shot to a badly wounded comrade begging to have his misery ended. Carson was aware of an emptiness of soul as he rode Pulver cross-country to his aunt's house about ten miles away. He felt, now that his father was dead, that he no longer belonged. Although he had a fierce pride in and loyalty towards the ancient home of the Woodvilles it was a long time since he'd really lived there. When Agnes appeared on the scene he moved to a cottage on Uncle Prosper's estate, and soon after that came the war and a succession of camps and billets in a number of different countries for almost the next five years.

Short leaves had mostly been spent at Pelham's Oak or his Aunt Eliza's, that is aside from periods in hospital and convalescent homes. But he had always longed to get back to the war because it was where he felt he should be. Each time he returned to the front he was convinced he would never see England again. It seemed incredible that, when so many around him, including many good friends, were dying he should survive, practically unscathed. His wounds had been superficial, mostly caused by shrapnel.

Towards the end of the war Carson had decided to continue his life as a soldier, a career which, many years before, his Uncle Prosper had urged on him, to be rudely and peremptorily rejected. Because Carson was rude in those days: ill-educated, uncouth and lacking altogether the refinement that one would have expected of the son of a baronet. The last thing he anticipated from service in the army was polish, especially in such conditions of chaos and carnage which epitomised the breakdown of civilisation. He had observed deeds of great bravery as well as cowardice. He knew how low it was possible for a man to sink; how incredible were the heights of nobility and self-sacrifice reached by some.

Yes it was an education, an education in life, and thus he had acquired that essential experience that turned a boy, a callow youth, into an adult and gentleman.

Carson regretted that part of his life before the war which, in retrospect, seemed so wasted, so reprehensible. He had been a good-for-nothing. He had caused his parents much pain, especially his mother whose death, his father claimed, he had helped to hasten.

And maybe he had ruined the life of a gentle, sweet, understanding young woman by proposing to her, when he knew he did not love her and never could, in order – at his family's instigation – to get her fortune to save Pelham's Oak from the auctioneer.

Subsequently he had fallen in love with his cousin Roger's wife when she was still only twenty-one, a spoilt young woman scarcely old enough to know her own mind. He had seduced her and carried on an affair under the nose of her mother-in-law, Aunt Lally. But then Carson had always suspected she had thrown them together.

And now Roger had died in the war and his grief-stricken widow apparently refused even to recognise her former lover. She had avoided him at the funeral, she had left the gathering at the house afterwards, early. It was obvious that she wanted nothing to do with him. Maybe she felt weighed down by guilt. And yet Emma's image remained lodged in Carson's heart. It had seen him through some very dark and dangerous days and nights.

He reined in his horse as Eliza's house came in sight through the trees and he sat there for a moment or two, trying to adjust his thoughts from visions of Emma to his family. Upper Park was a splendid residence and Carson always enjoyed visiting it. Unlike Pelham's Oak it was in first-class condition and beautifully kept. When, during the war, his stepmother had been at Pelham's Oak, he had spent some of his leaves with Eliza whom he had always loved. His Uncle Julius was Eliza's second husband and on their marriage he had bought this mansion which was considered a fine example of Georgian Baroque architecture. It was built of Dorset brick, faced with Chilmark stone and stood on an incline, facing north/south, with magnificent views of the surrounding countryside.

Julius was his godfather as well as his uncle (his mother's brother), but he had always found him a cold fish. He was thirteen years older than Eliza and for him too it had been a second marriage, his first wife having died. He was a stern, taciturn man, a successful businessman, head of the Martyn-Heering business empire. Now seventy he had virtually retired, though he still kept a close eye on the business. He devoted most of his time to gardening pursuits, horticultural developments and the cultivation, in his specially built and heated greenhouses, of exotic plants that were brought to him by company ships from all over the world.

In many ways the marriage of Eliza and the solemn Dutchman had been one of convenience. Both had needed a mate, as people who have been married seldom have the inclination to live alone. There had been affection and respect but not passion and, over the years, instead of coming closer together they had grown further apart.

This process had been accelerated when Eliza's son Laurence had fallen into financial difficulties and, despite her entreaties, her husband had refused to bail him out. Laurence had committed suicide, and in Eliza's heart there remained a profound core of bitterness towards Julius. Occasionally, during his leaves, Carson would also see Dora or Hugh, also on leave at the same time, and the cousins had become close. Dora was three years older than Carson, Hugh two. Today he was looking forward to seeing them again.

Carson's reverie was broken by the sound of laughter from beyond the trees and he urged his horse forward. Though not so spectacular as Pelham's Oak the house was beautifully situated. The front lawn sloped to meadows and paddocks and in the distance were the rows of greenhouses which Uncle Julius seemed to add to fanatically every year.

Carson emerged from the copse and saw his cousin on her horse in the paddock watched by her brother Hugh and a woman beside him, both of whom were laughing. One of the practice jumps was lying on its side which was a probable reason for their laughter. Hugh limped over to it and, joined by the stranger, righted it while Dora sat on her horse watching them. At that moment she looked up and seeing Carson raised her crop.

"Hello!" she called out. Carson sprang off his horse and went over to Dora, who leaned down grasping his hand.

"Carson how *very* good to see you. We wondered if you'd gone back to France."

"Is this goodbye, then?" Hugh came up to him leaning on his stick.

Hugh had lost a leg on the Somme and had spent many months in hospital. He had been left lying, helpless and in pain, in crossfire for many hours before being rescued and consequently suffered much psychological trauma as well as physical distress. Hugh had had an academic career before the war, but it was felt that it would be many months before he was fit to resume it again.

"I'm not sure," Carson replied. "I've a lot I want to talk to Aunt Eliza about."

It was always Aunt Eliza, never Uncle Julius, but maybe this time he could be useful in view of his acknowledged financial expertise. "I wondered if I could stay here for a few days?"

"Why, I'm sure you can." Dora looked pleased. "Have you and your stepmother had words again? By the way," Dora pointed her crop at the woman standing behind Hugh, "this is May. May Carpenter. We nursed together. May, my cousin, Carson. Colonel Woodville, I believe we should call him."

"How do you do, Colonel?" May said, taking his hand.

"Oh please drop the 'Colonel', Dora's just pulling my leg." He looked angrily at his cousin. "Dora, you know I hate that sort of thing."

"Relax she's only teasing you." Hugh put an arm round his shoulder. "Shall we go and give Pulver some oats? Mother will be delighted to see you."

"See you back at the house," Dora called, cantering off.

35

"What about May?" Carson looked at the young woman who had helped Hugh right the fence.

"May will come in with Dora."

"She seems rather nice."

"She's very nice. She and Dora went through a lot together. Right up near the front."

"How's the leg?" Carson looked anxiously at his cousin. They hadn't really been close as boys, having little in common. Carson was always regarded as a bit of an outsider by the younger members of his family. He never sought their company and they seldom sought his, as though they rather disapproved of the wild company he kept. But the war had changed all that. During his leaves he had seen fewer of his older friends and more of his family, just in case he never saw them again.

As a soldier he had managed to be of help to Hugh, understanding some of the trauma he had gone through, the depressions, the nightmares, the fear.

"The leg's coming on," Hugh said. "What's left of it. I have massage which also helps me to sleep better. I feel I'm a trial to Mother."

"I'm quite sure you're not," Carson said reassuringly, then raised his hand as his aunt appeared at the top of the steps leading up to the house, shading her eyes with her hand as she looked towards the paddock. When she saw Carson she gave an exclamation and ran down to him, flinging her arms round him and embracing him.

"What a *lovely* surprise." She kissed him hard on both cheeks and then, her hands still on his shoulder, searched his face. "Not to say 'goodbye' I hope?"

"Not just yet, Aunt. I wondered if I might stay a few days?"

"Oh I expect you and Agnes have been fighting."

"Well," Carson gazed down at his feet, "let's say the situation is a tricky one. An awful lot has happened, I'm afraid, to do with Father's will. I need advice."

"Well then you shall have all the advice you want." Eliza

tucked her arm through that of her nephew and, with Hugh now holding Pulver's bridle, they went round the side of the house to stable him.

The meeting took place in the library after dinner. This had been an amiable, pleasant occasion with the young people enjoying one another's company and the older ones relieved and happy to have them all safely home again.

After dinner Hugh, Dora and May went off to the snooker room where Carson promised to join them later.

Uncle Julius kept a good cellar and produced a fine brandy to drink with coffee as they sat round the fire in the library. The curtains were drawn and it was very cosy.

"You said you'd tell us what the lawyer said," Eliza prompted Carson. "You were with him a very long time."

"And you said you'd tell me about Elizabeth."

"I'll get to that in a minute," Eliza said. "Tell us first about the debts."

"Oh debts!" Julius sat back, puffing at his pipe. "I know whenever there are Woodvilles there are debts."

"Please Julius do *try* and be helpful." Eliza frowned at him. "Carson needs your advice not censure."

"The debts had nothing to do with me, Uncle Julius."

"No, they would have to do with your father." Julius stretched his legs comfortably before him, puffing away at his pipe. "A leopard doesn't change its spots." He gave a mirthless chuckle. "The fact is that your father never had the slightest idea about money, which was why the family were anxious to see that he didn't get all of your mother's. He would have thrown it all away on that woman."

"He means Agnes." Eliza raised her eyebrows at Carson.

"Well, he threw it all away on her anyway," Carson said, "or what little he had left. There is no money to pay for the upkeep of the estate, for the thousands of pounds worth of repairs that need doing. Apart from that there are bills from creditors amounting to several thousand."

"The estate is bankrupt," leaning forward Julius knocked out his pipe on the hearth, "and that is the end of the matter."

"But what can Carson *do*?" Eliza, pained and exasperated by her husband's response, which she might have expected, looked anxiously at him.

"Sell up." Julius addressed Carson. "You could get a good price for the house and land. The London house also should be worth a bit, and you have land there too. And then if it is not enough to pay the bills you will have to declare bankruptcy."

"But I don't *want* to be a bankrupt!" Carson exclaimed, angered by his uncle's response.

"Not you, the estate. The estate of the late Guy Woodville."

"But it will be in all the papers."

Julius shrugged and began to draw tobacco from his pouch to fill a fresh pipe.

"Your father is not alive to feel the shame so what does it matter?"

"But *I* will feel the shame. It will affect us all."

"You may come to an arrangement with creditors. It does happen. They take so much in the pound. They are not likely to get any more anyway."

"I don't find you very helpful, Julius," Eliza said coldly. "Not for the first time when it comes to money you show such insensitivity. Such lack of understanding."

"My dear, I *do* understand because I understand money." Julius looked at her sharply and then rose from his chair. "So if I can be of no further help, and I doubt if either of you will take any notice of my advice anyway, I shall go to my study. Please do call me if I can be of any use." He paused and looked at them. "That is my advice. But first you have to talk to Agnes. Is *she* not a wealthy woman?"

"She says the estate should pay. She refused to discuss the matter but started, rather like you, Uncle Julius, to heap abuse on the Woodvilles."

"I do *not* heap abuse on the Woodvilles . . ." Julius began indignantly but Eliza waved a hand at him.

38

"Oh be off with you, Julius, to your study, your books and your plants, and let me talk to Carson."

"I don't know why I asked him," Eliza said as the door closed behind her husband. "He can't see sense where money is concerned, or perhaps it is sense; but he only sees in straight lines and not round corners. And people *are* concerned with corners, aren't they, Carson dear?" She reached over and took the hand he held out to her.

He put hers to his cheek. It was warm and pliant and he was reminded of the few times he'd been close to his mother. He had always adored her but, except occasionally, she had been a rather remote, undemonstrative person, little given to kissing or hugging, whereas his aunt had those instincts in abundance. Aunt Eliza was tactile and, from what he had heard, it had much to do with her impetuous youth when she and Uncle Ryder had defied their families and eloped.

It was very difficult to think of Uncle Julius doing anything so foolhardy or impetuous as eloping, even when young. Indeed it was hard to imagine him ever being young.

"I love you, Aunt Eliza," he said impulsively, kissing her hand. "And I don't know why we asked Uncle Julius. I don't even know why you married him. You're so unalike."

"Ah!" Eliza shook her head. "There are many reasons for that. There is a great deal of kindness in Julius, but he is not warm. He can't help it, and when it comes to money he can understand nothing but the need to hang on to it. He could have saved my son from suicide but he didn't. I asked him to help Laurence when he got into debt, and he wouldn't, so you can be sure he won't help you."

"I don't know why you go on living with him."

Eliza shrugged.

"Because I have known poverty. It was very unpleasant after Ryder died. He too left very little. He didn't think he was going to die, and he hadn't taken Julius's advice either in making provisions in case he did. You see . . ." as she leaned forward the firelight played on her still beautiful, but rather careworn, face, "unfortunately, Julius does have a habit of getting things right. And it may be that you should do what he suggests."

"But I don't *want* to sell Pelham's Oak. It has been part of our family for centuries."

"But how can you keep it with no money?"

"I'll find a way," Carson said. "For instance I'll try and make the farming pay. I'm sure I can borrow money on the strength of our assets. I will certainly sell the London house and land. That should fetch a bit and . . . I've decided I must leave the army, Aunt Eliza. I finally made my mind up as I rode here this morning."

"Oh dear," Eliza squeezed his hand, "but you wanted to make it your career. You seemed so suited to it."

"The career will have to go."

"Maybe Agnes *has* got some money. Maybe we can prevail upon her. Maybe *I* should go and talk to her." Eliza concluded thoughtfully. Then she looked at Carson as if weighing something up.

"And I was going to tell you about Elizabeth."

"What has she to do with Agnes?"

"Quite a lot," Eliza glanced at the door. "I'm glad Julius has gone because he doesn't know this. Hardly anyone does."

"About what Aunt Eliza?" Carson was aware of a mounting sense of excitement as if an important family secret was about to be revealed.

"Elizabeth is Agnes's daughter," Eliza murmured almost inaudibly. "That was the reason she fled abroad after the baby was born."

"She just left the baby?" Carson looked incredulous.

"Yes. Elizabeth was born in Weymouth. I helped to arrange the whole thing. Beth went to look after her and one day after she and the baby returned from a walk Agnes had gone and we didn't hear from her for over twenty years when she suddenly turned up in Blandford, staying in some style at the Crown. There she was seen by Sophie and her mother who were in town that day."

"So *that's* how she came back here. I wondered." Carson tapped his fingers thoughtfully on his knee. "And Father . . ."

"Guy was Elizabeth's father, Carson." Eliza's hand stole towards his comfortingly.

"But how could she . . ."

Eliza's hand pressed his.

"They had an affair many years before. Agnes was always a discontented girl. She felt that she was better than anyone else. Too good to marry a local man, a farmer or a builder or such. She went to London, but failed to find a mate there. She came back and was employed as nursemaid to the daughter of Lord and Lady Mount. I'm afraid Guy seduced her and used to visit her there in secret."

"Then Father was as bad as everyone said?"

"He certainly liked women. And they liked him. Agnes had set her cap at him. He found it hard to resist, but I can tell you this Carson. Your father did love your mother. In the end very much. He repented of his misspent youth and he loved her. He also knew that Elizabeth was his daughter and begged Agnes to acknowledge her, but, being Agnes, she refused."

"She refused to have anything to do with Elizabeth?"

"She insisted on it. She made it a condition of marrying Guy. She was ashamed that Elizabeth was working as a servant in the Crown."

Carson put his head between his hands. "What a dreadful story. Agnes Elizabeth's mother! What a hard-hearted creature she is," his voice was contemptuous, "not to wish to acknowledge her own daughter. She's even worse than I thought."

"Agnes was always a very hard woman. As a girl she was self-centred and she remained so. She will only think of her own interests and no one else's. Guy wanted to acknowledge Elizabeth and do the right thing by her."

"Did she know he was her father?"

"Oh no." Eliza vigorously shook her head. "She was told that her mother died at her birth; that the mother was Beth's sister, and Beth and Ted adopted her and brought her up. Obviously

41

Beth couldn't pass her off as her own, having shown no signs of pregnancy. Seeing that Elizabeth was so tiny she has always thought of them as her natural parents. In fact Beth, knowing her from birth, has been more like a real mother to her."

"Doesn't that seem unfair? She is my half-sister, a Woodville. Really I find it hard to understand all these lies, Aunt Eliza."

"Oh, I know you might think that what happened was wrong, Carson. Maybe you feel *I* should have given Elizabeth a home. But how could I have explained adopting a child? In those far-off days there was a different standard, a different code. I loved Elizabeth and kept a close eye on her. I don't see as much of her as I did, but she was and is very dear to me, even though she is rather like her mother."

"Oh, how so?" Carson was curious.

"You know . . . well, perhaps you don't. She is always a bit discontented. Always wanting something better. Nothing quite good enough for her. Just like Agnes. Strange, isn't it? Like mother like daughter . . . you know the old saying." Eliza got up and began restlessly to pace the room. "I don't know what you are going to do about Agnes, Carson." She threw a couple more logs on the fire and, as the flames shot up the chimney, rubbed her hands to warm them. It seemed suddenly cold in the room. "In many ways I think Julius may be right. Perhaps you should accept the inevitable. Sell Pelham's Oak and stay in the army. Maybe that would be the best way, to make a fresh start? Cut the ties with the past and begin all over again."

Carson leaned back, linking his hands around his knees.

"That's not the only problem we have, Aunt Eliza. Father has left Elizabeth a legacy. She's got to know about it." He paused and gazed thoughtfully at his aunt. "And that means she has to learn about her parentage. It's time this deceit was finished anyway. That poor woman has got to know the truth."

"It will cause awful trouble." Eliza, suddenly weary, shook her head. "I wish now I had never told you."

Carson rose and went to stand by her side. He too stood looking into the fire. "You couldn't help it, Aunt. You had to tell me. Father might have had his own reasons for his legacy. He might have wanted to tell Elizabeth about her origins, even from the grave."

"Perhaps you're right." Eliza looked over at him. "You have a very good head on your shoulders these days, Carson. You have matured so much. I agree, but I think that in my own way and in my own time I should be the person to tell Elizabeth. You must understand that the repercussions will be enormous on us and on her and her family. No one can possibly know what the consequences will be."

Chapter Three

Agnes lay in bed, her breakfast tray in front of her, the morning papers scattered around her. But she had little appetite, either for food or for reading the papers. The aftermath of war was not quite what everyone expected. Sporadic unrest, even revolution, continued in parts of Europe and the Balkans and war still raged in Russia. Soldiers returned from the front with no jobs to go to and there were rumbles of unrest at home. An epidemic of influenza had ravaged Europe and killed hundreds of thousands, maybe millions, so that many who had survived the war did not live to enjoy peace.

Not that world affairs preoccupied Agnes Woodville very much, except insofar as they affected her or her wellbeing. She was not one to concern herself about what happened to other people. Her abiding interest was herself, and it always had been. Her whole life had been given to self-gratification, to the pursuit of her own ambitions, which had seemed to reach its triumphant apogee in her capture of the thirteenth baronet, Guy Woodville. When she finally got him, though, he was a pathetic shadow of the fine figure of a man he'd been when she'd first set her cap at him when they were both young.

There was also the undoubted shock that he had no money; but his title, his fine ancestral home and her own barefaced cheek in conning money out of the banks had ensured they had survived, just.

But what was to happen now that Guy was dead and that wretched Carson was buzzing around causing trouble? She was sure that in no time at all he would have people crawling round

45

the house valuing it. There was no doubt that he intended to dispose of it as soon as he could, and where would she be then? Incarcerated in that rabbit warren of a place in Wenham, a small provincial town that she detested and where she would surely suffocate and die.

Agnes had dined with friends the night before at Quaglinos and then they'd gone on to the Cavendish where there was drinking, and the Savoy to dance, so that the sky had been streaked with the pink of dawn when she finally climbed into her bed. But her sleep had been fitful and now it was nearly noon. Even then the day ahead, though half over, still seemed to stretch tediously before her until she joined her friends in the evening for a trip to the theatre followed by cards or, maybe, dancing again at Chez Victor or Ciro's.

It was the end of July and London was muggy. Normally by this time Agnes and her friends would have retreated to the cool of the countryside, but everyone had been in London for the victory parade headed by Lord Haig, and the celebrations that started then had continued without respite. But soon her friends would go away and she would have little alternative but to return to Pelham's Oak, though it had even fewer charms for her now that Carson had suddenly resigned his commission and taken up residence there.

Every night was the same for Agnes – eating, dancing, drinking, late, very late to bed. Her friends had the same hedonistic principles as she had. Although none of them were young, and thus most of the men had avoided the war, they danced and partied as though there would be no tomorrow and indeed at one time, in the black days of 1916 and 1917 with the awful never-ending carnage of the war and news from the front, it had seemed there might not be. Fading belles and ageing roués now vied with young people for who could last the longest, who would go home with the milk float.

Agnes moved with a rather louche, hard drinking set on the furthest periphery of London society. Among the women, as well as a few widows, such as Agnes, there were a number of divorcees,

still socially unacceptable and barred from the Royal Enclosure
at Ascot. There were several very bored married women, and
one or two of questionable reputation whose status was not
known, with no apparent means of support.

The credentials of some of the men were even more dubious.
There were younger sons of earls who had been banished to
the colonies in their youth for some misdemeanour and had
come home when their parents were dead, to die themselves
in the old country. There were raffish business men who had
made fortunes in the arms trade and generally profited from the
war while remaining out of harm's way themselves. There were
retired military men; men who lived on their wits, and loafers
who preyed on rich widows.

Agnes knew how to steer clear of them all while enjoying
their company and how to take advantage of a man with money
without compromising herself.

Some of them had been friends of Guy's in his youth and
the cachet of Lady Woodville was a valuable 'open sesame'
when she had first come to London. In the early days of their
marriage Guy had come with her, delighted to see his darling
shine, marvelling at her qualities as a hostess, the brilliance
of her social skills. There had been lavish parties and money
seemed to gush as though it came from a deep well, and no one
questioned the source.

Even after Guy became ill the entertaining continued without
him, the bank offering continuous credit on the strength of the
Woodville name.

Now it seemed the reckoning might be near.

Agnes, roused from her reverie by a shaft of afternoon sun
stealing across her bedroom carpet, threw back the bedclothes
and summoned her maid, determined to banish unpleasant
thoughts.

At three, bathed, refreshed and conscious of a new lease of life,
Agnes sallied forth for a stroll in Hyde Park, a short distance
away. These days she spent a lot of time on her toilet, especially

on her face, to disguise the blemishes of age. Invariably she had a rendezvous with people she knew, also taking the air, and they would discuss plans for the evening's entertainment either for that night or the future and sometimes, to kill a little more time, she would invite them back for tea at Chesterfield Street.

There had been a half promise made very late at night, or rather in the early hours of the morning, to meet her friend Dolly McGill, once a chorus girl and now the widow of a peer, to take a stroll round the Serpentine or sit and watch the riders in Rotten Row. It was a long time since Agnes had declined to venture into the park without her maid. There was now nothing wrong, she felt, for a woman of a certain age and social accomplishment to take a stroll in an open space within a stone's throw of her home; but still it was nice to be meeting Dolly and she strolled briskly in the direction of their rendezvous – a gardener's hut somewhere near the centre of the park.

The park was thronged this summer's afternoon: lovers lying in the grass, families picnicking in the shade of the trees, children running about with balls and hoops pursued by the family dogs. There were loafers and idlers, couples arm in arm, single women with parasols to shade their eyes from the sun. A vendor was burning horse chestnuts over a brazier, and a flower seller offered posies to the young men, maybe freshly returned from the war, who were strolling with their sweethearts.

In the distance Agnes spied Dolly, who raised her hand in greeting and, as she hurried her steps, she could see that Dolly was with a little group of people, most of whom she recognised. After embracing Dolly, Agnes turned and greeted the others: Maud Featherstone whose husband had been a diplomat, Edith Shiff the wife of a retired Army general, and Matthew Parker who had never done very much in particular except hang around women who were married and therefore "safe". Much younger than most of her regular set, in his forties rather than fifties or sixties, he was a particular friend of Edith's, and frequently accompanied her on walks in the park or escorted her to parties or dances while her gloomy old husband remained at home staring into the fire and reminding himself, helped by copious quantities of port or brandy, of days long gone.

As Agnes greeted her friends, one man remained on the fringe looking on. He wore a light grey suit with pearl grey tie and an elegant gold watch and chain hung across his waistcoat. His well-polished black shoes were encased in spats and there was a carnation in his buttonhole. As Agnes turned towards him he removed his bowler hat with his left hand, which carried a cane and, bowing, shook her hand.

"Lady Woodville," Dolly suddenly became aware that Agnes didn't know the stranger, "may I present Sir Owen Wentworth? I suddenly realised that perhaps you hadn't met."

The stranger, Agnes's hand still in his, bowed again. He had a full, waxed moustache and twinkly black eyes. He was slim and not very tall, only an inch or so taller than Agnes, and strands of black hair were combed with exaggerated care over a large bare patch on his domed head. The overall effect was of someone rather dapper, possibly, God forbid, in trade, with a fondness for nifty dressing and, judging by the twinkle with which he greeted Agnes, perhaps an eye for the ladies.

"Charmed, Lady Woodville."

"How do you do, Sir Owen?"

"Sir Owen has not long been back from India," Dolly bestowed on him an approving smile.

"The army?" Agnes enquired.

"Tea, Lady Woodville. A tea planter from Assam."

"How very interesting." Agnes gave him a detached smile and then, as if dismissing him from her mind, tucked her arm through Dolly's and suggested a stroll round the Serpentine followed by tea back in Chesterfield Street, Sir Owen apparently forgotten and relegated to the back of the small procession that set off slowly through the park and half an hour or so later wended its way back again to where afternoon tea awaited them.

The Woodville town house was a substantial double-fronted, eighteenth century dwelling which formed part of a terrace in an exclusive part of Mayfair built for the wealthy land-owning classes in search of a London residence. The front door led directly on to the street, and black iron railings fenced off the basement area with a steep flight of steps to the servants' quarters and the tradesmen's entrance.

The drawing room was on the first floor and ran the length of the house. It was a very beautiful room only recently redecorated in cream and gold to Agnes's exacting specifications. The cornices, quatrefoils and lozenges in the ceiling had been newly picked out with gold leaf, and a splendid central oval showed Diana the huntress, gilded bow and arrow at the ready, in hot pursuit of her prey.

On the walls hung portraits of Woodville ancestors painted by various famous artists, together with bucolic scenes in which Pelham's Oak could be seen from various angles. The Adam mantelpiece was adorned with a magnificent Viennese ormulu clock that had been a wedding present to Guy's parents, and figurines made from Meissen or Dresden china. The furniture was Chippendale or French eighteenth century – there were two magnificent, tapestry covered Louis XV bergère armchairs – and rugs brought by an adventurous Woodville early in the nineteenth century from far off China and Persia adorned the highly polished parquet floor.

Agnes's guests sat in a semi-circle sampling the wafer-thin sandwiches and delicious cakes baked by cook that very morning. They ate off plates and drank tea from cups made of the finest Spode bone china. They were waited on by a maid and a footman, a butler had admitted them at the door and the whole atmosphere was one of elegance and wealth. It seemed positively to ooze through the walls.

Sir Owen Wentworth, plate in hand, obviously feeling a little out of place, wandered round the room inspecting the portraits on the walls as the rest of the guests chatted to their hostess. Although she joined in the animated conversation Agnes watched Sir Owen out of a corner of her eye noting every scrutiny, every gesture as he peered at the portraits, the family photographs and the delicately wrought figurines on the mantelpiece and scattered on the side tables. It was clear that he was impressed, and he paused before a rather fine painting of Pelham's Oak by Sir James Thornhill, the eminent Dorset-born artist whose mansion also happened to be not far from Pelham's Oak.

This coincided with a lull in the conversation and, as Sir Owen turned enquiringly towards her, Agnes, excusing herself and putting down her plate, rose and joined him.

"Rather fine, don't you think?"

"There are a number," Sir Owen's hand vaguely indicated the other paintings of Pelham's Oak on the walls. "The country seat?"

"Pelham's Oak," Agnes nodded. "The Woodville home in Dorset."

"It looks very handsome." Sir Owen was obviously impressed.

"Do you know Dorset, Sir Owen?"

"Not at all I'm afraid." Sir Owen ran a finger across his luxuriant pair of moustaches. "Spent most of me life in India."

"And your family came from . . . ?"

"Yorkshire." Sir Owen repeated the gesture, his hand caressing his moustache, and Agnes noticed that his face was very faintly beaded with perspiration. But of course it was a very hot day.

In the background Dolly and Maud, smoke spiralling from their cigarettes, were discussing the latest fashions, the return to soft patterned summery materials – crêpe-de-chine, ninon, chiffon and art silk – after the rigours of war. The raising of the hemline to show silk stockings and daring high-heeled shoes. The wearing of large-brimmed hats and the jettisoning of the head-hugging toque. Altogether there was a liberation of fashion, welcome after centuries of long skirts even to an older generation such as they. From time to time Edith, who was the oldest person present, joined in. As usual Matthew listened, smiled from time to time and said nothing.

Meanwhile Agnes conducted Sir Owen round the room giving him a running commentary on the portraits and pictures until she rested, perhaps deliberately, in front of a particular one.

"And this is my late husband Guy, thirteenth baronet, painted by John Singer Sargent."

It was a particularly good portrait of Guy by the distinguished American artist who had settled in London in the 1880s. Youthful and handsome, it bore little resemblance to the decrepit remnant of humanity they had laid to rest only a few months before.

Was it really only a few months? Momentarily Agnes felt a stab of guilt at the thought of all the parties and dances at which she was a willing and enthusiastic participant. But what was the point in mooning about in widow's weeds? Nothing would bring Guy back.

Sir Owen composed his features into a suitably solemn expression and murmured something inaudible.

"Are you married, Sir Owen?"

"Also a widower, alas, Lady Woodville. My wife died of a tropical disease. She was quite unsuited to the Indian climate."

"And have you children?" She put her head enquiringly on one side.

Sir Owen shook his head. "I'm sorry to say Lady Wentworth and I were not so fortunate."

"So, no heir to the title?"

Again he shook his head. Then, after a moment's pause: "And you, Lady Woodville?" He looked at the picture on the wall a few yards away. "No heir to that magnificent house?"

"Oh yes, indeed. My stepson, Carson, is the heir. He has just left the army. Sir Carson Woodville, *Colonel* Sir Carson Woodville, twice decorated for gallantry in the field."

"And how long since Sir Guy . . ." Whatever Sir Owen was about to say was lost as there were sounds of movement behind them, voices raised and chairs carefully scraped back as the rest of the party prepared for departure.

"Oh, but you're not going so soon . . ." Agnes looked at the clock on the mantelpiece. To her surprise it was nearly six.

"My dear we must *fly* home and change," Edith exclaimed as if she too hadn't realised the time. "Remember we're dining with the Woods, and afterwards at the Embassy Club."

"I hadn't forgotten."

"We'll pick you up, dear." Edith looked at Michael Stansgate who nodded his confirmation. "At about eight?"

Agnes rang the bell, and a moment later the door was opened by Edward the butler, who stood back to allow the company through. Agnes and Sir Owen brought up the rear. In the hall the ladies were handed their sun parasols and one or two parcels they'd been carrying, the men their hats, Sir Owen his cane. He stood slightly apart from the others and looked at Agnes.

"Thank you *so* much, Lady Woodville, for a most delightful and instructive visit."

"It's a pleasure, Sir Owen." Joining her hands together, head to one side, Agnes gave him one of her most charming and practised smiles. "I do hope we meet again."

"I do hope so, Lady Woodville," Sir Owen said fervently. "I hope we meet again very soon."

"Telephone for you, madam." Stella, Agnes's personal maid, popped her head round the bedroom door. Agnes grunted and her face appeared above the sheet.

"Who is it at this hour?" She looked at the clock on her bedside table.

"Sir Owen Wentworth."

"Tell him to ring again. It's much too early."

"It's nearly midday, madam."

"Do as I say, Stella."

"Yes, madam."

Stella was about to withdraw but Agnes called her back sharply.

"Say I am engaged. Don't tell him I'm in bed."

"Of course not, madam."

"And tell him to ring back in an hour."

"Yes, madam."

"And run my bath."

"Yes, madam. Shall I bring your breakfast madam?"

"You can bring me a cup of tea." Agnes glanced again at the bedside clock. "I'm lunching out. I shall be late."

Once again Stella withdrew and Agnes, now fully awake, stretched her arms above her head and gave a luxurious yawn.

Sir Owen Wentworth. There was something *parvenu* about him, not quite right. She couldn't exactly put her finger on it, but did it matter? She knew he had been taken by her, she was far too experienced in the ways of the world, and particularly the habits of the male sex, not to know that. She had known a number of men like Sir Owen during her many years in America where she ran a business specifically for the entertainment of the opposite sex.

Sir Owen seemed to her like a middle ranking businessman perhaps, she would have said, had she still been in America, something to do with railroads or commerce of some kind. Yet he said he was a tea planter from Assam. Perhaps.

She got out of bed and went and stood at the window of her bedroom, which was above the drawing room, overlooking the street. There were very few people about at noon. She went over to her dressing table and, sitting on her stool, gazed at herself long and hard in the mirror.

She was fifty-eight. Sir Owen was probably quite a bit younger, not much more than fifty; but then she knew she didn't look her age. She'd taken great care of herself except, perhaps, for being a bit careless about her diet. But then she liked food, and she liked to drink. She imagined that Sir Owen, with his slightly florid complexion, liked to drink too. Probably little else to do in India. All those tea planters drank. But those tea planters were also usually very rich. They'd nothing to spend their money on and, if there was something about Sir Owen that made Agnes think he lacked breeding, there was also about him the whiff of money, perhaps a lot of it, a commodity of which she was greatly in need.

Agnes got into her bath which Stella had by now run, as well as delivering her tea, and wallowed there for some time. Then she got out, dressed, did her hair and made herself up with her usual care and, just as she finished she heard the phone ring and a moment later Stella popped her head around the door again.

"It's Sir Owen, madam. Shall I tell him . . . ?"

"No," Agnes said sharply and, crossing the room, picked up the telephone by her bed.

"What a *nice* surprise, Sir Owen!"

"I hope you don't mind me calling you so soon, Lady Woodville?"

"Not at all."

"It was such a pleasure to meet you. I wondered . . ."

"Yes, Sir Owen?"

"I don't suppose you're free for dinner this evening are you? I thought the Trocadero . . ."

"Oh!" Agnes gave an exclamation of regret. "I'm so sorry. Not tonight."

"Of course I understand, your diary must be very full. Perhaps tomorrow?"

"How about Thursday?" she said, mentally counting the days on her fingers. Thursday seemed just about far enough away to show distance without rebutting him. One didn't want to appear too keen. In a game played for high stakes timing was essential.

"Thursday? Thursday is fine." Sir Owen seemed to swallow his disappointment bravely. "Shall we say eight o'clock, Lady Woodville? I'll call for you, of course."

"I'll look forward to seeing you, then. Goodbye Sir Owen." She gently replaced the receiver and remained staring at it for some time, aware of a sense of anticipation, of excitement such as she hadn't felt for many years.

If she had been a religious woman she might have thought that, just possibly, Sir Owen would be an answer to her prayers.

* * *

Carson Woodville stood on the brow of the hill, arms akimbo, hat on the back of his head, watching with satisfaction as on one side of the field the hay was bailed after scything by the workers on the other. And how they'd toiled! Many farm workers had not returned from the war and a whole new army of helpers, men, women and children, had been recruited to help with the haymaking.

Carson worked with them too from early morning until dusk and his reward was to see the neat bales of hay that would be used to feed the cattle through the winter.

Scything, however, was hard work, his hands were blistered and his back ached; but hard work of this kind was sheer joy when he recalled that this time last year he had been engaged in fierce, sometimes close, combat with a still stubborn foe, inching up on swampy ground near the town of Neuvilly as the near victorious allies pressed determinedly across northern France, at last driving back the enemy.

The Crook family had been tenants of the Woodvilles for generations and ran the farm nearest the house, supplying them with eggs and milk. Old Martin Crook had never forgotten the kindness of Carson's mother when she helped to restore the farm and put it on a sound financial footing after years of neglect. The farm was now run by Martin's son, David, and his wife, who also made delicious bread which she supplied to the big house. David had not gone to the war because his work as a farmer was of national importance, but his brothers Sam and Ned had gone and neither of them had come back. Almost every family, every community in the district had lost someone in the war. A whole generation had been almost obliterated.

At the moment it was difficult to know for what, Carson sometimes thought, as rumblings of discontent continued even after the peace. Had all that sacrifice really been worthwhile?

Below him in the valley David Crook looked up and, seeing him, waved. Carson waved back and was about to continue his descent to join him when he heard a voice hail him and, looking back, saw his Uncle Julius striding across the lawn towards him.

It was such an unexpected sight, Julius was such a rare visitor, that at first Carson was apprehensive that something had happened to his Aunt Eliza, but Julius reassured him.

"No, your aunt is perfectly all right. I wanted to see you and have a chat."

"Oh I see," Carson tipped his hat back and scratched his head. "I was about to return to the fields, Uncle. We want to get the hay in before it rains." He looked doubtfully up at the sky. His uncle grunted his approval.

"You've been taking a hand cutting hay yourself have you?"

"I learned to use a scythe in the old days when I worked at Sadlers' farm. I don't think I've lost the knack."

"I'm sure you haven't." Julius laid a hand on his nephew's shoulder in a gesture of approval. "You're a good lad, Carson. I think you're more of a Heering than a Woodville. You've inherited your mother's temperament."

"I suppose *that's* meant to be a compliment, Uncle Julius." Carson looked at him good-humouredly.

"Of course it's a compliment. Your mother restored the fortunes of this place. In the years that have elapsed since her untimely death they've gone downhill again, that is until your return." Again he looked at Carson approvingly. Then he turned to take in the aspect around him. "What a fine sight it is. The bales of hay drying in the sun. The fertile land of England, at peace once again, thank God."

Carson looked curiously at his uncle. "If you've something to say you'd better say it. I'm needed down there." And he pointed to where David Crook and his helpers were hard at work. "I don't want them to think I'm shirking."

"Well, I'll not keep you." Julius glanced around. "I'd quite like to sit down. I'm not a young man, you know. Shall we go inside?"

"By all means." Carson led the way indoors to the study which he now used as an office. "Excuse the untidiness," he gestured round clearing a space on a dusty chair for his uncle.

"I see you've been busy." Julius nodded towards the ledgers on the desk, the clutter of paper on either side.

"I'm trying to do a complete inventory of our assets and liabilities. This includes the farms on the estate, various tenanted properties, rents receivable and so on." He pointed to an open ledger in front of him.

"It seems unbelievable but these were last brought up to date by my mother not long after she married Father. She went round every property promising to do them up providing the farmer could guarantee a good yield. Old Martin Crook says he has never forgotten her kindness or the way she helped him keep the family home."

"It's a great pity your mother was taken so young," Julius had a catch in his voice. "She would never have let the estate go to ruin." He looked meaningfully at the paint peeling from a corner of the ceiling.

"No, Mother's death was a tragedy in more ways than one. But we now have to make the best of it." Sadly, Carson shook his head. "However, with the best will in the world I don't think I can hang on here, Uncle Julius. There is too much to do. I thought maybe I would move into one of the farms and manage that. I've always liked the land, and after the war I appreciate it more than ever."

"You really are serious?" Julius kept his eyes on Carson as he pulled a ledger towards him on which there were rows and rows of neat figures. Then he turned the ledger towards his uncle.

"Look, Uncle: credit and debit. What we owe and what we're owed. Add this to Aunt Agnes's extravagance, the bills that were laid at Father's door. It all shows I could never make ends meet."

"Not even if someone took care of her debts?" Julius, who was a tall man, stretched his legs and gazed at his boots.

"Who would do that?"

"I might." Julius's gaze travelled slowly from his feet to his nephew's face. "I have reconsidered what I said to you a few months ago. No no . . ." he held up a hand, "your aunt had nothing to do with it; but I have searched my conscience and found it wanting. It is quite true that had I offered Laurence more help he probably would not have taken his life . . ."

"I have no intention of taking my life, Uncle, I assure you."

"No, I'm sure of that. But I could have been more under-standing, more humane. Anyway, it caused a rift between your aunt and myself that has never been repaired. I do this partly for her. She was born in this house and it and her family mean a lot to her. But it would be a foolish gesture – and everyone knows I am not a man to throw his money about – were I not so impressed by what you have done since your time here. It has not gone unnoticed, I assure you, how hard you have worked. All this," the sweep of his hand included the papers and ledgers round him, "is a credit to you; but with your father's debts you are shackled. Would it be possible, for instance, for you to carry on if I relieved you of that burden? After all, they're not your debts, nor are you in any way responsible for them. If I settled the bills run up by Agnes do you think you would be able to avoid selling up? Obviously," looking round the room Julius shook his head, "I can't take over everything for you. This house needs a fortune spent on it; nor, I'm sure, would you want me to. But if you go carefully, taking one step at a time in the cautious, careful way you are, you might be able to preserve the home you love so much, which your Aunt Eliza loves and which you deserve to keep."

For a long time Carson sat silently, staring at his uncle while warring thoughts raced through his mind. It was difficult to think that Uncle Julius would be capable of an act of such altruism were not Aunt Eliza at the back of it. On the other hand he had always known Julius to be a straight man, mean but honest. He didn't think he'd lie to him or dissemble. Without the burden of Agnes's debts it might be possible for him to contemplate the future with more optimism.

"I can't promise you you'll be all right," his uncle said as if he was aware of what Carson was thinking, "but at least you're in with a sporting chance." He looked at his watch and made as if to get up. "By the way any news of Agnes? I don't think she's been here all summer has she?"

"She's travelling on the continent I believe," Carson said offhandedly. "I think she's keeping out of my way in case I try and get some money out of her. She's also nervous about my plans for the London house." Carson ran a hand through his hair. "So far I have been too busy to think of it, but it is in my plans and it will come to a sale, very soon, I'm determined on that."

Julius got to his feet and shook his head. "That woman will always be a problem. Sometimes I think it almost seems as though the Devil himself has got into her. Somehow she makes me more nervous when we don't know what she's up to than when we do. Travelling on the continent, indeed!" He then turned towards the door but Carson stopped him and held out his hand.

"Thank you, Uncle Julius. I can't tell you what this means to me. Ever since I came home I've seen nothing but clouds. Now at last I feel I see some sunshine between them."

Chapter Four

Suds up to her elbows, her hair plastered over her forehead from the rising steam, one child tugging at her skirt while the baby howled in its basket on the floor, Elizabeth Sprogett felt close to breaking point.

"Frank," she bellowed, "Frank." But Frank, she knew, would not budge. He remained all day either in the bedroom gazing at the ceiling or in the front room staring at the floor.

The bright lad she'd married in 1913, only twenty-four years of age, who had gone so enthusiastically at the call to arms, willingly to serve King and country, had returned in 1916 a broken reed. Badly gassed, suffering from shell-shock, Frank, the cheerful brewer's drayman, was scarcely recognisable. He was treated in hospital, discharged from the army and sent home to the ministrations of his wife. It seemed that the army didn't really care about soldiers from the rank and file. They took much more care of officers, cosseted them and put them into convalescent homes where they were ministered to by doctors and psychiatrists, fellow professionals from the upper classes.

It was very difficult not to feel irritation with someone who seemed to make no effort to help himself. Sometimes he didn't even want to dress, but just dragged himself around puffing on endless cigarettes and gasping for breath. He also had a hacking cough and was almost blind in one eye.

How Elizabeth rued that day, so full of promise, that she'd married him.

They lived in a house in Blandford that had belonged to the brewery and still did. Theoretically they could be asked

Nicola Thorne

to leave at any time, but Frank's former employers had shown themselves to be generous to an ex-serviceman and allowed the couple to stay on. It was a small house built on a sloping road leading out of Blandford with two bedrooms, a sitting room and kitchen, no bathroom and an outside lavatory.

Blandford was a pretty country market town, much larger than Wenham, surrounded by beautiful countryside, and so much more attractive than areas of the industrial north or large cities to which so many wounded veterans returned.

It was possible to go out of Blandford to the country, to Elizabeth's mother and father who still worked for Mrs Heering and lived in a pleasant cottage on the Heering estate about ten miles away.

Mrs Heering had been kindness itself about Frank, had even offered them a cottage near Elizabeth's mother and father; but people had their pride, and Elizabeth didn't want to go back to a state of dependence on her parents and their employers unless she had to, though she sometimes wished that Frank would go back to his and she could start all over again.

But with three children that was clearly an impossible situation. Elizabeth loved her children and was a good mother. And although she had once dearly loved Frank, or thought she had, it was a stranger who had come back from the war, a man whose constant whining, complaining and cantankerous moods had turned him into someone she no longer loved and couldn't even like.

It had been a white wedding at Wenham Parish Church which had been packed with family and friends, there to wish the handsome young couple well. Sir Guy and his new wife had not attended and nor had Carson, but then one would not expect them to. But Mrs Heering was there with her daughter and son, Elizabeth's proud parents with her elder sister Jenny and younger brother Jo, Jenny's husband Clifford and assorted relations. Mrs Heering had had a reception at the big house and her wedding gift had been a honeymoon on the Isle of Wight, which was the happiest time Frank and Elizabeth had

62

ever spent together and where little Jack, now five years old, had been conceived. Mary, now tugging at her skirt, had come along a year after Frank got back from the war, and the baby, Betsy, bawling away in her cot was nearly nine months old.

It was Elizabeth's pious hope that there would be no more. Frank's creative urges appeared not to have been affected by his injuries in the war, which was a pity really. Elizabeth would have preferred that they had gone, and his wits and eyesight had remained so that he could have got a good job, and maybe left her alone. Also one child was so much easier to cope with than three. If only one knew how to stop them coming. Maybe she should ask her mother, except that it was always such a difficult subject to talk about, even to kith and kin.

Elizabeth finished her washing, emptied the tub down the sink, slapped Mary's hand, wiped the baby's permanently dripping nose and carried her basket of damp clothes into the garden. It was a cold, blustery winter's day and they wouldn't dry, but it was better than having them hanging damp all over the house. Mary, still grizzling, still hanging on to her skirt, had followed her mother into the garden, but little Betsy had settled down to sleep. In a while Elizabeth would put her in her pram to go to the shops. Sometimes she saw a friend and it was a nice way of getting out of the house which, these days, seemed permanently filled with gloom.

Sometimes she thought that really to give in and go and live near her mother would be the best thing. Certainly they would have to do that if the brewery wanted the house back. Elizabeth was a determined, stubborn sort of person who had always nursed an ambition to be something different than what she was – better, grander.

When she was in her teens she had worked as a milkmaid on Sadlers' farm where Carson Woodville had also worked. She had rather fancied Carson and knew he quite fancied her; but she had played hard to get, thinking this was the way to trap him. However, she left it too late. Her parents found out about it from her sister Jenny, who was always a jealous, snoopy

63

sort of person, always prying into other people's business, and promptly moved her away to work as a chambermaid at the Crown Hotel in Blandford, where she'd met Frank Sprogett who used to deliver beer at the back door. As well as being an engaging sort of chap Frank Sprogett had seemed a way of getting out of a life she detested, running after wealthy, selfish women like, for instance, the present Lady Woodville whose maid she had briefly been when she first arrived back in Blandford from America.

What wouldn't she give to exchange that for the life of drudgery, servitude and misery she now led?

Elizabeth went back into the house, Mary still whinging, still clinging to her skirt. At least the baby remained asleep in her crib and Elizabeth wished she could leave her there and creep out into the town. How nice it would be to be able to leave the children with Frank and have an hour or two to herself; but he couldn't be trusted to keep an eye even on his own flesh and blood.

In the old days when he was normal, when she had first loved him, Frank Sprogett was one of the nicest, least selfish of men. Now he had completely withdrawn into himself and seemed to care for no one else.

Elizabeth climbed the stairs to the bedroom and stood in the doorway contemptuously regarding her supine spouse. He had several days' growth of beard, he was abnormally thin and his eyes were sunken in his withered cheeks. He was only thirty and he looked fifty, more. You couldn't help feeling pity for him at the same time as you despised him, because it just seemed as though he'd let himself go, hadn't made an effort, hadn't even *tried*. A kinder woman might have made more of an effort to understand the nature of her husband's condition and the terrible experiences that had brought it about, but Elizabeth had an innate streak of selfishness which had been fostered by the way she had been brought up, never quite like her siblings, but as someone apart. Besides, she felt terribly let down and betrayed; all the hopes of her wedding day completely dashed. It didn't matter that the dreams of thousands of other women had been similarly destroyed. Like her natural mother, Elizabeth had a tendency to think only of herself.

The doctor had tried to explain that mental illness was just as real as physical illness, only it didn't show. But it was still difficult not to believe, in one's heart of hearts, that Frank wasn't really making an effort.

"Frank," she said sharply and he half sat up in bed.

"What is it?" he croaked wiping his bleary eyes. "Wassermatter?"

"I'm going out to do a bit of shopping," she said, taking her hat out of the wardrobe and bending down at the dressing table so that she could see in the mirror to fit it. "Do you think you're capable of looking after the baby?" She glanced back at him witheringly across her shoulder.

Frank didn't reply but sank back on the bed again his eyes staring at the ceiling.

"Of course you're not," she cried, securing her hat firmly on her head with a sharp pin. Then she straightened up and turned to stare at him, hands on her hips. "You're good for nothing that's what you are, Frank Sprogett."

"Can't help it, Bet," Frank said in that whining tone she so hated. "Can't seem to help it."

"Course you can, if you tried," she said contemptuously getting her coat out of the wardrobe and shrugging it on, struggling to do up the buttons in the front. Elizabeth was a good-looking woman, fair-haired, blue-eyed with strong features. In her youth she had been fine boned, almost fragile, but now the years of childbearing had given her a rather plump, matronly figure, big breasted. In addition she was worn out with looking after Frank for the last four years and producing and caring for three young children, and she looked older than her twenty-nine years.

"Wouldn't trust you anyway," she retorted, going to the door where she stood and glared at him. "Can't look after your own children. If you ask me it's a pity we had them and, what is more," she leaned towards him and raised her voice, "there ain't going to be no more! Do you understand *that* Frank?"

For answer he pulled the bedclothes over his head and disappeared under them, possibly because he didn't dare tell her that sex was one of the few pleasures, perhaps the only pleasure, he had left.

Downstairs the baby was awake and gurgling. Elizabeth got her out of her crib and strapped her in her pram. Mary had stopped grizzling at the prospect of an outing and as her mother got her into her coat and did up the buttons she even managed a smile.

"That's better!" Elizabeth grunted, wiping her daughter's runny nose – all the children had perpetually runny noses these days – and was about to put a woolly cap on her head when there was a tap at the door.

"Blast!" she said getting up and glancing at the clock. If she didn't hurry it would soon be dinner time and the kids would start grizzling again.

She opened the door and stood looking impatiently at the man who stood there diffidently, carrying a briefcase. Dressed in a dark grey overcoat, a bowler hat on his head, Elizabeth's first thought was that he was someone from the brewery.

"What do you want?" she asked rudely half closing the door in his face.

"Mrs Sprogett?" The man politely removed his hat.

"Yes."

"I wonder, Mrs Sprogett," the man tentatively put a foot across the threshold as though to prevent her slamming the door, "if I may come in?"

"You may not!" Elizabeth said firmly banging the door against his foot.

The man winced.

"If you're from the brewery it's not convenient . . ."

"Oh, I'm *not* from the brewery, madam." The man carefully, gingerly withdrew his foot. "I am a solicitor and, I hasten to say, that I am here only with good news. That is I have to tell you something that will be to your advantage. Now do you think I might be allowed in?"

Elizabeth continued to look at the man, her face dark with suspicion, but opened the door a fraction wider. "How do I know you're a solicitor?"

The man put a hand in an inner pocket and produced a card which he handed to Elizabeth.

"Graham Temple, Mrs Sprogett, of Pearson, Wilde and Brickell, Solicitors of Blandford. You've probably heard of us."

"Well," Elizabeth stood grudgingly aside, "you'd better come in, but I warn you my husband is upstairs . . ."

"You need have no fears on that account, madam," Mr Temple said frostily. "I assure you I shan't detain you a moment longer than is necessary." Then, once inside the door, "Would you like Mr Sprogett to be in on this meeting, madam?" As he spoke he produced a document from his well-worn briefcase. "It concerns a legacy, you see." Though clearly ill at ease after his reception, he looked up with a rather false smile. "I have the pleasure to tell you, Mrs Sprogett, that you are a beneficiary under the will of the late Sir Guy Woodville."

"Sir Guy Woodville!" Elizabeth sank on to a chair while Mary, mouth agape, went and stood by her side, clutching her mother's hand, staring wide-eyed at the stranger.

"It is not very much, I hasten to say." Mr Temple, having observed the humble nature of the dwelling, didn't want to raise her hopes too high.

"And is my husband a beneficiary too?"

"No, Mrs Sprogett."

"Then I don't see any need for him to be here. Proceed with what you have to say, Mr Temple. I cannot believe that Sir Guy would leave *me* anything. I hardly knew him."

"Nevertheless he did." Mr Temple began to read from the document in a sonorous tone.

"To Elizabeth Sprogett (née Yewell) the sum of one hundred pounds and a diamond and sapphire ring that belonged to my late mother."

"One hundred pounds!" Elizabeth gasped, rapturously clasping her hands together and immediately beginning to think what such a large sum of money would buy: new clothes for the children, a new dress and hat for her, perhaps a new coat ... Even then there would be some to spare. Suddenly her eyes narrowed suspiciously. "Why should he leave this money to me?"

"I have no idea, Mrs Sprogett. Nevertheless he did and I have a cheque drawn out in your favour with me this very minute." Once more he reached into his inside pocket and, producing a cheque, handed it to Elizabeth who gazed at it unbelievingly.

"And can I just go and cash this?" she asked taking it from him.

"Well you have to ... you don't have a bank account, Mrs Sprogett?"

"No."

"Well, I'm sure someone would cash it for you, a tradesman perhaps."

"I don't want any Tom, Dick or Harry to know about this. People gossip."

"Naturally," Mr Temple nodded understandingly. "Then I am quite sure that if you would care to call into our offices in the Market Place they would gladly provide you with cash, in exchange for the cheque endorsed in the name of my firm. Everything will be explained to you," he added noting a frown on Elizabeth's brow. Then, delving into his briefcase, he withdrew a small box which he handed to her.

"I think you will find this a very fine piece of jewellery, Mrs Sprogett. Worth more, I believe, than a hundred pounds."

"Well I never!" Elizabeth, face flushed with excitement and disbelief, opened the small velvet covered box and gazed at the jewel inside. It was indeed very fine, a large central sapphire surrounded by a double tier of small diamonds.

"I believe the band is platinum," Mr Temple explained, looking over her shoulder, "that is, even more valuable than gold."

"Well I never ..." Elizabeth exclaimed again and tried to

squeeze it on her finger, but Guy's mother's hand must have been smaller than hers and it didn't fit.

"You could have it enlarged," Mr Temple said encouragingly. "I believe it was the late Lady Woodville's engagement ring from Sir Guy's father, Sir Matthew Woodville, so it is of great sentimental value."

"But why *me*?"

"I have no idea, madam," Mr Temple said as patiently as he could, doubtless echoing the sentiment that had passed through his own mind at the bizarre nature of the bequest. "Maybe your mother or father would know. Was your father not once in the employment of Sir Guy?"

"But that was many, many years ago. My mother and father have worked for Sir Guy's sister, Mrs Heering, for over thirty years."

"Then maybe she or your mother will be able to help you." Mr Temple was now anxious to get away and his voice had a trace of impatience as he headed for the door. "She is the one to ask."

Paris in the spring of 1920 was like every other European capital struggling to recover from the aftermath of war. The Germans had never reached the city but it had reverberated to the sounds of Big Bertha, the 420 mm mortar, the 'secret weapon', of the mighty German army pounding away on the outskirts.

Paris had seen the Peace Conference of 1919, and its famous hotels had spruced themselves up for the occasion.

The Grand Hotel occupied a splendid site on the Rue Scribe near the Paris opera, a square courtyard leading into a sumptuously painted salle des fêtes.

It seemed fitting to complete their European tour, during which they had stayed in many fine hotels, at one of the most luxurious. There had been times when Agnes thought she would indeed prefer to live on the Continent, especially, if she had the opportunity, the Riviera. There they had stayed at the Riviera Palace in Menton and the Palace Regina in Nice,

69

where a wing with a private lift had been specially reserved for Queen Victoria who had regularly stayed there. They had been guests at the Grand Hotel du Lac in Lucerne, the Amstel in Amsterdam and the Imperial in Vienna, which had previously been the town palace of one of the Dukes of Württemberg.

They had dined in the best restaurants, danced in the smartest clubs, taken tea in the finest cafés, carefully sidestepped the ruins and avoided battle-scarred places altogether. The north of France was given a complete miss and so was Germany, the Baltic states, most of Holland, Austria and, of course, poor little Belgium.

But if you avoided the beggars on the streets, and the vacuous gazes of blind ex-soldiers selling matches, it was possible to forget there had ever been a war so quickly did Europe settle down to try and put its house in order. There was food in plenty in the grand hotels even though shops were bare and at home sugar, meat, butter and other essentials were still rationed.

They travelled by train or hired car; they travelled in luxury, and by the time they reached Paris they were loath to go home again.

Owen was an entertaining companion. He knew his way round, how to handle people and money. He was an adequate lover but that sort of thing had never meant very much to Agnes except when she was young and in love with Guy Woodville, who used to visit her secretly at the country home of Lord and Lady Mount, which gave the adventure added spice.

The bloom faded when Guy left her pregnant and alone. She had the humiliation of being sent away from the Mount home like some errant serving girl, banished to Weymouth, Guy neither seeming to know or care. When her baby was a few weeks old Agnes had taken to her heels and set out on an adventure, in the course of which she was to change her lifestyle and way of life many, many times.

Agnes had made other discoveries about Owen Wentworth during the months they'd been together. He was a gambler, a drinker, possibly not altogether honest about money but certainly not a thief, at least she didn't think so. But above all he was a rough diamond, an adventurer, rather like herself, with a veneer of polish that was easily rubbed off if he was thwarted or annoyed. In short, Owen and Agnes recognised each other; like for like.

She attributed his rough edges to the fact that he had been brought up abroad and lacked the refinement of an English public school education. He had gone to school in India and even though he told her it was a public school run by Englishmen for the benefit of expatriates and the sons of wealthy Indians, somehow it was not quite the same thing. In his holidays he had run wild with the natives. His mother had died when he was young so he lacked the civilising influence of female nurture. He had no brothers or sisters. His father had been a lonely rather severe man who beat him, and a drinker too.

Agnes gave Owen an edited version of her life story which included the lie she had put about in Wenham when she returned in 1912, that she was the widow of an American railroad millionaire. So firmly was this fiction anchored in Agnes's mind that she almost believed it and had managed almost entirely to forget the truth, which was that she had been the owner of several successful brothels and real estate in the heady climate of New Orleans in the expansionist years of America before the war. Reading in the papers of the death of Sir Guy Woodville's wife she sold up, came home and, much sooner than she thought she would, persuaded him to fall head over heels in love with her all over again and marry her.

Agnes looked up from her reverie, aware that Owen was gazing at her over the rim of his brandy glass.

She gave a fleeting smile and raised hers towards him.

"Here's a toast, Agnes."

"To what?"

"To our future."

"Oh!" She glanced quickly down at the table aware of the strains of the orchestra playing quietly in the background, the smooth passage of waiters between tables, trays held high above their shoulders.

"We do have a future, don't we, Agnes?"

"I hope so." She looked tremulously up at him. "But I should hate to live in India, Owen."

"Oh there is no question of going back to India." He reached over and put a hand on hers. "That is all over and done with."

"I wasn't sure. Have you sold your estate there?"

"How do you think I financed this trip, my dear?" He smilingly put his head on one side. Her heart gave a little jolt. It was true the trip must have cost a small fortune. It was like the honeymoon before the wedding. Was that, in fact, what Owen had had in mind?

"More brandy, monsieur?" the waiter intervened, hovering by his side. Owen shook his head and looked across at Agnes.

"Would you like a stroll, my dear? I think it's warm enough."

Agnes nodded, drained her glass and stood up as the waiter drew back her chair. She made her way towards the entrance to the dining room and then she turned to wait for Owen, who was having a word with the waiter and putting some coins into his palm.

There was no doubt that Owen looked very good in evening dress, she thought, gazing at him critically: crisp white shirt, black studs down the front, winged collar, neatly tied bow-tie.

It was not that he looked distinguished. He could have passed as the maître d'hotel, or some hotel functionary with his waxed moustaches and the carefully combed strands of hair plastered across his bald pate. He looked like someone in trade rather than a member of the professional or leisured classes; but at her age she couldn't be too choosy, and there was no doubt he had the money. He didn't spend it like water, but you could tell it was there. He was sybaritic rather than cultured and didn't like art galleries, historic monuments or churches, but then neither did she.

That much she had discovered in her continental sojourn. They were two of a kind. They liked travel and the things that money could bring including good food, good wine and the comforts of first class hotels. They liked spectacular sights like the Alps, deep gorges and the broad sweep of the bay at Cannes. Things you could gaze at, admire, and then pass on.

Owen escorted her through the lobby of the hotel which was thronged with people on their way in to dine or emerging from the dining room. Except for new arrivals checking in at the desk they were mostly in evening dress either going perhaps to the opera, a music hall or to some nightclub for drinking and dancing. Or, perhaps, some too were out for a stroll and a coffee and brandy at one of the boulevard cafés.

They reached the impressive carriage entrance to the hotel in the Rue Scribe where vehicles of all descriptions were jostling for position, either entering or leaving. The doorman asked if he should call them a cab, but Owen shook his head.

"Warm enough, my dear?" He looked solicitously at her.

"Plenty warm enough," Agnes said pulling her stole around her shoulders. In fact she was a little chilly, but instinct told her that Owen had something to say and she didn't want to do anything to interrupt the moment.

Some moments, once interrupted, never occurred again.

He took her arm and they strolled along the brightly lit Avenue de l'Opéra, bustling with the flotsam and jetsam of humanity. There were couples like themselves clearly bent on pleasure, dressed for the opera or the theatre, the men with starched white fronts, the women with ornate coiffures, fur stoles draped over *couture* evening dresses. Horse-drawn carriages still fought with automobiles along the busy street. A drunk waved a bottle at them through the window of a cab, until an unseen companion drew him back out of sight.

Vendors of all kinds ran among them hawking their wares: papers; elaborately packaged bonbons tied with bright ribbon; cheap souvenirs of Paris; glittering Eiffel Towers and models of Notre Dame. On a street corner an accordionist played listlessly while a tired little monkey on a string perched on his shoulder rubbed its eyes. A lone singer, not young, warbled a current

73

popular number holding out a plate to all those who passed, her eyes desperate.

Ladies of the night walked by, their bright, darting eyes ever alert for clients and, when successful, they separated wordlessly from their female companion, linked arms with their customer and disappeared into the warren of small streets that ran through Paris like little capillaries joining up the main arteries.

They passed the garden of the Tuileries and strolled along the quay in the dark shadow of the Louvre until they reached the Pont Neuf. In front of them rose the massively forbidding Conciergerie, the tall spire of the exquisite Sainte Chapelle.

They crossed to the middle of the bridge and gazed across at the Île de la Cité, and then down into the river twinkling with the lights of passing boats.

The diamonds of the ring which Owen held towards her with his fingers sparkled in the romantic glow cast by the street lamps, and Agnes caught her breath as he held out his hand for hers and gently, carefully, ran the ring along her finger.

"Yes," she breathed, "yes."

Then, drawing close to her, he took her in his arms and sealed their troth with a practised kiss. No blushing teenager could have wished for a more romantic proposal.

Chapter Five

Lally Martyn, Carson's aunt by marriage, had always been a great favourite of his. She was an astonishingly beautiful woman who in her youth had been a dancer. She had captivated his Uncle Prosper, his mother's brother, then a wealthy man about town, who had first made her his mistress then married her. For a while they had been very happy even though Prosper was twenty years her senior and now in his eighties. The marriage however had been marred for Prosper by the couples' inability to conceive a child, for which Lally had seemed to want to compensate by adopting unwanted orphans.

The first was Roger who had been taken from a poor home in Kentish Town. He had been educated and groomed until he became a successful businessman and married a very beautiful woman called Emma. Carson had fallen in love with Emma, and their affair continued until the war in which Roger had been killed, during the third battle of Ypres, in 1917.

The second orphan was Alexander who had been left on Lally's doorstep in London in the year 1910. Her adoption of this foundling caused much friction between her and Prosper, and from then on they led increasingly separate lives, Lally at the house in Dorset and Prosper at the London house in Montague Square.

It was very sad that such a love match should end this way, but there was no doubt that Prosper had been jealous and also found his wife's predilection for orphan boys hard to understand.

Carson had always considered Uncle Prosper stern, a strict disciplinarian who had little time for him when young. However, everyone loved Aunt Lally who was understanding, kind and gentle. Though now in her sixties, she still retained her beauty, her elegance, the graceful figure of a dancer. Her life had been completely shattered by Roger's death and a melancholy had possessed her that was not there before.

In the year since he'd been back, Carson had frequently been over to see Aunt Lally, to try to comfort her about Roger's death. He was very fond of Alexander and, although her name was seldom mentioned, he always nursed the hope that one day he might see Emma again.

Carson considered himself fortunate that, in his aunts Eliza and Lally, he had two women whom he not only loved but upon whom he depended as replacements for the mother he had lost when he was a young man.

Lally lived in the house that Ryder Yetman had built for Julius Heering in 1894. It was a very beautiful house on which no expense had been spared and had incorporated in it all the most modern devices of the time. After Ryder's death in an accident on the estate, Julius felt unable to live in the magnificent house which he had sold to his friend and business partner Prosper, who was a Dorset man.

It was in a cottage on the estate that Carson had lived for a while after Agnes married his father, and it was a place for which he felt deep affection. It was also there that he had fallen in love with Emma.

Carson rode through the gates of the house and, as he alighted from his horse the front door opened and Alexander, closely followed by Lally, sped out and hurled himself into Carson's outstretched arms.

He was now ten, a sturdy lad too tall to throw up in the air as Carson used to when he was a baby, but Carson hugged him for a brief moment and then, Alexander's hand in his, he leaned forward to greet Lally, who gave him one of her soft, perfumed kisses. Always exquisitely turned out she could have stepped straight from a Mayfair drawing room. She kept her hair in the old-fashioned style she had worn before the war, swept up from the nape of her neck with bouncy little curls on top. She made no concessions to age and was as blonde as she had been as a girl. That and her cornflower blue eyes made her seem much younger than her sixty-one years.

A groom appeared to take Carson's horse, and the three of them then walked into the house, Alexander's hand still in Carson's, Lally's arm through his.

"To what do we owe the pleasure, Carson?" Lally enquired as they reached the drawing room, whose French windows were open to reveal an acre of rolling lawn leading down to a lake.

"I thought it was a long time since I was here," Carson replied. "I should have rung."

"Not at all. I'm very glad you came. It is a long time since we saw you and we miss you, don't we Alexander?"

Alexander, his face still red with pleasure, grunted. He not only loved Carson; he hero-worshipped him and, as he grew bigger, he had followed all his exploits in the war with maps and charts as the British forces either advanced or retreated in the course of those four terrible years.

"And how's school?" Carson asked looking fondly down at him. Alexander shrugged.

"No scholar I'm afraid," Lally said, regret in her voice. "But he excels at sport. Like you."

Alexander blushed anew.

"It's great about the sport." Carson got out a cigarette and lit it. "But you mustn't neglect the studies. It's very important in life, Alex, to have some scholarship. I would not have had quite such a misspent youth if I'd had more learning. We can't all be saved by war."

"How do you mean 'saved by war'?" Sounding puzzled, Alexander looked up at him.

"Well, in the war I found myself as a person, as a man. I can't quite explain but . . ." Carson paused, seeking the right words, rubbed his cheek and then he looked up as the door silently swung open and a beautiful young woman, dressed entirely in black, stood there gazing solemnly at him.

"Emma!" Carson gasped. "Aunt Lally you didn't say . . ."

"You didn't give me the opportunity." Lally laughed awkwardly. "You were too busy talking about your misspent youth."

"Oh that," Carson laughed dismissively and crossed the room towards Emma. She politely and with formality held out her hand.

"How do you do, Carson?"

"How do you do, Emma?" He gravely took her hand, as if she were a perfect stranger. "How long have you been here?"

"A week," Emma said with composure and, letting go his hand, walked into the room.

"A week!"

"I must order tea." Lally, clearly flustered, signalled to Alexander who seemed unsure what to do.

"Oh do let me come with you, Mother." Emma hurried over to her but Lally held up her hand.

"No, dear, there is nothing for you to do. You stay here and talk to Carson." She put a hand on Alexander's shoulder.

"Darling, would you go and get chairs so that we can have tea in the garden? It's such a lovely day." Alexander sped off to do as he was told.

After Lally and Alexander had gone Carson and Emma stood looking at each other. He felt very awkward but thought she seemed perfectly composed, detached.

"So," Carson nonchalantly relit his cigarette, "you have been here a *week*."

"Yes, and I may stay another." Sounding offhand she walked over to the open French windows. "It really *is* very beautiful down here."

"Are you still living with your parents?" Carson walked slowly after her admiring the curve of her back, her beautiful legs encased in black silk stockings. Even the cut of her mourning dress was fashionable. Like her mother-in-law, her hair was very fair but her colour was natural and softly waved in a fashionable bob. One of the most glorious features of Emma was her skin

78

which was practically translucent, and her deep, almost violet, blue eyes.

"Yes." She turned and gazed at him. "Daddy has been very ill."

"I'm sorry."

"And Mummy was *very* shocked at Roger's death. We all were. Terribly."

"Yes." Carson bowed his head. "It was very bad luck." No one quite knew how he'd died except that it was near the Bremen Redoubt on or about August 1. "I'm very sorry." Raising his head he was shocked to see on Emma's face an expression of such hostility that one might have thought he, personally, was responsible for Roger's death.

"Emma . . ." he gestured helplessly. "I still love you."

"Don't even *speak* of it," she snapped turning her back on him. "With Roger dead."

"But it wasn't my fault and . . . Emma you didn't love him, you know you didn't. You told me you didn't. You loved me. Why pretend it wasn't the case just because now Roger's dead?"

"How can you!" Emma rounded on him, her face contorted with anger. "How *dare* you speak like that!"

"Because it's true. You can't change the past. I'm very sorry that Roger's dead. Frankly it was the last thing I expected. I always thought he would survive. I don't know why, but I did."

"I suppose *you* thought that if he died I would fall into your arms," Emma said contemptuously.

"I thought no such thing. That's a dreadful thing to say. All I did say is that whether Roger had lived or died you and I might have had a future together after the war."

"Well, we haven't," she said.

She then became extremely agitated and began wringing her hands, pacing backwards and forwards, her tone of voice hysterical as she burst out: "Carson you have no idea how guilty, how *dreadful*, I feel about Roger. It was a terrible thing to do to deceive him the way we did . . ."

79

Nicola Thorne

"But Emma you had been married nearly two years and you were still a virgin. When you and I became lovers you were bitter and frustrated. You said it was awful to be with a man who could never love you as a woman . . ."

"That's all in the past," she said struggling to regain her composure. "Roger couldn't help it, and it doesn't make it any better for me. Before he went abroad he made up for it."

"Do you mean that before he went away . . ." Carson drew in his breath. "Do you mean . . ."

"Before he went away we became lovers, and he loved me," Emma said firmly. "It all came right and we looked forward to the future. And then . . ." Suddenly she put her head in her hands and burst into tears. "I shall never, ever be able to live with the grief and despair I feel about Roger. The sense that I betrayed him. Why couldn't it have been *you* who were killed, Carson, and Roger spared? I really feel now that I can't stand the sight of you."

A few moments later when Lally reappeared she was surprised to see Emma on her own, apparently upset and drying her eyes.

"Where's Carson?" she enquired looking around.

"He left."

"Oh! Is there something wrong?"

"Don't ask Mother, please don't ask." Emma blew her nose vigorously. "And please excuse me if I don't come to tea. I have a headache."

"You'd better go and lie down, dear," Lally said calmly. "I'll come up later to see if you're all right." She put her arm round Alexander, disconsolate that Carson's visit had been such a brief one. Then, her brow puckered, Lally watched her daughter-in-law as she left the room, aware of a deep sense of unease. She knew quite well that what had happened so long ago between Emma and Carson was partly her fault. They had met at her house and she had thrown them together because she knew that her son, whom she loved so much, could never be a proper husband to Emma.

80

Once, in his misery and chagrin before he left for the front, Roger had confided to her that he was unable to love Emma because his sexual preference had always been for men. He had been bullied into marrying Emma by Prosper who, perhaps suspecting his inclinations, had hoped to change him. How Lally now wished she'd never thrown Carson and Emma in each other's paths by feigning a cold which had kept her to her room. She had been sorry for her daughter-in-law, anguished on her account. How she wished she'd left well alone. But the follies of the past could never be undone, and that was her punishment.

Carson felt a sense of despair as, yet again, he walked round Pelham's Oak with Ivor the bailiff. It was true that Agnes's debts had been settled by Julius, for which he was truly grateful, and he now owed no one anything. Even his father's death duties had been paid. He had concentrated on getting the tenant farms in working order and making the most of the land to produce food and provision that not only was sufficient for him and the staff at Pelham's Oak, but a sizable proportion of which went to market.

Little, however, had been done to the house itself, and sometimes when he looked at it or wandered through its large, empty rooms, he wondered if he should after all not sell up and start life anew? Maybe go abroad and seek his fortune overseas where he would have enough money to buy a farm, or start some kind of business perhaps in Australia, South Africa or one of the other colonies? If only his cousin Laurence had not killed himself there would have been the Yetman building business to help him out, but that had been sold and broken up after Laurence's death. If only he himself were equipped to do something useful he could at least make a start somewhere but, due to his misspent youth, he was good for nothing except soldiering, and the further away from the war he got the less the army seemed attractive. Also if he went away, far away, there would be no possibility of seeing Emma again, because the thought that when she visited Lally she was so near and yet so far away was a torment to him. Carson threw up his hands, his expression one of dejection.

"I don't know where to start, Ivor. Maybe . . ."

"I thought," Ivor looking towards the house ran a hand over his cheek, "one way, Sir Carson, might be to close part of the house and do up the rest. Then when things change, or improve, for you financially, you can start on the other half. It would also mean, sir, that you would need fewer staff . . ." Ivor paused and looked at him thoughtfully. "I hope I am not speaking out of turn, Sir Carson."

"Not at all." Carson looked gratefully at the bailiff who had served his family so well for so many years. "It's a very good idea."

"You wouldn't let it go to ruin, of course. The fabric would remain intact, but it would spare the need to decorate and . . . well, it is already too large a house for yourself and the small staff you have left, Sir Carson."

"I would hate to part with any of them."

"Arthur, I think, might be quite pleased to go, sir. He is full of rheumatism and I'm sure you would be generous with him."

"Well," Carson looked doubtful, "as generous as I can be. That goes without saying."

Ivor seemed to have something else on his mind and stood there kicking the pebbles at his feet.

"I hope you don't mind me mentioning it, Sir Carson, but did you not say your problems might be eased if you sold the property you own in London?"

"Yes they might be eased," Carson said, "and I don't mind you asking. But the fact is that if I take a roof from over my stepmother's head in London she will want to come and join me here, so, until I can solve this problem it's something I'm hesitating about. Also house prices are low and everyone seems to think that as the economy improves and the effects of the war diminish, they will rise. By that time we may have sorted out just what to do about Aunt Agnes. Well, now, let's make a start on drawing up plans."

This decision having been taken, already Carson felt more cheerful as if a great weight had been lifted from him. "And then as soon as possible we can begin."

But it was very slow work and Carson soon realised that he and Ivor alone were unequal to the task. It was a very big house and had been so constructed that it was difficult to know where to make a division. For one thing the great drawing room, with its spectacular view over the countryside, ran from one side of the house to the other. How to divide that? And then if a division was made from front to back all the domestic services, the kitchen, scullery, pantries and so on would be separated from the rest of the house. The house had been designed in an integrated way, so that division was difficult.

One evening Carson, having finished dinner which, as usual, he took by himself, was yet again seated at his desk fretting over the plans when there was a knock at the door and Arthur put his head round. Thinking he had come to enquire about his future Carson invited him in and asked him to shut the door.

"I daresay you've heard rumours . . ." Carson began, but the servant interrupted him.

"Sir Carson, there is a gentleman at the door asking for you. I took the liberty of inviting him in, sir, as it was cold outside, but he is in rather a dishevelled state."

"Well, then can you find him some soup and maybe a bed for a night in one of the old servants' rooms?"

"No sir, not *that* sort of gentleman, I mean not a tramp, sir. He says he is acquainted with you from the war and happened to be passing . . ."

" 'Happened to be passing'!" Carson exclaimed looking at the clock. "At this time of night! Did he give you a name?"

Arthur, looking embarrassed, mumbled:

"He appears to be a foreigner, a French gentleman, sir. He gave me his name but I'm afraid I didn't quite catch it. Part . . . Part something . . ."

"*Parterre!*!" Carson exclaimed. "I simply can't believe it's my old friend Jean Parterre," and he hurried to the door and flung it wide open.

There standing in the hall, a rucksack at his feet and looking footsore and weary was a man of about Carson's age and height, with a few days' growth of beard. His dark hair was tousled and in need of a wash and comb, he was hollow-eyed as though he had not slept, or had slept badly, and he was dressed in walking clothes: thick trousers, a combat jacket and sturdy leather boots with thick socks turned over at the top.

Carson held out his arms, throwing them round his friend and holding him close while Arthur looked on in some astonishment not ever having seen his master, normally so restrained, give vent to such emotion.

"Jean, Jean," Carson stood back holding firmly on to his companion's shoulders. "It is so good to see you. Why didn't you tell me you were coming?"

Jean Parterre shook his head.

"I don't know, my friend. I wasn't sure. I have simply been walking, walking, walking, unsure of my direction."

"I see." Carson let fall his hand and turned to Arthur. "Maybe some sandwiches for my friend? A bottle of wine?"

"Of course, Sir Carson." Arthur bowed and went in the direction of the kitchen while Carson ushered his friend into the drawing room at one end of which a fire still burned.

"My goodness," Jean looked around, "this is some place you have here, Carson." He scratched his head. "It was hard to find. Such a huge place." He glanced at his companion in arms. "I didn't realise, Carson, that you were the owner of a vast chateau . . ."

"Alas, my father died last year," Carson replied heaping logs on the fire as Jean looked so cold. "I inherited it from him."

"I'm sorry." Jean sat down and extended his hands towards the blaze.

"It needs a lot doing to it," Carson gestured round. "It has been allowed to fall into disrepair. The last years of my father were sad ones."

"I'm sorry," Jean said again and looked up at Carson. "And you, my old friend, saviour of my life, what of you?"

"I resigned my commission after the death of my father. I found he had left nothing but debts, but these were run up by my stepmother. The house has been in my family for generations. It is very precious to me. An uncle has partly helped me by paying off my father's debts, but the rest is up to me. It is a challenge."

"It is," Jean Parterre nodded and looked up as Arthur entered bearing a tray with a large plate of sandwiches, a bottle of wine and two glasses.

"Thank you very much, Arthur," Carson said relieving him of the tray. "I think you can go to bed now."

"Thank you, Sir Carson. I expect Mr Parterre will be staying the night, sir?"

"I hope so." Carson looked over at Jean who nodded. "Yes of course. If I may?"

"I have had the bed made up in the old nursery wing, sir."

"That's very kind of you. Thank you, Arthur."

"Not at all, Sir Carson. Good night, sir."

"Good night Arthur."

Arthur bowed to Jean, who nodded his head and watched him thoughtfully as he left the room.

"You have a title of some kind? You are a lord? I didn't know."

"My father was a baronet. It is a bit like a lord, not so important."

"Well mon vieux . . . had I known."

"It would not have made any difference," Carson said firmly. "It does make no difference."

"We have a bond that no one can break," Jean agreed. "You nearly gave your life for me."

"It wasn't as bad as that."

"I was inches from death. It *was* as bad as that."

They both fell silent looking into the fire as if seeing again the scene where Carson had, indeed, rescued Jean from a certain death. It had been at the Battle of the River Ancre, a tributary of the Somme, in 1916. Jean Parterre had been a liaison officer from the French forces attached to the British Fourteenth Brigade, two companies of which had fallen back upon the Serre trench. They were pressed hard by the enemy until the 1st Dorsets came up from the rear, lobbing bombs, and saved the situation. During the fighting many were killed or wounded and among the latter was Jean Parterre, who had been hit in the shoulder and thigh. Those who were left were exposed to a German counter-attack of great severity and many were killed. Carson had been about to withdraw his men when he saw a soldier lying in an exposed position between trenches, obviously still alive and in great pain. Telling his men to cover him he went out and drew him back to safety just a second before a bomb fell in the spot where Jean had lain, demolishing the terrain completely.

When he recovered Jean had returned to his unit with the French forces, but he managed to trace Carson and thank him, and the two had remained in touch, never knowing if they would see each other again, until the end of the war.

In the silence, Jean munched his sandwiches as Carson opened the wine and poured them each a glass. Then, as he held his aloft, the light shining through the crystal reminded him powerfully of blood, all the blood that had been shed in that most futile and senseless of wars. The same idea seemed to have occurred to Jean.

"Santé, to peace," he said raising his glass.

"To peace, indeed."

They both drained their glasses, which were refilled by Carson.

"This is very good wine." Jean looked appreciatively at his glass.

"My father enjoyed the good things of life. He built up a fine cellar. We'll have a few bottles more before you go. I hope it won't be for a while." He looked down at Jean who, having finished his sandwiches with the speed of a man on the point of starvation, was now gazing again at the fire.

"Tell me, Jean, how goes it with you? Your wife? Your children?"

"My wife left me for another man during the war. He was not a combatant but had one of those mysterious 'reserved' occupations where people seem to make a lot of money, no one quite knows how. I think he was able to operate on the black market very profitably and became very rich."

"I'm sorry."

"If she was that sort of woman she was not worth bothering about. It is my children I miss. They went with her too. Of course, they were so young."

"And have you seen them?"

Jean Parterre shook his head.

"With the money I had left from the war I travelled and, eventually, I came here. Maybe I thought I would see you and talk about old times." Jean looked up and gave Carson a grateful smile. "Thank you for receiving me so well. You are very kind. You saved my life and now you offer me hospitality."

"For as long as you like." Carson leaned down and put a hand on his shoulder. "Believe me I would be glad of the company too."

Carson got more pleasure in his friend's company than he could have imagined possible. It was the companionship that was important, as well as the revival of old memories. Although the war was hideous it had also been important, the most momentous event, not only in his life but in the lives of millions. It had also radically altered his outlook, his philosophy.

Those things which hitherto had been of such importance were important no longer. Faced with the carnage he had seen human life seemed infinitely precious. He had been twenty-seven when the war began, already mature and yet, in many ways, his behaviour had been that of a youth, his outlook undeveloped and insular. He had been trained for nothing, did nothing. No wonder his parents had despaired of him and considered him a wastrel. He wondered what his life would have been had the war not occurred? The only regret he had was that, had that been so, the consequence of his affair with Emma might have been very different. He might have succeeded in persuading her to leave her indifferent husband and marry him.

Jean too had suffered in the war, not only physically, emotionally and mentally but he had lost his wife and children. Like Carson he was adrift, and as the two tramped or rode round the Woodville acres they discoursed long and deeply about the meaning of life.

For Jean it had no meaning. It was pointless. Yet why had he lived when so many others had died? To what purpose? He was the only man to live from the bombardment he had been in and, had not Carson been there to save him he would have sunk in the mud of the banks of the Ancre to have disappeared for ever.

Jean, however, was able to be of help to Carson in another, practical way. He had trained as a builder and pointed out many modifications that could be made to the house so as to save costs. He made a lot of technical suggestions which Carson and Ivor noted down and studied at the end of each day.

However, after a week or so of this pleasant life, Jean decided it was time to move on. He confronted Carson over breakfast one morning, saying he had packed his bag and stripped his bed.

"But you can't go just like that," Carson looked at him in surprise.

"I have to move on, Carson." Jean rose and began to pace the floor of the breakfast room. "I can't stay here forever. I feel like Ulysses' men and the Lotus Eaters . . ."

"I don't know what you mean," Carson grimaced. "Don't forget I have not the benefit of a classical education."

"Ulysses' boat was driven on to the land of the Lotus Eaters as he journeyed home from the Trojan war. The taste of the lotus made men forget all desire to reach home. Ulysses resisted the fruit and managed to rescue those of his men who had eaten it. I too know how delightful it would be to linger here where the company is so good, the countryside so beautiful. But I must go."

"Where? Why?" Carson demanded.

"To tell you the truth I don't know." Jean slumped in his chair again and lit a cigarette. "All I know is that I can't stay here."

"But I *want* you to stay here." Carson's tone was insistent. As Jean was about to speak he held up a hand. "Please don't say anything, but I have been doing some serious thinking during the past few days. Not only do I enjoy your company, your presence takes me out of myself, but you have given me much valuable advice due to your training as a builder. Well," now Carson got up and began to stride excitedly back and forth past his friend, "I want to offer you a job."

"A job!"

"What say you take charge of restoration at Pelham's Oak? You can oversee the rebuilding programme. I can't offer you much money, but I can pay you something, plus your board and lodging. Say it takes you six months or a year or even longer? That way you can think about your future, as I can think about mine? You can have your own quarters. The place is big enough. We don't have to live on top of each other or in each other's pockets. Neither of us would want that; but I think we get on well enough to be able to endure this kind of close contact and if we find we don't, then we can agree to part and remain friends."

"Well," Jean leaned back scratching the back of his head, "I don't know what to say."

Yet it was true he felt refreshed and rested from his short stay. He loved the house, the countryside, and Carson was one of the finest men he had ever met, as well as the bravest. He liked and respected him; in a way he loved him.

"It's very tempting," he said after a pause. "Can I have a little time to think about it?"

"How much time?"

"An hour. Two hours?"

"Take all the time you want," Carson said extending his hand. "I, meanwhile, will go and have your bed made up again. I shan't let you go unless the answer is 'yes'."

Chapter Six

The woman moved quietly among the graves, a large bunch of
flowers clasped in one arm. She stopped before one at the far
end of the churchyard and, placing the flowers on the grave,
stood there for a few moments, head bowed, hands clasped.
Momentarily she rested a hand on the cross at the top of
the grave as if reluctant to leave, and then she moved on,
stopping every now and then to examine the inscriptions on
the tombstones as she passed them. Some she lingered by and,
again, that curiously touching gesture with the hand.

She moved in a graceful, arresting way rather like a mannequin,
as if she were used to showing off herself and her clothes. She wore
a white linen coat over a pretty belted floral dress with a large
white collar. She was of medium height but this was enhanced
by a pair of high-heeled white shoes, and a broad-brimmed,
white straw hat shaded her eyes, lending her an air of mystery.
A white handbag was slung casually over one arm and, in her
right hand she carried a pair of long white kid gloves.

Strangely out of place in Wenham churchyard, Carson thought,
watching her progress with no small degree of fascination from
the gate which he had been just about to open when he saw her.
A stranger, yet something about her was familiar, although he
couldn't think he'd ever seen her before. Suddenly she raised her
head from the tombstone she was examining, but appeared not to
see him and walked on again, her coat swirling gracefully about her.
She seemed to know where she was going because when she came to
the Woodville family vault, surrounded by high iron railings, she
paused again carefully scrutinising the names inscribed on it.

More intrigued than ever Carson opened the gate, went through it and, as he started along the path towards the vault, the woman turned, raised her head and from beneath the brim of her hat looked directly at him. Then she looked quickly back the way she had come, as though she was searching for a way of escape. But the moment of panic appeared to pass and she confronted him, a faint smile on her lips.

"May I help you?" Carson enquired politely. "Are you looking for something or, perhaps, someone in the churchyard?"

"That's very kind of you," the woman murmured in a low musical voice, shaking her head. "I think I know my way about." She raised her head as if to see him better and he saw that she had a rather fine pair of eyes, if a little close together, as if suggestive of a very slight squint, but this was not unattractive. She had a frank, engaging smile which showed white even teeth. There was definitely a hint of mystery about her, but once again Carson had felt his memory jar, as if he knew her and the way that her eyes expressed merriment, rather as though she too knew him.

"Do we know each other?" he enquired, stooping towards her in order to try and see her better.

The woman now laughed openly in a frank, good-natured way and put out her hand.

"I see you don't remember me, Carson . . ."

"Connie!" he exclaimed. "Constance Yetman."

"Exactly."

"But Connie I would *never* have recognised you. I thought there was something familiar about you but I couldn't place it. It must be the hat, and yet you're taller and . . ." he was going to add "smarter", but pulled himself up in time.

"Different," she suggested as he took her hand and shook it warmly, murmuring "Connie Yetman, well I never. When did you arrive?"

"Two days ago but . . ." Seeing the question in his eyes she looked down at herself. "Oh I see you think I've just arrived because of the way I'm dressed? I am just on my way back from Yeovil where I had business, and I was anxious to put flowers on the grave of my parents. While I was here I took the opportunity to look at the other stones to our departed loved ones. It's been a long time, Carson." She realised that her hand was still in his and swiftly removed it.

"It has." He took her gently by the arm and led her to a bench on which he sat down, facing her.

"It must be, well . . ." he paused awkwardly, but Connie's expression didn't change as if the memory of what was troubling Carson amused her. He was struck by her composure, her *sang froid*, so unlike the timid child-woman he'd known, or thought he knew. She seemed to have nothing at all in common with that extraordinarily shy, plain, myopic, desperately insecure young woman he had so nearly and, possibly disastrously, married.

"It must be eight years, Carson."

"It's all of that."

"A very long time ago."

Again that awkward pause. Then:

"Have you forgiven me, Connie? I behaved disgracefully."

"Forgiven, and forgotten," she said dismissively. "We were both pawns in a silly family game. My aunt was most to blame, but she meant well." She gave a deep sigh. "However let's not dwell on the past." She brushed his hand lightly with her finger. "You know that Miss Fairchild died?"

"I'd heard she was dead."

"She died in Venice and we buried her there. Of course I had to because of the war."

"You spent the war years in Venice?"

"Yes. It was almost impossible to get back here. We had a very nice apartment in a palazzo on the Grand Canal."

"And do you still live there?"

"Yes. I think I shall settle in Venice. I have made a lot of friends, and it's such a beautiful place."

"And your singing?" He sighed nostalgically. "Do you still have that beautiful voice?" If he had once been in love with any part of her it was her voice.

She laughed, for the first time showing embarrassment. "Well,

93

I like to sing, thank you for remembering. I also play the violin, and a group of friends and I meet frequently to play trios or quartets. Oh yes life in Venice is wonderful with all the museums and the opera and various other cultural activities."

"And you never . . . married, Connie?"

"No." She smiled again, openly and cheerfully. "Not yet anyway. And you Carson, are *you* married?"

Carson shook his head.

"I'm very surprised." There was a note of mockery in her voice. "You were such a catch. I suppose the women are all over you still?"

"I was in the war, Connie. I went right through from the beginning to the end and it changed me. Believe me it changes a man."

"Of course!" Momentarily she looked nonplussed. "How could I forget? But at least you survived. We had several friends who lost sons or husbands." Her eyes veered towards the Woodville family vault again. "I am sorry to see the name of your father, Carson. He died a year ago?"

"Thereabouts. After that I left the army and came home to shoulder my responsibilities. I had thought I might make a career of soldiering, but it was not to be."

"And your stepmother, my dear half-sister Agnes?" Connie's tone contained just a hint of sarcasm. "What news of her?"

"Very little. I haven't heard from her for months. She seems to like to appear and disappear. Let's hope one day she'll disappear for good, but I rather fear not. Like the bad penny she will always turn up again. She lives in London at the family house, but I understand she has been on the continent for some time. Frankly we never got on, and little good she did my father."

"I must say my half-sister *was* rather strong medicine. I was not over-fond of her either." Connie got to her feet. "Well, I must go, Carson." She pulled her coat closer to her. "Besides it is rather chilly here."

"I apologise," Carson hurriedly got to his feet. "I shouldn't have kept you."

"Not at all. But my purpose in visiting Wenham is to dispose of Miss Fairchild's property. There is no point in hanging on to it, especially if I am to live abroad. I shall also probably sell our house in Bath, as I make so little use of that." She gave him a frank, impersonal but friendly smile and once more held out her hand. "It was very nice to see you again, Carson. I'm glad we met."

"I am too, Connie." He took her hand and held it for a minute, somehow reluctant to let it go. She had used the past tense. "How long will you be here?"

"Oh, that's undecided." She tossed back her head, a gleam in her soft brown eyes. "Maybe a week or two. I may have to go to London on business, but I'll be back. I have a car."

Carson gulped. She was so much the woman of affairs it was hard to take it all in. This time it was he who felt the country bumpkin.

"Well, then I hope we shall meet again."

"That would be nice," she said with the same composed smile, but really the implication was that she didn't much care. Once apparently so in love, she had obviously put him firmly at the back of her memory.

"Did you have some purpose in coming to the churchyard, Carson?" she asked as an afterthought, as they began to walk slowly towards the gate.

"I have a friend who is discussing some work for the Rector. He is an old comrade of mine from the war who is staying with me. He is a master builder and he's advising Hubert Turner on some repairs to the church. I introduced him and then left him. I often come to visit the resting places of my parents and my dear sister Emily, who died so young of the scarlet fever."

Connie's expression was sympathetic.

"We share some very sad memories, Carson, do we not? I remember little Emily well and your dear mother and father too of course." She paused by the side of the gate and looked back towards the far side of the churchyard. "Today I saw, as well as the graves of my own dear father and mother, those of

Ryder Yetman and his son Laurence. But what a lovely place
for them to lie." She looked around at the pretty churchyard
on the banks of the Wen with the trees newly clad in the fresh
greenery, the blossom of late spring. "Sometimes I feel sorry I
shan't rest here myself."

"Connie, that will be a long time off," Carson exclaimed
seizing her hand. "Look, I shall be very sorry indeed not to
see you again. You too are a link with the past and bonds such
as these are so important. If I may I shall call on you in a day
or two and maybe you'll come and dine with us at Pelham's
Oak before you go?"

"Oh, I would like that enormously, Carson," she said warmly
as they finally stopped outside the Rectory. "I too shall look
forward to our next meeting."

"I can't get over the change in her!" Carson had hardly been
able to stop talking about his meeting with Connie. "I didn't
recognise her."

Listening to him burbling on, Sophie permitted herself
a smile.

"She used to wear most unbecoming spectacles." Carson
looked at her abruptly. "What happened to them?"

"I think she found she didn't really need them. She only
uses them now for reading. She is indeed a very self-assured
young woman. I scarcely recognised her myself when she
appeared on the doorstep. It's wonderful how travel broadens
the mind."

"She seems to bear me no grudge," Carson murmured looking
at the others in conversation on the far side of the room. But her
husband and Jean Parterre were engrossed in an examination of
some new plans for the church.

"I'm sure she doesn't. In fact what happened may have been
a very good thing."

"Oh, in what way?" Carson looked at her curiously.

"She might not have developed her potential, as she undoubtedly has, but remained subdued by her status as your wife, sharing

the house with Agnes and so on. In those circumstances I don't think it could possibly have been a happy union, Carson, and doubtless Connie now thinks that too."

"Well . . ." Carson was about to proceed when the door opened and a maid appeared carrying a tea tray while behind her another followed with sandwiches and cakes.

In the background Hubert Turner rubbed his hands.

"Good, I spy tea," he said and again Sophie smiled as she took up her position by the table on which the tea things were being laid.

"Hubert is always very happy when food appears. You would think one kept him permanently starving."

She looked fondly at her husband who, in fact, in the years since they'd been married had put on at least a stone and was beginning to resemble the rubicond stereotype of a fictional clergyman, a sort of Friar Tuck character with thinning hair and ruddy cheeks. The Rector's wife was herself the opposite, being slim, taller than her husband and having kept her robust good looks. Though never a beauty she had always been considered handsome and remained so. Her brown hair, which she wore in a roll, was thick and luxuriant, her brown eyes clear and intelligent, her expression alert but at the same time not lacking humour. She had been the daughter of the previous Rector of Wenham and had first married the heir to the Woodville title, George, a marriage which pleased no one except the participants. George and Sophie, both inflamed with love of the Divine, had gone as missionaries to Papua where George died of fever leaving Sophie to return to Wenham with her two daughters. Now she was the mother of two boys as well, and in her role as the Rector's wife much admired for her charity, compassion and good works, a lynchpin of the community.

Hubert and Jean continued with their deliberations while Sophie poured the tea. She handed a cup to Jean and one to her husband.

"How is it all coming on?"

"Very well," Hubert said helping himself to a second sandwich.

"The belfry has to be reinforced and also parts of the sacristy. Mr Parterre thinks it will take about six months."

"As long as that?" Sophie grimaced. "I hope Mr Parterre will be able to supervise it. I understood his work at Pelham's Oak takes up much of his time?" She looked enquiringly at Jean, who stirred his tea thoughtfully.

"I think I can fit them both in, if Carson permits. I have the help of some good men . . ."

"It's also a question of money," Carson pulled a face. "It always is. Sometimes I think it is a task which will never be completed. I'm sure the church has more money than we have anyway."

The Rector said nothing. It was known that he was a man of substantial private means, not forced to rely solely on his church stipend. He had already put much of his own money into refurbishing the rectory with its twelve bedrooms and large reception rooms, built at the turn of the nineteenth century for a rector with a large family. In the weeks he had been there Jean had already proved himself an asset in helping with the reconstruction of Pelham's Oak. He knew how to save time and cut costs. The fabric of the outside had been made secure, was repointed and repainted. The reroofing had begun. Without physically dividing the house they had managed to close the rooms which were not needed and secure them against damp and cold.

"I'm sure we can work something out," Jean said tactfully. "I don't think the task is as big as the Rector thinks. I'm sure I can manage both. Now if we could have a look at the belfry, sir . . ." He then picked up the architect's plans they had been discussing and took them over to the window to point something out to the Rector.

"What a charming and helpful man Mr Parterre is," Sophie murmured *sotto voce* to Carson as the two men proceeded with their discussions. "Nothing is too much trouble for him. And he is so good with the children. Has he children of his own?"

"He was devoted to them," Carson nodded. "But his wife deserted him for another man."

"And does he see them?"

Carson shook his head. "Not, I think, for a long time."

Carson finished his tea and replaced his cup on the table. He crossed to the window and stood looking in the direction of Miss Fairchild's house.

"I wonder how long Connie Yetman will stay with us?" He turned and smiled at Sophie. "Frankly she was so nice with me, I shall be sorry to see her go."

Sophie joined him by the window. Miss Fairchild's house, just out of sight, was a substantial dwelling, the last big house in the village. Her parents had owned the draper's store in the town which had passed to her after their deaths. Her father had also invested money wisely in stocks and shares as well as property, and had left her well off. But her real fortune came from apparently worthless shares in a South African mine which had suddenly struck a rich vein of gold. When she died she left her ward not simply well off, but an extremely wealthy woman with the power and ability to do with her life exactly what she pleased.

Sophie craned her head forward as she saw her elder daughter coming round the church in the direction Connie would have taken.

"Here's Deborah," she said. "I wonder if she's been paying a call on Connie?"

"Deborah is not returning to school?" Carson asked, following the progress of his niece, whose beauty it was hard to exaggerate. She was tall, like her mother, slim, blue-eyed with fair hair which she still wore in her girlish, but becoming, ringlets as though she was reluctant to grow up.

"She's eighteen in January, and has finished her schooling. The problem now is what to do with her."

"She's so pretty," Carson murmured. "You won't have that problem for very long."

"You think she'll marry?" Sophie laughed. "I'm not sure she's in any hurry. She has much admired what Dora did in the war and has ambitions to be a nurse."

"And should you mind that?" Carson looked at her enquiringly.

"Not in the least. You know we have a tradition in our branch of the family of service to the community. Hubert and I would not in the least mind if she took up nursing, and I'm sure her dear father would have approved."

Surreptitiously Sophie and Carson clasped hands. The great bond they shared was love for the late George Woodville. He had been a mentor and example to Carson who could never forget that, but for George's untimely death, Sophie would now be mistress of Pelham's Oak and the problems that beset him now might never have happened. He would have been a carefree soldier, enjoying life to the full.

On their way out, Carson and Jean stopped in the hall where Deborah was playing with her small brother Timothy, who had just been bought his first bicycle. When she saw Carson Deborah ran up to him and flung her arms round his neck. He jumped back, startled, aware of how grown up she had suddenly become, not as tall as he was but tall nevertheless. He was very fond of his niece and she adored her father's younger brother. To her he was such a glamorous figure with his war record and his reputation for wildness as a young man. She didn't know which aspect of him she found more attractive.

"Uncle Carson," she exclaimed, standing back to gaze at him, "are you going to stay for tea?"

"We've just had tea. You're too late."

"Oh!" Dejectedly she looked in Jean's direction. "And, Mr Parterre, how long have you been here?"

"Almost all afternoon. I had business to discuss with your father."

"I wish I'd known." Deborah stamped her foot angrily. "I missed all the fun."

"I assure you there was no fun," Jean replied looking at her kindly. "It was all talk about building with the reverend."

"*And* you saw Connie?" Deborah looked archly at Carson. "You heard?"

"Yes, I heard. I was on my way home from seeing a friend and I saw Connie Yetman go into Miss Fairchild's house. She paused and waved to me so I went in for a chat."

"Surely you didn't remember Connie?"

"Oh, I remembered her. Of course I remembered her."

"And you recognised her?" Carson appeared amused.

"Of *course*, but she came to the house when she first arrived. Didn't you recognise her?"

"I thought she'd changed."

"She thinks *you've* changed too."

"Oh really?" Carson's eyes twinkled. "For better or worse?"

"She didn't say." Deborah paused. "She just looked thoughtful. I can see that she's forgiven you."

"Now, now," Carson looked uncomfortably in Jean's direction, "that was a long time ago."

"She said that she was glad she didn't marry you."

"Oh did she?"

"Yes. She said that now she had a very full and happy life, and invited me to visit her in Venice."

Connie drove through the narrow lanes of her native county, Dorset, her hair ruffled by the breeze blowing in through the open windows of the car. It was a glorious summer day and it was surprisingly good to be home.

Connie was a Wenham girl, born of an elderly father and a mother who was nearly forty and who died giving birth to her. Her father John Yetman had been a widower when he wooed and married Euphemia Monk, a wealthy, but extremely shy and withdrawn spinster of the parish. In the care of her grieving father Connie had had a sheltered, narrow upbringing and this inevitably continued after her father died and she was adopted by Victoria Fairchild, another wealthy spinster to whom she had become extremely attached.

Connie clung to Miss Fairchild as she had clung to her

father. She was a plain, nervous child who wore glasses and took little interest in her appearance, in anything except music at which she excelled. Indeed it was her only passion until she met Carson Woodville and he began to take a kindly interest in her. It seemed impossible that this godlike creature could love her enough to propose to her, but he did.

Even now she could blush at the memory of her chagrin when she discovered that Carson had been talked into marriage by his father in order for Connie's fortune to save the family estate.

Connie, not surprisingly, had had a breakdown and Miss Fairchild, as overprotective as ever, had whisked her away, first to Bath where she bought a house then, just before the outbreak of war and as Connie recovered, to the continent.

Connie had loved Miss Fairchild but, especially after the fiasco of her broken marriage plans, she also came to resent her. As she grew older Miss Fairchild became cantankerous and over-possessive. Looking at the situation with the gift of hindsight Connie realised that Victoria had almost deliberately kept her back, encouraging her childish attitudes and behaviour. She paid for everything and gave Connie little spending money of her own. She supervised her wardrobe continuing to choose styles for her that were far too young.

Small wonder, then, that when Victoria died shortly after they had settled in Venice, Connie took stock of her life and found it wanting. Being alone, far from home, friends or family, she had only her own resources to fall back on.

At first she was terrified, but then she discovered a sense of freedom, the ability to choose and make her own decisions. If she was to remain a dreary spinster all her life, singing in the church choir and scuttling around the narrow alleyways of Venice, keeping out of sight, it seemed that the choice was up to her.

Luckily at that stage, before she had time to settle once again in a rut, she was taken in hand by a worldly Venetian woman, the wife of the Italian lawyer who was the administrator of Victoria's estate. Francesca Valenti was only a little older than Connie and she took an interest in her, especially when she discovered the extent of her wealth. However the Valentis were not poor and there was nothing mercenary or self-seeking in Francesca's altruisim. She had seen the potential Connie offered, so to transform her was a challenge.

She took her shopping and to the *couture* houses which flourished even in wartime. She encouraged her to take a pride, not only in what she wore, but how she looked. For instance it was possible to see without her spectacles, except for reading. Connie realised that she had worn them as much to protect herself from the world as anything else. They were a shield.

Francesca taught her what exciting things she could do with her money. How it enhanced life. In no time she had transformed the ugly duckling into a swan.

Connie was still only thirty-three, and if she regretted the wasted years of her former life she made up for it in enjoyment of what she had discovered, and the prospect of the years that lay ahead when she returned to Venice, to the companionship of the Valentis and all the wealthy, talented, cultured and exciting people they had introduced her to.

She passed the open gates leading to Pelham's Oak and drove up the drive conscious only of a tiny qualm. She had not been as indifferent to Carson Woodville as she had pretended in the churchyard. Her heart had actually performed a somersault when she saw him again and mentally she had reverted to being the shy spinster, seeking a way of escape. But none offered itself and when she confronted him at last – the man she once thought had ruined her life – it was to test the woman she had become, and throw aside the naive person that she used to be for ever.

Eliza had always felt a special affection for Connie. She had held her in her arms after her difficult birth, thinking that the child was dead and the mother dying. She had baptised and willed life into her and she always thought that God had answered her prayer, though He had taken her mother to Himself. Eliza was

103

not formally religious. She seldom went to church, but now that she was older she was convinced that mankind was not alone in this cosmos, but governed by some form of superior intelligence or being.

From the day of her birth, and ever after, Eliza felt a deep bond which was reciprocated by Connie, who never failed to keep in touch with her, even during the war.

When Connie had been engaged to Carson Eliza looked forward to having her as an even closer relation, but at the same time she was deeply apprehensive about the wedding, and the reason for it, even though she had connived to bring it about with her brother, to persuade Carson to ask Connie to marry him.

It was an event of which Eliza had not been proud, but now, watching Connie energetically playing croquet on the lawn with the rest of the lunch guests, she felt that what had happened had happened for the best. Connie had indeed developed in a way that no one could possibly have expected. It was almost like knowing two completely different people.

The big lunch party at Pelham's Oak had been a happy occasion. Not only Connie, Eliza and her children, and Dora's friend May, had been there but also Sophie and Hubert Turner, Deborah (the young boys had been left behind with the nursemaid) and Mr Parterre.

Eliza shifted restlessly in her chair, shielding her eyes from the sun. She was the only one to opt out of croquet, preferring to take her ease in a chair on the terrace which overlooked the lawn and the tree that Pelham had planted, now a mighty oak, and beyond that the town of Wenham shimmering in the afternoon haze.

Eliza experienced a sensation of ease at the beauty of the day, the pleasure of the occasion with all the family gathered together, including Connie, all related to one another in some way except for May, Dora's seemingly inseparable companion, and Mr Parterre, now nowhere to be seen.

The game was coming to an exciting conclusion. There was

much running about, punctuated with laughter, as a mallet cracked against the ball which slid through the hoops in the ground. Hubert, overweight and perspiring profusely, partnered with his wife, seemed to be losing, while Connie and Carson, partnered together, were winning.

Eliza noted that Carson was never very far from Connie and kept on glancing at her; but Connie was intent on her game bending eagerly forward, her eyes on the ball as it was chased round the lawn, scarcely looking at him.

Eliza sighed and leaned back in her chair trying to banish a slight, curious feeling of unease. She couldn't understand the reason for it and, besides, wasn't it lovely to have all the family together in the home where she was born and which she had loved all her life?

Then, from the corner of her eye Eliza was aware of a movement up the drive and, by slightly turning her head, she saw a stately car travelling slowly along it.

They had all gawped in fascination at the Pierce-Arrow in which Connie had arrived, a magnificent car she'd bought in Paris and in which she'd driven over to England. Now here was something equally grand, if not grander. In the front was a chauffeur with a peaked cap and in the back two shadowy figures.

Eliza sat up and leaned forward but the car swept round a bend and out of sight in order, presumably, to pull up by the front door.

"Carson," she called.

"Hush, Aunt." He made a gesture of annoyance with his hands. "This is a very tense part of the game."

"You've got some visitors." She gestured towards the drive. "Important ones too, by the look of it. Are you expecting anyone?"

Carson halted the game and looked up. "Visitors? No."

"Well I saw a very grand car."

"Maybe Uncle Julius has come to collect you?" Julius had preferred his greenhouses to the family party at Pelham's Oak.

105

"Of course he hasn't! I'm going back with Dora." Dora had a small Ford of which she was immensely proud.

At that moment Arthur appeared, looking flustered, doing up the collar of his shirt as though he'd been caught having forty winks.

"Sir Carson . . ." he called, a tremor in his voice. "Sir Carson!"

"Pray, Arthur, don't trouble to announce us," a loud, haughty voice interjected behind him. "Give us the pleasure of announcing ourselves."

Everyone on the lawn seemed simultaneously to stop the game, heads raised, some mouths agape as, as if making a stage entrance, Agnes, in a long silk afternoon dress and huge picture hat, half veiled, swept through the French doors on to the verandah followed by a moustached gentleman in a sporty check suit, a colourful bow tie, yellow spats, and clasping a cane in his hand.

Carson rapidly crossed the lawn and ran up the few steps to the terrace.

"Aunt Agnes!" he gasped. "Why didn't you tell us you were coming?"

Agnes appeared at first to ignore him, intent on gazing at the concourse of people on the lawn. "How delightful," she cried, looking around, "to find a family party in progress. Carson, *dear!*" She then turned her attention to him and, in a gesture worthy of the stage, threw her arms round him and planted a robust kiss on his cheeks. "I wanted to surprise you."

She sprang apart from Carson and gestured dramatically towards the man who stood diffidently, apparently ill at ease, a few paces behind her. "And to introduce you to my husband, Sir Owen Wentworth. Owen dear," she said placing an arm proprietorially round his shoulder, "behold, in front of you, most of my family assembled to greet us."

The silence from the onlookers was every bit as tense, as explosive, as if there had been a loud thunderclap.

Chapter Seven

Agnes yawned and looked restlessly about. The air was perfectly still, the silence complete. They were sitting on the terrace after dinner and she was bored. Owen, quietly smoking a cigarette, gazed in front of him, replete, almost asleep. He was not a hard man to please.

But it was very hard to please Agnes, as he had quickly discovered. No sooner in one place than she wanted to be in another. She was a restless, dissatisfied woman yet she mesmerised him, captivated, frightened him. She tied him to her with a bond of terror. Like many men in thrall to powerful women, he perversely enjoyed, nay thrived, on being dominated.

The effect of Agnes's arrival in Wenham had been rather like that of a stone which, thrown into a calm pond, sends ripples spreading out towards its edges. No member of her family had remained unaffected by her arrival, and none seemed the better for seeing her again.

"I think it's time we went back to London, Owen," Agnes said in that flat resolute tone of voice he knew so much and dreaded.

"But dearest we have only just arrived," he timidly reached out to take her hand.

"We have been here a *week*," she said truculently not bothering to stifle a fresh yawn. "I never remember being so bored. Wenham is *such* a boring place."

"But I thought you wanted to spend the summer here, my dear?" That wheedling tremor in his voice.

She pouted disagreeably.

"That *was* the idea, but as soon as I got here I realised my mistake. I'd forgotten what a bore it was living here and what drove me to London in the first place. I *so* miss my friends. Dorothy, Emily, Clara."

"I find it a heavenly spot." Owen sighed and looked up into the night sky. They had dined with Carson and Jean after which, as always, the two men found something to occupy them. The barrage of criticism they each endured during the course of the meal was more than either could bear. It went on night after night, and day after day when she got the opportunity, ever since Agnes's arrival. She picked at the state the house was in, its sheer lack of comfort, the time taken to carry out the repairs, the poor quality of those repairs, the sparsity of servants, the quality of the food. It was very hard for the men to take and Owen, who secretly sympathised with them, thought they bore up well even though at times Carson seemed close to boiling point.

"It *is* a heavenly spot," Agnes agreed, "for a day or two, but I much prefer the city." Suddenly her attitude changed and placing a hand on Owen's arm her tone became kittenish. He was used to these swift, and somewhat disconcerting, changes of mood when she wanted anything which she thought might be hard to get. Over the months since he'd known her, and particularly since he'd been married to her, he had come to dread them almost as much as her rages and unprovoked personal attacks.

"Owen, dearest, Carson talks again about selling the London house. Why don't we buy it?"

"*Buy* it?" Owen stammered.

"Then we needn't ever come back here again except for a brief visit. That will also give us some security, dear. We can't go from hand to mouth living in hotels."

"No, we certainly can't."

"Well, what do you think?"

"I think it's very pleasant here." Owen nervously cleared his throat. "It's a lovely spot, it's a beautiful house . . ."

"A beautiful house!" Agnes exclaimed. "It's falling apart, and you call it beautiful?"

"Yes I do. It's a lovely place. Besides, the countryside is so delightful, and I think . . ." He shifted in his chair and nervously cleared his throat again. "I think we could be very happy here, Agnes, surrounded by your family and friends."

"Oh you think that, do you?" The kittenish tone had been replaced by one of sarcasm. "Did you notice how swiftly my 'beloved' family cleared off as soon as we arrived? They stayed long enough to gawp at you and satisfy their curiosity; then off they went, never to be seen or heard of again. Eliza I could never stand! Sophie is a prig. The children I hardly know, and don't much care for what I see. Dora is so mannish and as for that woman who hangs about her . . . if you ask me it's an unnatural relationship."

"Agnes!"

"It is my dear, don't pretend you don't know what I mean."

"I know what you mean, but I can't agree. I thought Dora charming. I mean you don't *know*."

"I do know," Agnes nodded her head emphatically. "I am wise enough to the ways of the world to know a Sapphist when I see one. As for that little mouse, Connie . . ."

"I thought her charming too, and not in the least a 'little mouse'."

Agnes gave him a forbidding look. "Please don't argue with me, Owen. I know what I'm talking about. You don't know Connie as I do; after all she is related to me. We had the same father but, thank God, that is the only thing we have in common. I'll grant you she has *slightly* improved," Agnes added grudgingly. "She's done something about her looks, discarded those awful spectacles, tidied up her hair. She used to look dreadful, frumpish. Appearances might have changed, but once a mouse always a mouse. She nearly married Carson. *What* a misalliance that would have been!"

"Why did she not marry Carson?" Owen asked, puzzled.

"I think it was because I came along," Agnes gave a chortle. "They were after her money to restore Pelham's Oak – she's a very wealthy girl, and even wealthier now that her dreadful old spinster of a guardian has died; she left her everything."

Owen felt a cold shiver trickle down his spine.

"And . . ." he began and stopped.

"And what?" She looked enquiringly at him.

"Why should that have affected their marriage?"

"Because they thought *I* had a lot of money. That *I* was the one who was going to restore Pelham's Oak. I tell you I had far better things to do with my money than waste it on this old heap."

So, still he didn't know the position of her finances. Had he been taken in by appearances – the title, the London town house, the mansion in the country? The jewels, the clothes, the ostentatatious atmosphere of wealth?

The object of his anxieties fast asleep beside him, Owen tossed and turned, wrestling with his doubts and uncertainties about the woman he had married so hastily in Rome in the spring. He had emptied his own pockets, blown the lot, to lull her into a sense of security about his own situation in the hope that there would ultimately be rich rewards. He was virtually penniless, and there had been the bait of the London house with its beautiful, expensive furnishings and artefacts, and now this veritable palace in the country to help him regain the vestiges of his solvency with the help of his few meagre investments.

And now she suggested buying the London house! That 'we' buy it. All Owen Wentworth wanted to do was settle down somewhere and, for the foreseeable future, live in the greatest comfort while spending as little money of his own as he could. Of course he had never thought through the consequences of marrying Agnes, a formidable woman with a fierce and, occasionally, uncontrollable temper, at times insatiable demands. He had been swept along on the magic of her personality, her charm and, most important of all, what he took to be her wealth. Here was the woman of fortune, the rich widow he had been looking for.

Gradually, little by little, he was beginning to realise that all was not what it had at first seemed, appearances had been deceptive. Guy Woodville, though the thirteenth baronet, had been a veritable pauper, the ancestral home was in a state of terminal disrepair and required thousands of pounds being spent on it. Why had Agnes's money not been forthcoming if she, in turn, really had been the widow of an American railroad millionaire?

He had noticed she was close, but in his experience rich people invariably were tight-fisted. Besides, a woman liked to be pampered, fêted, bought flowers and jewels, lodged in the best hotels. In exchange she gave certain favours and in this regard Agnes had not failed him. Her plump, perfumed body was eminently desirable and during her lifetime's experience she had learned the art of pleasing a man, even at the expense of her own enjoyment.

But there was a lot about Agnes he did not know. She seemed to tell him the essentials and keep the rest to herself. He knew she was born in Wenham, had hated the place, had gone to America and married Wendell Gregg, a multimillionaire some years her senior who had died and left her his fortune.

With this she had returned to Wenham to meet up again with Sir Guy, also now a widower, and there had been a happy but comparatively brief marriage, only six years.

He knew she didn't like her stepson; indeed the undercurrent of mutual hostility between them was palpable, but things like this happened in the best regulated families. She thought her own family provincial and they were; but they were also charming, at least Owen thought so. He had considered Eliza delightful, a person for whom Agnes reserved most of her rancour. He had thought all the young people quite charming. He would have been utterly happy to have stayed in this delightful, if dilapidated, place pottering about, not doing very much, certainly not spending very much, in the company of his Agnes, feared but adored, for the rest of his life.

Agnes turned and moaned in her sleep as if she were having a bad dream. In the light of the moon that shone through the window Owen looked at her in concern.

Maybe she was and, maybe, for them both the bad dream would be the reckoning that at the moment they were only postponing. Somehow now over him he felt there loomed a dark shadow.

Carson had begun to experience a sensation of happiness that had been absent from his life for some time, until the sudden and unexpected return of Agnes complete with new husband. His father's debts had been cleared through the generosity of Uncle Julius; the repairs to Pelham's Oak were in hand due to the timely arrival of his old comrade Jean Parterre, also unexpected but, in this case, delightful.

And finally another arrival had awakened, deep inside him, emotions that he thought had gone ever since his rejection by Emma. This was also unexpected, to have ideas of romance reawoken by a woman towards whom he had once behaved shamefully: Connie Yetman.

Seeing her in the churchyard, moving about so gracefully, like the woman of one's dreams, was a little like falling in love all over again.

And now she was leaving without giving him the chance to explore new opportunities. He re-read with horror the letter which had just been delivered in the morning post.

'Dear Carson,

This is to thank you for a most delightful lunch the other day. Forgive me for not writing to thank you sooner, but I had to go to Bath and then on to London on a matter of business. I now find that I have to return to Italy sooner than expected, so I am writing to say 'farewell', at least for the time being.

How are you faring with dear Agnes? (Rather you
than me!)
With sincere good wishes,
Yours affectionately,
Constance Yetman.'

Carson looked at the clock, jumped up and hurried from the
breakfast room leaving the rest of his post unopened. On the
way he passed Jean Parterre who was briefing workmen on
the morning's operations. Jean put out a hand as if to waylay
Carson, but he was brushed aside.

"Not now, Jean. I have an urgent errand. I'll see you when
I get back."

He then entered the stables, saddled his horse and set off at
a gallop over the fields towards Wenham.

Connie thought that in many ways she would be sorry to say
a final 'goodbye' to the place of her birth, the little town of
Wenham. She had been born just a short distance away in
a house practically opposite the Rectory, that had belonged
to her mother. Euphemia Monk had been the only child of
wealthy parents too, so that by the time Miss Fairchild died,
and another fortune thus fell to her, Connie was a very wealthy
young woman indeed, and could live the rest of her life doing
pretty much as she pleased but without a care in the world.

It was true that Connie had a call to go back to Venice. The
rest of the palazzo in which she had her apartment was on the
market and Guido Valenti, her lawyer, was suggesting that she
might purchase it and restore the palazzo to its former glory as
one of the great houses of Venice.

It would be an exciting and challenging thing to do. She could
become one of the city's celebrated hostesses with a salon for the
arts and music, entertaining writers, artists, politicians, anyone
she chose.

It was a very exciting prospect, and yet . . .

She looked out of the window across the fields leading down to the river where she had wandered as a child, seldom playing with other children because she was so solitary and shy that she found making friends difficult. Her young contemporaries avoided her because they thought she wasn't much fun, and indeed she wasn't. A plain, bookish, withdrawn child who, by her birth, had been responsible for her mother's death, and was orphaned early on, was indeed burdened with disadvantages when it came to spending time with healthy, carefree youngsters, many of whom came from large, jolly farming families. They thought she was a freak.

This sense of freakishness was enhanced when she first became engaged to Carson Woodville, an act that seemed unreal in itself, and then was subsequently jilted within weeks of the banns being called.

It was something that, at the time, she thought she would never get over, and yet she had. She had found a new life, *made* a new life for herself. Why then this reluctance to sever all her links with Wenham, to sell Miss Fairchild's house, in exchange for the glamour and excitement of Venice?

The answer at that moment appeared at the gate of the house astride a fine horse. The words of the lovely poem by Scott sprang to her mind: '*Young Lochinvar has come out of the west . . . and save his good broadsword he weapons had none, he rode all unarmed and he rode all alone . . .*'

Carson, astride his horse, was a splendid sight and once again, as it had done many years before, as it had done when she saw him so recently in the churchyard, her heart turned over with joy.

Carson was looking anxiously at the house and then, when she opened the door, his expression turned instantly to one of relief. He vaulted off the horse and tethered him to the railings of the house.

Connie, slightly bemused, hands on her hips, stood on the steps looking at him.

"Do you mind if I come in?" he called from the gate.

"Of course not," she replied stepping back.

"I wasn't sure if you were still here," he said, panting as he came up the steps. "I just got your letter."

Connie didn't know how to reply, so said nothing as she led the way indoors to the drawing room which was full of half packed cases and tea chests.

"When are you off?" Carson surveyed the scene with dismay. It all looked so final.

"Tomorrow," Connie replied. "I'm getting the Pullman from Victoria."

"And will you be back?"

"I'm not sure."

"Have you sold the house?"

"Not yet. I've had several people to see it, but that's no problem. The agent will handle it for me. I . . . I may never return to Wenham, Carson. I have the chance to buy the whole of the property where I now live. If I do that I will definitely spend the rest of my life in Venice."

Carson looked at her and wondered how he could ever have considered her plain. Despite her fashionably bobbed hair, her lightly applied powder and lipstick, her appearance was slightly dishevelled. She wore a silk blouse tucked into slacks, a sight in a woman he was still unused to. Few women, if any, in Wenham would dream of wearing trousers, but the war had changed everything. The previous year the suffrage had been given to women over thirty. The Liberal Party leader, Asquith, had just called for the opening of all professions and trades to women on the same terms as men. Connie's appearance was in line with the idea of the New Woman and, on the whole, Carson felt he approved. His had always been a family of strong women – his grandmother Henrietta, his mother Margaret and his aunt Eliza. They held no fears for him. As for Connie, she looked so adorable that it seemed incredible he could possibly not have loved her.

"I wish you wouldn't go!" he burst out. "You've hardly arrived, and now you're going again."

Connie stared at him, perplexed.

"But, Carson, I was *never* going to stay here for long," she said gently. "I left Wenham and I am never coming back, for good anyway."

"All because of me . . ." He flung himself dejectedly into the one chair that wasn't full of clutter needing to be packed.

"We've said it was a very long time ago. Anyway I like my life now, I'm very happy. It's so," she looked around as if searching for the right words, "so very, *very* different. You can't know how different it is."

"Yes I can. Don't forget I have been away for nearly five years too."

"Yet you have a home, roots."

"You have a home too. This is a very nice house. You have family here, friends, bonds."

"I hope you don't call Agnes family," Connie said with a note of amusement in her voice.

"No, I don't mean Agnes. Hopefully she won't be staying long. But Eliza, whom you always loved . . ."

"Do love still," Connie insisted.

"Sophie, your Yetman cousins. And me," Carson finished lamely. "I'm very fond of you Connie."

Connie perched on the arm of the chair opposite him, arms folded. Her expression was grave, thoughtful, composed. When she raised her eyes, she looked directly at him.

"You rejected me once," she said. "It was very hurtful."

"I know. But now it's not the same. *You're* not the same."

"It is the same. I am the same person only a little older. I've got the same feelings and the same fear of being rejected again."

Carson rose and went over to the window which overlooked the pretty garden at the back of the house on which Miss Fairchild had lavished such love and care. Now in high summer it was at its best. He turned to look at Connie, who was watching him carefully.

"I'm not quite sure how to say this, but put it this way. *I'm* not the same person. The war has taught me a great deal, changed

116

me forever. I think – I hope – it's made me a better person. I was selfish, superficial. I was also very unhappy without realising it. I was never clever or successful like my brother George. I also knew my mother loved him better than me, and my father adored Emily. I was the odd one out. I wanted my mother to love me and I think that, of course, she did, though not as much as George. But instead of pleasing her I hurt her, and then before I could make it up she died. I never really got over my guilt about not being a better son while my mother was alive."

"It's true that a blunder was made about our marriage in which both of us were really stooges to the wishes of my father and your guardian. You would not have wanted to be married to a man who didn't want to marry you . . ."

"Of course not!"

"Well," his expression was abject, "for me that's all changed. It's a different situation, a different set of circumstances. I can't ask you to marry me at this moment because I don't want to make the same mistake again. I want to be sure; but I do feel very strongly about you and I would like you to stay."

A wave of indignation welled up inside Connie and she said witheringly, "On approval."

"I beg your pardon?"

"Goods on approval."

"Not at all."

"Then *what*, Carson?" Her voice throbbed with anger. "You don't take account of *my* feelings in all this. I mean am I meant to hang around while you consider the situation? And then, if you decide in my favour, do I gratefully accept?"

"Not at all." Carson felt flustered. He realised he'd made yet another error. He flung out a hand towards her. "Look Connie. I'm a country bumpkin, an uneducated man. I've put it badly. I'm sorry. I want you to know I do feel—"

"And I want *you* to know that I have feelings too, Carson Woodville. They are feelings that are not to be trifled with. Put bluntly – and in case you think I am likely even to *consider*

117

hanging around waiting for you – there is someone in Venice to whom I am deeply attached. It is likely that when I return we'll get engaged."

Then she paused and gave him a smile of disarming sweetness.

"I hope that will enable you to make up your mind once and for all."

She then walked to the door and held it open, firmly indicating the way out.

"Now, Carson, if you would be so kind I have a lot of packing to do." She held out her hand and gave him a detached, impersonal smile that was more chilling than anything she'd said. He could see very clearly now that, contrary to his hopes, in Connie all love had died and there was no hope for him.

He took her hand, held it briefly to his lips and then stumbled down the steps towards his horse.

As he rode away he didn't look back.

Part II

The Prodigal Daughter

Chapter Eight

Agnes fretted out the summer in Wenham, unsettled, getting in everyone's way, wanting to be somewhere else.

As for Carson, having lost Connie his world became a dark place and he blamed much of it, somewhat unjustifiably, on Agnes. Now that Connie had gone he knew that he wanted her. Desperately. He knew that he was in love with her and that no one else would do. He toyed with the idea of going to Venice after her, but he too had his pride and, besides, his experience with women, which was extensive, told him that was not the way to capture anyone's heart. Best to lose someone for ever than have her despise you.

The family helped out as much as they could. Lally had Agnes and Owen for a meal several times, Eliza and Sophie were both generous with their hospitality. They all had to put up with Agnes's complaints, criticism and general dissatisfaction which she voiced freely among members of her clan as if it didn't matter what they thought of her.

Owen was quite liked but not much admired, pitied for being a stooge of Agnes, a butt for her unkind, remorseless jokes at his expense.

It was true that he cut an odd figure as a countryman with his waxed moustache, his shiny shoes encased in grey spats, his natty suits and soft, wavy, brimmed trilbys worn outdoors or at a rakish angle in the car. One of his accomplishments, doubtless perfected if not learned in India, was horseriding, and he often accompanied Carson on a morning ride well before Agnes was up, faultlessly attired in

121

highly polished riding boots, fawn jodhpurs and brown hacking jacket.

But the thing Owen knew most about was tea and, when Agnes let him get a word in edgeways, he talked about it with all the authority of his years as a tea planter, commented on every cup he drank as if he was tasting fine wine, and bored everyone to death.

But Owen's favourite pastime was to occupy a comfortable chair on the terrace, preferably alone and away from his wife, reading the morning paper with a cigar in his mouth and a glass of whisky by his side.

He was a very idle and, indeed, deeply boring man, with apparently few original views of any kind and a desperate desire to please. Carson, who got to know him better on the morning rides, still found him slightly effeminate, with his emphasis on "correct" attire, even if it was clearly out of place in the country. He couldn't understand how it was that such a man had captured the affections of his mercurial and demanding aunt who never passed an opportunity to demean or snub him, unless it was that, with advancing age, she was afraid of being lonely.

So the summer passed. It was not one enjoyed by Carson, irritated to death by his aunt and wracked with misery about thoughts of the women who had spurned him: Emma and Connie. But Emma seemed firmly rooted in the past now and was comparatively easy to forget. He had known that that love was dead. About Connie he was more optimistic. Eliza had given him some hope. Apparently she was not engaged to be married and in her frequent letters she always asked after him. However for a man who had always enjoyed success with women it was mortifying to be rejected by two in a very short time.

In days gone by Carson would have laughed it off and jumped into bed with the next casual woman who crossed his path, but not now. Real love had made him more selective, taught him the importance of an enduring relationship and shown him, yet again, that the war had changed everything; he was not the man he used to be.

Progress on Pelham's Oak remained slow. The problem was paying for the materials needed for repairs. Jean Parterre worked well and thoroughly and proved an amiable companion, a foil to Agnes, her frequently expressed boredom and her moods.

Yet sometimes Carson had the feeling that life couldn't continue for long in this unsatisfactory way. Things were bound to come to a head and, one afternoon, towards the beginning of September, he was proved all too prophetically right.

Carson had been down to one of the farms with Ivor Wendor to try and settle a boundary dispute with the neighbouring tenant. The mission had been successful and he felt pleased with his afternoon's work. Matters such as this justified his position as landlord, custodian of a centuries old tradition of service both to the land and the community. It made him feel magisterial, authoritative, mature.

It had been agreed to divide the disputed land so that one tenant got one half, the other tenant the other. It was not as difficult a judgment as that of Solomon, in fact it had appeared quite simple and obvious but, nevertheless, it was a grievance that had been simmering for years between two stubborn men who several times had come to blows.

Thus it was with a feeling of satisfaction, a job well done, a day well spent that Carson stabled his horse, bade goodbye to the bailiff who lived in a cottage on the estate and made his way back to the house.

The days were drawing in, the sun was setting. Autumn. He paused on the porch of the great house and looked over the earth, the quiet earth, he loved so much. The fields of cut hay stretched away into the distance, fodder for the stock in the cold coming winter months. Some trees were beginning to shed their leaves, the squirrels were busy gathering nuts for the long months ahead when the land was hard and barren. The cattle were still in the fields, but soon they would be brought in for the winter. In a few months snow, frost and ice would cover the landscape starkly outlining the skeletal trees against the horizon.

Carson loved the seasons. At times of utter peace, such as this, his mind involuntarily returned to the noise and carnage of war; the chaos, disorder and death that made it seem as though mankind suffered from some sort of collective madness. Then visions would come of men squirming in the mud in their death throes, sometimes their pitiable animals beside them. Carson shut his eyes to the images flitting across his mind. He knew they would never go away, never cease altogether, either as nightmares or as horrible interludes to torment him during the day. It was the price he had to pay for being a survivor, for living to see this day, this sunset and, hopefully, the morrow; to greet the dawn that so many hundreds of thousands of his comrades would never see.

Carson opened his eyes, jerked rudely back to life by loud voices coming from indoors, his aunt Agnes's the most predominant. He quickly ran up the steps and entered the hall to be confronted by a bizarre sight. Aunt Agnes on one side and Arthur and one of the maids, Maudie, on the other, the latter in tears. Aunt Agnes was stabbing the air in a frenzy and Maudie's sobs grew louder while Arthur's low voice occasionally intervened in an effort to make peace or, at least, reduce the temperature.

"And I absolutely *demand* that this girl is dismissed," Agnes pointed to the weeping maidservant, "but not before she has restored all my missing jewellery. I shall decide with Sir Carson whether to press charges or not."

"Oi bain't taken nothin' ma' am," Maudie sobbed, screwing up her white apron in her hands. "Oi bain't never seen your jewels, save what you wuz wearing ma'am. Oi swear . . ."

Agnes raised her arm and looked as though she was about to administer a blow across the face of the unfortunate girl when Carson ran across the vast hall and seized her arm in mid-air.

"Please, Aunt," he thundered, "whatever do you think you're doing? Striking a servant?"

The expression on Agnes's face matched his. Momentarily she struggled with him, finally capitulating and letting her arm fall.

"I have been listening to such a torrent of lies that I have lost all patience with this girl, and Arthur is not helping by defending her."

"All I am trying to say, Sir Carson," Arthur was visibly distressed, "is that Lady Wentworth has not a shadow of proof that Maudie has taken any of her jewellery. She says that certain items are missing."

"Do you doubt my word?" Agnes demanded rubbing the wrist that had been seized in Carson's strong grasp. "If *I* say something is missing you can be sure something *is* missing, and I am not making it up."

"I'm not doubting your ladyship's word," the tone of Arthur's voice seemed to indicate that that was just what he was doing, "I am just saying that there is no proof that, if the items are in fact missing and her ladyship has not mislaid them, that Maudie is responsible."

"Maudie is my personal maid." Agnes's voice began to rise again. "She knows where my jewellery is kept."

"Then don't you think it unlikely, Aunt, that she would steal it?" Carson interposed gently. "The finger of suspicion would inevitably be pointed to her. Maudie is a bright, intelligent girl," he paused to bestow on her a benevolent, kindly smile, "and I am sure she would be the first to realise that. Also I know her family well. They have worked for us for years. Her father is one of our tenant farmers. They're honourable and truthful people. Did you look in Maudie's room?" he enquired thinking that, once more, the role of judge was falling on him and, once more, relishing it.

"That thought occurred to me, sir," Arthur answered woodenly, "but I thought that your permission would be needed, that is if Maudie had no objection."

"Oi would be *glad* if you would look in my room, sir," Maudie put her apron to her face to dry her eyes. "Oi have no objection at all."

125

"Then let's do that straight away."

"There's no proof that if my jewels are not there Maudie hasn't stolen them," Agnes objected. "She could have spirited them away to her family."

At this fresh imputation of dishonesty Maudie began to bawl again, but Arthur put a hand on her shoulder and gently shook her.

"Now now, Maudie, Sir Carson has this matter in hand and he is a just man."

And with that they all trooped solemnly up to Maudie's room high in the attic where a thorough search was undertaken by Arthur while Carson, Agnes and the accused maidservant looked on. Nothing was found which gave Maudie fresh opportunity to recommence her hysterics and demand to be taken home so that she could tell her father and mother what had occurred. Carson persuaded her not to. In order to try and take the heat out of the situation he asked Agnes to apologise which, of course, she declined to do.

Maudie and Arthur returned to the servants' hall and Agnes and Carson retired to the drawing room where Carson immediately went over to a side table to pour himself a drink.

"Would you like one?" he asked Agnes who, still very angry, nodded.

"A *very* large whisky, please, Carson. I never remember feeling so angry and humiliated in my life. Fancy you, my stepson, taking the side of a serving maid, believing her word against mine. I can't think what your father would have said."

"It was only justice Aunt," Carson replied handing her her glass. "You really had no proof, and what exactly is missing?"

"A beautiful diamond brooch that Guy inherited from his mother, plus some rings and a valuable string of pearls."

"And you are sure you had them here with you?"

"Of course I'm sure, you impertinent young man!"

"I don't think I'm being impertinent, Aunt. Stealing is a very serious accusation and I just wanted to be sure they were not left in London or at your bank."

126

"*All* my jewellery is here with me," she said firmly.

"Then you had better give it to me for safe keeping."

"Indeed I shan't. I have secreted it in a place that now only Owen and I know of."

"And where is Owen?" Carson looked up.

"Owen is so upset by this commotion, so embarrassed, that he has stayed in our room. Of course it reflects so badly on the house when the servants steal . . ."

"Really Aunt I will *not* have this." Carson sat down and thumped the arm of his chair with clenched fist.

"Then who did take my jewels?" Agnes, her features rigid, her colour high, stared imperiously at him. "They don't just fly off in the air by themselves, you know."

"If they were taken I have no idea; but anyone in this house could be responsible. *I* could be responsible, being in need of money, which is well known. Or the alternative is that it may be someone from outside, a professional thief who gained access while we were out, or eating. It is a large house and with the workmen we employ frankly, Aunt, it could have been anyone. I am very sorry it has happened here, but if it has . . ." he paused and examined his fingernails. "Doubtless it was insured?"

"Insured in pre-war years for far less than it is worth. Then I have to prove that it is stolen and not simply lost or mislaid during my long sojourn on the continent. Indeed," looking visibly distressed, Agnes produced a handkerchief and vigorously blew her nose as though to ward off tears, "I am not even sure that the premiums are up to date. There has been so much on my mind. In fact I may not receive a penny for my loss."

With a heartfelt sigh Agnes drained the contents of her glass which she held out to Carson.

"Fill me up please, Carson."

"Certainly, Aunt."

He rose, replenished both their glasses and, giving Agnes hers, returned to his chair.

"There's another thing Carson," Agnes rather agitatedly sipped at her drink, pausing occasionally, "I think it is time we returned to London. Owen enjoys the country well enough but I am extremely bored. This business about my missing jewellery is the last straw."

Carson's heart gave a bound and a smile spread over his face.

"That sounds like a *very* good idea, Aunt Agnes."

"This place is appalling," she continued gesturing round as though she had not heard him. "Appalling. It is falling to pieces, despite the efforts of Mr Parterre, and very uncomfortable. The housemaids are slovenly and there is dust everywhere. In fact all of the servants are lazy, rude and for the most part ignorant. The—"

"When will you be going Aunt?" Carson asked, an edge to his voice. "And, above all, where? Have you made arrangements to stay somewhere in London?"

Agnes stared at him in astonishment.

"What do you mean? We shall be going to Chesterfield Street, of course."

"Ah!" Carson rose slowly and stood with his back to the fireplace. "I had intended to tell you, but somehow forgot. My financial position is such that I have been forced to put the house on the market, Aunt, and I would much prefer that you did not live there. Certain repairs have to be carried out in order to fetch a good price. I—"

"How *dare* you," Agnes snapped, rising and putting her empty glass on the table with a resounding thud that almost cracked it. "How *dare* you?"

"I dare." Carson lifted his chin defiantly in the air. "It is not your house. It is mine, and now that you have a new husband I do not feel I have any responsibility for housing you. I have tolerated you here with your outbursts, your rudeness and general unpleasantness because you were my late, esteemed Uncle Ryder's sister and my father's widow; but now, thank God, care for you has passed to somebody else. So now I think I have discharged my responsibilities, and generously. In fact, Aunt Agnes, I am so heartily sick of you that, family or not, my father's widow or not, I would be extremely grateful if I never set eyes on you again, because you are nothing to me but trouble."

Owen was lying on the bed in the room he shared with Agnes, his eyes closed. But he was not oblivious to the row going on downstairs, or the reason for it. He wished his ears could block out the sound, as closing his eyes blocked out the light. But it was not so easy. Simply sticking his fingers in them made no difference.

Then the noise stopped abruptly, only to begin again a few seconds later when he heard the reasonable tones of Carson intervening.

Thank heaven for Carson, a man of good sense if ever there was one. Carson would calm Agnes down, at least for a time. If only Agnes could be silenced for ever. Or if, somehow, one could get away?

Owen was aware that he was clenching and unclenching his hands, a man in the grip of extreme fear and nervous tension.

Then there was silence for a very long time and, thinking the warring parties had dispersed, he felt himself gradually drifting off to sleep when suddenly the door flew open and all hell broke loose again.

"Owen Owen wake up!" Agnes screamed going over to the bed and staring down at him with the expression of a demented fury. "And what the *hell* do you think you're doing *sleeping* when my very honour is at stake, my truthfulness and integrity being called into question?"

"What . . . uh?" Owen raised himself on one elbow and stared at her. He had never seen her looking so ugly, her features so grotesque and distorted by anger. Suddenly she looked like an old woman. An old, cantankerous bitch, he thought wearily closing his eyes again.

"Owen, do you hear me? Wake up," she bawled once more and Owen felt a blow on the side of his head, so forceful that it almost knocked him out. His hand flew to his head and he staggered into an upright position once more.

"Get up, you lazy bastard," she cried. "What use to me are you, lying down when I need your support?" She raised her hand again to administer a fresh blow, but he forestalled her by rolling off the bed and, lying on the floor, attempted to cover his head with both hands. He dared not open his eyes but lay there while his heart hammered painfully in his chest.

"Owen get up," Agnes urged, but now in a more kindly tone. He was aware of her fragrance very near to him and, opening one eye, he saw her squatting beside him gazing at him with an expression of concern. Another of her lightning, disconcerting changes of mood.

"Owen I'm sorry, I lost control." She reached out a hand, gently massaging his head. "Dearest Owen, do forgive me but you have no idea what I've been through in the past hour." She put both hands to her own head. "My poor nerves are in shreds. That wretched Carson actually doubted my word that my jewellery had been stolen. Thought I'd imagined it or misplaced it." She gave a shrill laugh and stood up as if she'd already forgotten her wounded victim. "Can you imagine misplacing thousands of pounds worth of jewels? Believing the words of servants over mine! The trouble is that Carson is a peasant. He has inherited the blood of his Dutch mother – after all, her family were in trade – and not the aristocratic Woodvilles. But, that is not all." She sat down heavily in an armchair and, as Owen slowly, reluctantly heaved himself up from the floor, she took out her handkerchief and dabbed delicately at a few moist patches on her face: above her lip, her temples. "We have been given notice to quit."

"Notice to *quit*?" Owen staggered over to the dressing table mirror and examined his head, tenderly touching the place where he'd been struck.

"We have been told to leave here. Well, to be quite accurate I told Carson we would *prefer* to return to London in the circumstances that it appears this house is full of thieves. Do

130

you know what he said?" She turned her head and found her spouse still gazing anxiously at himself in the mirror. "Owen are you listening to me?" Her tone sharpened again.

"Yes dear, of course." Guiltily Owen dropped his hand.

"He said he was selling the London house and would not allow me to live there. He said," she paused and swallowed hard, "he said that I was no longer his responsibility and he had no duty to house me. Now, did you ever hear of anything like that?"

"No dear." A fresh feeling of nausea assailed Owen and he sank on to the bed again.

"In other words we are cast adrift, without a place to lay our heads."

"Well, my dear Agnes, it's not as bad as that." Now Owen produced his handkerchief and began to mop his own brow.

"Of course it isn't. Now Owen," she looked meaningfully across at him. "*I* have suggested before that we buy the house. It has been decorated and furnished by me to a very high standard, as you know. It is a lovely house full of beautiful things. So I suggest that we make Carson an offer for it. He says he never wants to see me again and, frankly, I have little desire to see him. In fact I would not even consider buying his property if I did not regard it as, in some ways, my own. We need not offer Carson too much money. He is clearly in need of all he can get. In fact the notion passed through my mind that *he* may be the thief."

"Carson?" Owen looked shocked.

"Why not? We know he has no morals, no scruples. I wouldn't put it past him, knowing quite well that the young maid would be accused."

"But you said he defended the girl . . ."

"Oh, my dear, don't be so naive. Besides, he's short of money and a cache of valuable jewels is a temptation to anyone. I should have thought of it before." Agnes rose impatiently and began to pace back and forth across the room until she stopped, abruptly, in front of her spouse and subjected him to

131

a thorough scrutiny that induced in him nervous palpitations all over again.

"Owen, we have never discussed finances have we?"

"Not really, Agnes."

"Then I think it's time we both came clean. I mean *I* think it's time I knew how you were situated, what your financial circumstances are."

"Well . . . I spent a lot of money on the Continent, Agnes . . ."

"Yes, yes," impatiently she brushed his remark aside with a wave of her hand, "but that was a mere pittance, I expect, to what you've got tucked away?"

"Quite." Owen raised his handkerchief to his brow again.

"I mean you have considerable assets, have you not, Owen? Stocks, shares, money in the bank?"

"Of course, Agnes, no need to worry about that."

"Good, that is what I had supposed." She gave a smile of satisfaction. "You see, my dear, my own affairs are not in such a healthy state. Except for my jewellery Sir Guy did not leave me well off . . ."

"But Mr Gregg . . ." Owen began to stumble. "D-d-dd-didn't he . . . ?"

"Well, of course, most of my fortune, and it was considerable, was dissipated on Sir Guy, on the London house. And then came the war . . ." she sighed deeply. "It made great inroads into my capital. Vast sums were simply wiped out."

"I see." Owen grew reflective. "Then you have no money at all, Agnes?"

"Not really." She smiled bravely. "But it doesn't matter at all, does it dearest, if you have enough for both of us?"

Owen became thoughtful again then, once more, he rallied, took a grip on himself, came to some decision and raised himself from the bed.

"Of course it doesn't matter, my dear."

Agnes's smile was triumphant. "Well then in that case there is no reason why we can't make Carson an offer for the London house?"

"None at all, if that's what you wish, my dear."

"It is what I wish," she said smiling, and, obviously relieved, holding out her hand, drew him to her and pulled his head towards her to kiss. Then she held him away and stared steadfastly into his eyes. "Let's do it this very day."

"You do it my dear," he said. "You know Carson better."

"Very well, if you wish," Agnes nodded, her mind made up. "I shall do it this very day."

Agnes felt an enormous weight lift from her mind now that she and Owen had had a chat about finances. For someone who spent money like water as he had on the Continent and beyond, buying her furs, jewellery, it was obvious that he was a man of substance, a man of means, as she had always suspected. She supposed that a woman like her, used to business, should have examined him on this subject before they were married. But the state of her own finances being so precarious left her open to the charge of being a gold digger were he to suppose that she was marrying him for his money.

After this talk her whole attitude to life underwent a dramatic change, becoming sunnier now that she knew her future was secure. There had been things about Owen that worried her, and there still were. He was lazy, he was not overimbued with intelligence, and she sensed that her family despised him, probably wondered why she'd married him.

However the main thing was that he *was* rich, possessed of sufficient funds to keep her in the style to which she had become accustomed at no matter whose expense.

At dinner she decided to be especially nice to Carson, as if forgetting the conversation they'd had only hours before. Not a cross word passed her lips. In fact so pleasant and relaxed was the atmosphere that she decided to save the important negotiations for the morrow, and she left the men to their cigars, port and game of snooker while she went upstairs to read.

That night in bed she again made Owen grateful that he had married such a sexually deft and experienced woman.

*   *   *

133

The following day after breakfast, which she always had in bed, Agnes sought an interview with Carson to be told that he had gone to Dorchester and would not be back until late afternoon.

She decided to call on Lally Martyn, a person who was not related to the Woodvilles or the Heerings, other than by marriage, and whom she had always rather liked. Though Lally didn't know it, they shared a lot in common in the past.

She popped her head round the door of the drawing room to see if Owen wished to accompany her but he was, as usual, immersed in the paper and smoking his customary cigar. She patted him on the head, planted a kiss on his cheek and told him she would be out for lunch, that Carson would be back late in the afternoon, and she had asked for an interview with him.

He put his arm round her waist, drew her down, kissing her fondly. Then he lowered his hand and gave her soft, rounded buttock a squeeze, remembering the pleasures of the night before.

Still in good humour she tapped him playfully on the wrist, kissed him on the cheek again and told him to behave himself. With a broad wink she left the room and walked round to the front of the house where her chauffeur was standing by the car.

Lally, liking Agnes more than the rest of the family did, greeted her with affection and asked after Owen.

"I wanted him to accompany me, but he's so *lazy*," Agnes complained. "I left him smoking and reading the paper and, doubtless, after my back was turned he'll help himself to a large whisky. But," she put a hand on Lally's arm and gazed excitedly at her, "I have got wonderful news."

"Oh, do tell." Lally led her into the drawing room where a sherry decanter and two glasses stood awaiting them on the table, together with a plate of dry biscuits. The French windows leading into the garden were open and from the orchard beyond came the gentle sound of cooing pigeons. Lally poured them each a sherry, asked after Carson, Mr Parterre and the rest of the family and then sat opposite her guest, looking at her with an air of anticipation.

"And now do tell me your news."

"We are to buy the London house!"

"The London house?" Lally, in the act of raising her glass to her lips, appeared not to understand.

"Chesterfield Street. The Woodville house. Owen wants to give it to me as a present so that we have our own establishment."

"Oh that *is* marvellous news." Lally raised her glass triumphantly towards Agnes.

"You know it has been a wonderful year since I met Owen. For all his faults he is generous and kind. We toured the continent and stayed at all the best hotels, ate in the finest restaurants. But one gets *so* weary of travel and longs for a place of one's own." Agnes leaned confidentially towards her friend and spoke in a lowered voice as if afraid someone would hear. "It is no secret, my dear Lally, that Carson and I do not see eye to eye. It was a mistake to spend so much time at Pelham's Oak, but Owen is so happy there and one must give in in small ways don't you agree?"

"Oh I do," Lally answered, sighing.

"Anyway the upshot is that Owen *insists* we have our own home, and tonight I am going to talk to Carson about it."

Lally rose and crossing the room stooped to embrace Agnes.

"I'm so happy for you, my dear. What a treasure Owen is. Now finish your sherry and let's go into lunch. It's just the two of us. Alexander is at school."

"He will soon be off to boarding school," Agnes said as they walked together arm in arm towards the dining room.

"I dread it, but hopefully it will be one of the good schools in Dorset – Sherborne is a possibility – where my dearest darling won't be too far from home." Taking her seat at table Lally looked across at Agnes with an expression of sadness. "You have no idea how *precious* he is to me. Now with darling Roger no more, and Prosper always up in London I feel Alexander is all I have. You are singularly fortunate in your marriage dear Agnes. Believe me."

"Don't I know it," Agnes said. "Don't I bless the day Owen and I met?"

When Agnes got back to Pelham's Oak later in the afternoon after an agreeable visit to Lally during which they gossiped, inspected the garden and all the new clothes Lally had recently bought during a visit to London, Carson had already returned. She found him in his study sorting through the day's post. When he saw her he stood up and politely indicated the seat opposite.

"I have to apologise for my behaviour yesterday," Agnes came quickly to the point. "I became rather hysterical; but the fact that you did not believe me about the theft of my jewels . . ."

"My dear Aunt Agnes, I did not *disbelieve* you. I simply wanted proof. In fact Maudie was so upset she has returned to her family."

"Ah!" Agnes exclaimed with a glint in her eyes. "*There* you have the proof."

"Of what?"

"Of her guilt."

"Not at all. Really, Aunt, if this is to begin all over again . . ." Carson rose from his desk and walked determinedly towards the door.

"*Please*, Carson," Agnes held out a hand. "Don't go. I want to talk to you."

"Then you must not provoke me, Aunt."

"All right, I won't." She watched as he resumed his seat again and then sat forward in her chair.

"Owen wishes to make me a present of the Chesterfield Street house. Provided the price is right we are prepared to make you an offer for it."

Carson leaned back and crossed his legs, a smile flitting slowly across his face.

"Why, that is an excellent suggestion, Aunt."

"Providing the price is right, I said."

"Of course. That goes without saying."

"You are agreeable?"

"Perfectly agreeable." Carson rose and, crossing the room, reached for her hands and clasped them between his. "I have no wish to fall out with you, Aunt, but you have told me in the past it is difficult for us to live in the same house for too long. I agree."

"We are too alike," Agnes said.

"Well," Carson studied the floor, "I'm not sure about that. However don't let's argue. Shall I go and find Owen and see if we can come to an agreement now? I shan't haggle about the price. I think we can agree on an independent assessment."

He glanced back before leaving the room. "We'll have a bottle of champagne with our dinner to celebrate."

Agnes smilingly inclined her head and watched Carson leave the room.

She sat back in her chair conscious of a feeling of extraordinary peace and happiness. She was, she decided, lucky in life. Invariably she got what she wanted. Despite her many vicissitudes she usually came up smiling. She had had good times and bad times, some very bad.

She had started with little in life: the frustrated, dissatisfied daughter of a provincial builder in a small provincial town that no one outside Dorset had ever heard of.

She had fallen in love with a married man who had left her pregnant. She had had a daughter she didn't want whom she had abandoned. There was some guilt about that, but only for a time and not much. She had crossed to America and become a prostitute, pure and simple; but, by dint of hard work and not a little cunning, she had ended up running her own establishments. There had been no railroad millionaire. Mr Wendell Gregg had been invented to imbue her with some respectability as a married woman when she returned to her native land. Most of the money she had saved and secured from her investments had been used to entrap Sir Guy into marrying her; the rest she had frittered away, extravagance and a liking for the good things in life being among her besetting sins.

But now at last she had her just rewards, something that she had worked for all her life and which she richly deserved. A second husband who, although insipid, was both titled and rich. But what did insipidity matter in a man with these attributes? Besides, no two strong people could live together. An insipid man and a woman with her character and personality were well matched. The main thing was that he adored her and would give her everything she desired.

She sat back with a sigh, aroused from her pleasant reverie by the re-entry of Carson alone.

"Where's Owen?" she enquired.

Carson threw up his hands. "I can't find him anywhere, Aunt. It appears he might have gone out. If so he has not returned as far as I can ascertain."

"What do you mean 'it appears he might have gone out'?"

"Arthur thought he saw him drive off."

"But I had the car."

"Arthur thought it might have been a cab. He said he wasn't paying much attention."

"What nonsense!" Agnes rose and stalked over to the door. "He'll probably be asleep. Really that man is *so* lazy."

"I looked in your bedroom, Aunt . . ." Carson began, but she paid no heed to him and he could hear her high heels tapping smartly along the corridor.

Carson returned to his desk and went on with his paperwork putting letters on one side and bills, too many of them, on the other. There was no doubt the money from the sale of the Chesterfield Street house would be useful. He would expedite this as quickly as he could. It was true he might have got a higher price on the open market but, after all, Aunt Agnes was family and maybe she had a point in saying that, though not strictly blood relations, they had a lot in common: a stubborn streak, an overhasty temper.

Time passed and he looked at his watch. Agnes had been gone over half an hour. Doubtless searching the house. It was dark by now and he began to think it odd that if Owen had gone he hadn't left some message.

Carson got up and, going over to the door, opened it and stood in the hall listening. The house was very still. The servants would be getting dinner. Jean was undoubtedly in his room or still somewhere at work. Where was Aunt Agnes? And where was Owen? Carson crossed the hall and began to mount the broad staircase that led to the upper floors. It was one of the features of the house, the staircase, as it branched off on either side towards the first floor, the intention of the original architect being to construct a grand entrance to the imposing drawing room with its double doors.

It then continued as a single staircase to the second floor where the main bedrooms were. The servants' quarters in the attic were reached by a separate staircase at the back of the house.

Carson arrived at the second floor and passed by his bedroom, Jean's bedroom, two that were unoccupied – they had been his parents' adjoining bedrooms – until he came to Aunt Agnes's room. The door was closed. When he had been looking for Owen it had been partly open enabling him to glance inside. He stood outside the door and tapped lightly on it. There was no answer.

"Aunt Agnes?" he called, softly tapping again.

Still no answer. Feeling uneasy, rather like a thief, he slowly turned the handle and pushed open the door.

Aunt Agnes was lying face downwards across the bed which occupied the centre of the room. It was an imposing four-poster which had formed part of his mother's not inconsiderable dowry from Holland.

Filled with alarm, Carson swiftly crossed the room until he stood hovering by the side of the bed.

"Aunt Agnes?" he whispered again and then stooped to touch her on the shoulder which suddenly gave a great heave. Bending to look at her face he saw it was stained with tears, her eyes staring in front of her, as though she'd had a stroke or, perhaps, some form of seizure.

Thoroughly alarmed he sat beside her and took her hand. It felt cold but alive and he started to rub it briskly.

"Aunt Agnes what has happened? Has Owen gone?"

She nodded, gripping the heavy brocade counterpane with twitching fingers. Then she raised one hand and flapped it towards the dressing room.

"Gone," she murmured, still in a trance-like state. "Gone. Packed his things, his clothes, taken every scrap of my jewellery. Everything. Cleaned us out. If you've got any family silver left, Carson, you'd better go down and count it."

Then she closed her eyes and her shoulders shook with great, heart-rending sobs.

Chapter Nine

Walking back from the Fenice in the cool of the night with a
gentle autumnal breeze blowing in from the Adriatic, Venice
was a romantic place, the narrow streets and alleyways softly
illuminated by lamps glowing from the walls of the buildings
– the houses, shops and palaces – of that ancient and venerable
city. Here and there was the glimpse of water and, still, at this
late hour, gondolas gliding along propelled by huge poles that
sought purchase with the mud of the lagoon.

Connie had gone to dinner and the opera with Francesca and
Guido Valenti and Paolo Colomb-Paravacini, now strolling by
her side, who was increasingly her constant companion. It had
been a delightful evening in the company of interesting and
intelligent people. Good conversation at dinner and then the
stimulation of the opera, Verdi's *La Forza del Destino*, played
out in the magnificent setting of one of Italy's, indeed the
world's, finest opera houses.

Paolo Colomb-Paravacini was a scion of one of Venice's
oldest noble families, his palazzo occupying a commanding
position on the Grand Canal. He was an art lover, an expert
on the eighteenth century Venetian painter Tiepolo, but eclectic
enough in his tastes to embrace the Post-Impressionists whose
art had scandalised London at exhibitions held there before the
war. He was a widower, about fifty, who had been introduced
to Connie by the Valentis not long after the death of his wife
during the war.

He had two children; a son of fifteen who was at boarding
school in England, and a daughter of nineteen who was studying

art in Rome. He was a delightful, cultured man and made no
secret of his interest in Connie.

Connie was flattered by Paolo's attention because the fact
that any man admired her slightly amazed her. As she had told
Carson, whatever exterior changes may have occurred, inside she
was the same person she had been when her guardian attempted
to thrust a shy young woman into marriage with a man who did
not love her and who bitterly hurt her in the process, contributing
thus to a mammoth loss of self-confidence.

Connie frequently recalled that time when, tongue-tied,
unsuitably dressed in an unbecoming pink frock which was
far too young for her, Carson's father had given a dinner
party for the newly-engaged couple only to announce that he
was to be married again himself. It was then that her massively
egocentric, larger-than-life half sister Agnes, whom she had not
seen since she was a child, reappeared on the scene.

Experiences such as Connie had had needed to be lived down,
and she had done her best to suppress them with the help of
Francesca Valenti, who had brought out the best in her and
shown what money could do to accomplish such change. One
could buy beautifully styled garments that improved one's image,
one's own self-esteem; employ hairdressers and beauticians who
exploited one's natural assets, changed the colour of one's
hair, creating a new style, and exploited the potentials of
one's complexion by enhancing one's natural colouring.

To change her appearance, even in a subtle way, had made
her feel good. Gradually she came to realise that she was also
a natural conversationalist, able now to converse easily with
people who understood about art and music and literature and
all the things she had fed upon secretly for so long.

Ever since the debacle of her abortive engagement Connie had
always accepted that she would be a spinster like Miss Fairchild,
that no man would desire her and she would never marry.

Now everything was different. Paolo had for a long time been
quietly courting her – at least Francesca had assured her his
intentions were honourable – and a situation had arisen between

her and her former fiancé that, to say the least, was interesting, but from which she had fled.

Yes, she had fled from Carson, too nervous, too much in dread of history repeating itself in that cruel way of long ago.

They crossed a bridge across the Rio de San Luca, passed the Campo Manin and the church of San Luca, and came again to the Grand Canal and the palazzo which contained Connie's apartment.

They stopped in front of the heavy door and Connie produced her key.

"I shan't ask you in," she said glancing apologetically at him, "it's terribly late."

"There was something I wanted to ask you," Paolo replied.

"Could it wait?"

"Well, I'd rather it didn't wait too long. Maybe we could lunch tomorrow?"

"That would be nice."

"I'll pick you up. About one?"

"Come in and have a drink beforehand."

"That would be lovely. Say twelve-thirty then?" He leaned towards her and lightly kissed her cheek. A hand fluttered near her breast but did not touch it.

"I'm terribly fond of you, Constance," he murmured in her ear brushing it with his mouth.

She knew he was restraining himself and had been for some time. But maybe tomorrow everything would be different.

They broke away and, without another word, Connie turned and went into the apartment shutting and bolting the door behind her. Inside a solitary lamp glowed in the hall. Lights still burned in the drawing room overlooking the canal. She felt strangely ill at ease, restless, and, removing her coat, putting down her bag and gloves, she went over to the window. She stood there for a long time looking over the shining waters of the canal to the palazzi on the other side, some in darkness, some with lights still blazing.

She employed two indoor servants, a husband and wife, who

shared the housework and chores with another daily maid who did most of the cleaning. It was already a large place, five bedrooms, and if she bought the whole palazzo, which the Valentis still wished her to do, it would be huge. What, in fact, would she do in it or with it? Once again the thought of what Paolo might want to ask her made her decide that it was best to hear what he had to say. His own palazzo was huge, one of the great palazzi of Venice, and if she became his wife, the Contessa Colomb-Paravacini, what need would she have of two palaces?

The Contessa Colomb-Paravacini. It seemed quite awesome even to contemplate it.

And yet . . . there was that word he had used . . . *fond.* Paolo had said he was terribly *fond* of her. Carson had said the same. But what did 'fond' mean? Did it mean sex, passion, or did it mean what she sometimes suspected it to mean, just friendship, a deep abiding friendship which was also a kind of love, but not the kind she wanted. She wanted the other sort. The sort that bowled a girl off her feet and, when eight years before that had happened to her, she knew just what it meant and what it felt like.

Only the feeling, the passion, had not been reciprocated and had ended for her in humiliation and tears.

Connie turned away from the window, closed the shutter and put out the lights in the room, a long beautiful room that had been furnished with antiques by the previous owners who had fallen on bad times. At a time when she and Victoria did not know what to do with their money all theirs had gone, and they had been forced to sell everything and retire to a small apartment near the Arsenal, leaving all their beautiful things behind.

Connie walked through the hall putting out lights and then slowly climbed the stairs to her bedroom. This was over the drawing room and shared with it a lovely view across the canal. After getting undressed, but still feeling restless, she put on her dressing gown and stood by the window thinking of the difference between where she was now and the place where she was born. The difference too between the heir to centuries of Counts Colomb-Paravacini, and the fourteenth baronet, successor to the equally ancient Woodvilles. One was a deeply cultured, elegant man of the world, at home in salons and opera houses, art galleries and Venetian palaces. The other, despite his heritage, was a son of the soil, an unlettered man who could not discourse about Dante or Tiepolo, Verdi or Mazzini, even supposing he knew who they were. He was plain and simply a countryman turned into a brave soldier by the war. In many ways a simple man. Yet Carson was not a simpleton and, for her, he still possessed the enormous power to attract.

It was perhaps fortunate that a woman in her position, a spinster in her thirties, even if a wealthy one, could even contemplate marriage to two such different men.

But if the opportunity were given her which would she choose?

She slipped off her gown and climbed rather wearily into bed where she lay for a long time, hands beneath her head, gazing at the reflection made on the ceiling from the lights that still burned on the water. But her last thoughts as she drifted off to sleep were not of the grandeurs of Venice, but of that small town so far away, and Young Lochinvar.

Connie slept fitfully, perhaps not surprisingly as she had a lot on her mind. If, as seemed possible, Paolo intended to propose marriage to her, how would she respond? She could hardly ask for more time as he had virtually been courting her for over three years. But was it what she wanted? At the risk of spending the rest of her life as a spinster did she really want to be Contessa Colomb-Paravacini with all the duties and responsibilities that that entailed? But, really, the most important thing was whether or not she was in love with Paolo, and she thought she knew the answer to that.

Despite the lateness of the hour at which she went to bed she was up early and she took a walk through the streets as far as the Rialto Bridge before returning home. Winter was fast approaching and the wind blowing in from the sea was keen. When she got back her maid Elena had laid breakfast in the small sitting room, much favoured by Miss Fairchild when she was alive as in size and its atmosphere of cosiness it reminded her of Wenham to which she probably remained more drawn than Connie.

As Connie sat down, Elena breezed in with a coffee pot and the morning's post which she accompanied with a patter of gossip and news from the locality. Each little area of Venice was in its way a counterpart of Wenham being just as preoccupied with trivia and banalities, the doings of the neighbours, the innuendoes and speculations of small town life.

Elena poured coffee while Connie buttered her bread and covered it with a smooth layer of apricot jam. Connie's mastery of the Italian language was by now complete. For days, even weeks sometimes she spoke nothing else, so she was able to understand even the nuances of what was going on in and around the campi Manin and San Luca. As Elena spoke, Connie idly looked through her mail and was delighted to see a letter from Eliza. Tearing open the envelope she held up a hand to Elena with a smile and fluttered the pages of the letter at her. It seemed to be a surprisingly long one. Elena understood, knowing the importance of letters from home, ceased her torrent and made her departure, closing the door gently behind her.

Connie loved her letters from England. If anything they increased her nostalgia, and this one was no exception.

Eliza started conversationally enough, apologising for taking such a long time to answer Connie's last letter, giving her the news of Dora, Hugh and Julius. Alexander Martyn was to be sent to Sherborne school when he was older and, meanwhile, would attend a prep as a weekly boarder.

Connie turned over the pages absorbing it all, feeling she was there. She read on hurriedly, subconsciously eager to have news of Carson.

"I have saved my most important news until last, dear Connie, because I suppose I still have some difficulty understanding what has happened. In a way it is so heartbreaking that, whatever one thinks of Agnes, one cannot help but pity her.

At the end of last month Owen suddenly disappeared from Pelham's Oak. He apparently stole not only every piece of jewellery, some of it very valuable, that Agnes possessed, but also part of the Woodville family silver, small items but all of great value. Obviously he was limited by what he could physically carry.

He left no letter and no explanation and has not been heard of since. Arthur actually saw him drive away in a cab some time in the afternoon while Carson and Agnes were both out, but thought nothing of it. Carson managed to trace the cab to Blandford and ascertained that Owen had called it earlier on in the day and wished to be taken to Blandford station where he caught the train to London. He was accompanied by a quantity of heavy luggage.

Agnes was left in a state of prostration and Carson had to call the doctor.

It appears that only the day before Owen had offered to buy the Chesterfield Street house for her as she told him she was tired of living in the country. I think also that she and Carson had had quite enough of each other! I should have written to you about this before – it happened over a month ago – but I wanted to wait and give you all the news I could as Carson engaged a private investigator to try and find Owen or, at least, what happened to him.

He found no trace of Owen after he left Blandford, bound for Waterloo, and of course he may have alighted at any station on the way.

However he did find some most interesting facts about him.

Owen apparently had no right to the title 'Sir'. He does not appear in the *Baronetage and Knightage of the*

United Kingdom and Ireland, or on any list pertaining to India or the rest of the Empire. As Mr Wentworth he worked on the tea plantations in Assam as manager for Sir Cuthbert Moran for many years, but left under a cloud before the war on a charge of misappropriation of funds! He was apparently a heavy gambler, a condition which got worse after the death of his wife from some tropical illness. They had no children.

No one seems to know what happened to him during the war until he resurfaced in London in 1918, calling himself "Sir" and giving the impression of being a wealthy gentleman of leisure. He met Agnes some six months later. (We all here, of course, thought there was something not quite top drawer, rather phoney, about Owen; but said nothing for fear of being accused of snobbery. Maybe now, with the gift of hindsight, we were wrong).

The rest is speculation, but it is likely he might have been on the lookout for a rich widow and Agnes seemed to fit the bill. She told Carson she and Owen did not discuss money until after they were married, in fact until very recently.

She realises she was very foolish but as he did not bring up the subject, nor did she. When they did discuss it, she was honest about her circumstances, and thought that if she'd asked him earlier he might have thought her a gold digger! He lied to her and gave the impression he was very well-off.

What also puzzles us is what happened to all the money Agnes was supposed to have inherited from her American railroad millionaire husband? That, as much else about your sister, still remains a mystery.

However, for Owen obviously the crunch came over the question of the house and he realised he would be exposed. Some of Agnes's jewellery had disappeared a few days before and it is not known if Owen was the thief, and he had been planning his escape all along, or if it gave him an idea and, faced with an impossible situation, he decided to do a bunk.

This business has preoccupied us considerably as you may guess. Poor Carson, who has behaved *terribly* well, and generously, has offered her a home for as long as she wants in Pelham's Oak, but he says the London house has to go.

Agnes now finds herself in the distressing situation of being legally married to a rogue and a thief whose whereabouts are unknown, and she is not even "Lady Wentworth", a matter which exercises her almost more than anything else!

Dearest Connie, I wish I could be with you to tell you all this because I know how upset you will be. As I said, whatever we think of her Agnes is, after all, your half-sister and my sister-in-law.

In a way she is the responsibility of us all, and we must rally round her and Carson and help them all we can.

Dora has come back from riding and it is time for lunch. Her friend May is still here. She seems to have become rather attached to a local farmer, Bernard Williams, who farms at Anstey. I think Dora is a bit upset because she thinks May too good for him. However it is a rather odd situation here, between ourselves, and I wouldn't be too sorry to see the back of May as she can be a *little* bit of a trouble-maker between me and Dora. But please keep this to yourself.

Do write soon,
Fondest love from us all,
Eliza."

Paolo Colomb-Paravacini, clutching a huge bunch of flowers in his arm, a broad smile of anticipation on his face, politely removed his hat as Elena opened the door.

"Good morning, Elena."

"Good morning, Count," she replied with a respectful bob.

"Is Signorina Yetman . . ."

Before he could finish his sentence she stood back and, with a sweeping gesture, ushered him inside saying, as she closed the door:

"Signorina Yetman had to leave suddenly for England. She had some bad news by post this morning concerning a member of her family. She sent her apologies, Count, and left this."

Elena handed Paolo a letter and, the flowers still in his arm, he tore open the envelope and extracted a single sheet of paper:

'Dear Paolo,

I do hope you will forgive me for not letting you have notice about cancelling our lunch date, but I received some very bad news this morning from Eliza Heering, my half-brother Ryder's widow.

I felt I had to be with the family as soon as I could, and the train for Milan leaves in an hour.

I will contact you on my return.

With kind regards,

Constance Yetman.'

Elena, hands linked in front of her, watched the visitor critically as he read through the letter once and then twice. Finally he shook his head and stuffed it back in his pocket.

"Well that's that, then. Did she say when she hoped to be back?"

"She gave no indication, Count. By the amount of luggage she took I think she expects a long stay."

"I see."

Paolo put on his hat as Elena opened the door and ushered him outside looking questioningly at the bunch of flowers which, however, he hung on to.

"Shall I give the signorina any message if she telephones, Count?" Elena enquired on the doorstep.

Paolo shook his head. "Just say I called. I'll be in touch with her. Good day, Elena."

"Good day, Count."

Elena watched him as he walked off down the street and then shut the door, wondering what he was going to do with the flowers.

Poor Count Colomb-Paravacini. He might be in love with Miss Yetman but Elena, her personal maid, knew she was not in love with the count but, she suspected, with the very handsome English gentleman whose photograph she had on a dresser in her bedroom, along with other members of her family. It was a happy picture taken, the signorina had said, earlier on in the year and showed them all playing croquet on the lawn of a country house. It had caught the couple glancing at each other and, in Elena's view, that look spoke volumes.

At the waterside Paolo stood for a long time contemplating the ripples made by the traffic that plied busily along the Grand Canal. Something told him that he had left it too long. He should have proposed much earlier. But how could one be sure that one's feelings were reciprocated by a cool English miss, seventeen years one's junior who, moreover, according to the Valentis, was also a woman of exceptional wealth?

He had bided his time and now he felt that the moment had passed. If she had been in love, if she had been anticipating his proposal, as he thought she had, she would surely have put that before any problems to do with her family. After all she was an only child and her mother and father were dead.

Raising his arms Paolo tossed the beautiful and expensive bunch of flowers far out into the canal, watching them separate and drift slowly away as if marking the site of a watery grave and the end of his dreams.

"Miss Yetman to see you, *Mrs* Wentworth." Arthur's plummy tones dwelt somewhat longer on the title than seemed necessary. Agnes looked round angrily but Arthur had slipped out of the door leaving Connie standing looking at the woman she hardly knew, but was now her closest surviving blood relation. There were two half-brothers, with families, but she had not seen them since her father's funeral in 1895, when she was only eight years old.

"Constance!" Agnes exclaimed in a weary voice, putting down the book she was reading, or attempting to read, so preoccupied were her thoughts with other matters these days. "Constance, no one told me you were coming."

"No one knew," Connie said walking slowly up to her half-sister. "As soon as I heard from Eliza about your misfortune I came at once."

"Well," Agnes rose and stretched out her arms to embrace Connie, kissing her lightly on both cheeks, "that was *very* kind of you."

"I'm terribly, terribly sorry, Agnes." Connie took her by the hand and led her back to the chair by the fire where she'd been sitting. "It must have been a terrible shock to you."

"It was. It was indeed." Agnes sank into her chair and nodded her head vigorously. "I can't tell you what a shock. I was completely deceived and taken in by a blackguard." She looked up at Connie piteously. "He has made off with every piece of jewellery I possessed and left me penniless. I am a beggar, at the mercy of Carson and the kindness of friends. Owen liked me to think he was a man of substance. He spent a fortune trying to impress me when we travelled the continent. I must say, to my shame, he succeeded. I thought I knew the opposite sex very well, but I deceived myself.

"It now transpires Owen Wentworth was *merely* the manager of a tea plantation in India, dismissed years ago for dishonesty. Heaven knows what he had done with himself since then. Somehow he had the money to spend. No expense spared, of course, just to trap *me* into marriage. He thought *I* was the one with the money." Agnes gave an unsteady laugh.

Knowing as much as she did, through Eliza's letter, Connie thought it unnecessary to probe further.

"But to claim that he had a title! That was monstrous. I am now reduced to being *Mrs* Wentworth, something the staff here don't let me forget."

"That's a very trivial matter to the harm that has been done you." Tentatively Connie put out a hand and gently stroked Agnes's brow. It was, she thought, the closest she had ever come to this woman who was capable of inspiring love and hatred in extreme measures. People fell under her spell and then, when they discovered her true nature, they hated her although, from what she had heard, Guy had adored his fickle, spendthrift wife to the end.

Agnes leaned back in her chair and closed her eyes. At the roots of her blonde coiffeur, Connie was shocked to see that her hair was grey. Her face was more lined than she had ever imagined possible and she found she was looking at a prematurely aged woman. Her mind flew back to the dazzling impression Agnes had made when she had returned to Wenham in 1912. All eyes turned as she came into the room, her hair piled high, with a fringe and a cluster of ringlets behind one ear, a sapphire-blue, full-skirted evening dress with a rather daring neckline displaying a glimpse of her voluptuous breasts. Although she was not tall she seemed to tower over everyone and all eyes turned to her. Not a glance had been spared for Connie – ostensibly the star of the evening – dowdy, frumpish, ill at ease in the ridiculous dress Miss Fairchild had had made for her. A more unflattering contrast to Agnes could hardly have been imagined.

Now, Connie fancied, a mere eight years later the boot was on the other foot, and Agnes seemed to realise it. She was staring at her young sister with a puzzled expression.

"I can't get over the *change* in you, Constance. It is as though you were another person. I used to think of you as a little mouse, but now . . ."

Still hurt by the term Connie removed her hand from Agnes's forehead and slumped into a chair beside her.

"I used to be a little mouse," she said.

"I think Miss Fairchild *liked* you that way." Agnes pursed her lips grimly. "But she came unstuck when she tried to marry you off to Carson . . ."

153

"Please, Agnes," Connie said urgently, gripping her arm, "please don't refer to that ever again."

"I hope you haven't really come to see Carson?" Agnes gave her a sharp, shrewd look. "Not trying to throw yourself at him again, are you?"

"Of course not!" Connie riposted angrily. "Don't be so cruel."

"I am being realistic, child. You have been hurt once and I don't want it to happen to you again. After all, we are sisters and I have some care for you, though you may not think so."

Now Agnes reached out and the palm of her hand curled round Connie's cheek, lingering there for a moment. "Carson is not to be trusted. He is a womaniser and they never change. He is also as short of money as his father was when I came on the scene and unwisely married him, thinking I should have a home and security for life. If Carson can get his hands on you he will, but I'm afraid it will be for your money and not for any other attribute you may think you have."

Connie got to her feet and stood looking down at her sister.

"Agnes that is a perfectly *horrible* thing to say."

"Nevertheless it is true." Agnes met her eyes with equanimity, rather as though the chance to needle Connie and cast aspersions at the hated Carson had cheered her up. "I want you to take care. I understand you are a wealthy woman, very wealthy indeed as you had three fortunes left you. Your mother left you all her money and estate, so did my father and so did Miss Fairchild. Would that I had had the chance." Agnes interrupted her flow with a deep sigh. "Life might have turned out very differently for me if our father had shared his fortune with his two daughters, instead of leaving it all to you."

She gazed reproachfully at Connie who, once again, was overcome by that complex emotion of anger, revulsion and affection her sister invariably engendered in her at the same time. Somehow she always managed to turn the tables to her own advantage.

"Agnes," she said trying hard to keep her voice under control, "the reason I am here is *not* to see Carson as you unfairly suggest – I have no interest in him and I'm sure he has none in me – but to offer you assistance." Taking a deep breath she sat down again next to her and looked into those rather mean, calculating eyes which always seemed to be assessing someone's worth or truthfulness. This being the case it was strange, as well as a pity, she hadn't been more astute about the husband she had not long ago married.

"Go on," Agnes said encouragingly as if her inspection of Connie's face was complete.

"I am fortunate, as you say, in having sufficient funds to do what I want in life. I know that when our father died you had disappeared and no one knew where you had gone . . ." She paused and looked at Agnes who sat up stiffly.

"I had my reasons."

"I'm sure you had. But whatever they were I feel convinced he would have divided his fortune between us, because he was a good and generous man and his other children were provided for. I have come from Venice where I have a home to see what I can do for you, how I can help you."

"Well . . ." Agnes seemed nonplussed by Connie's words and her expression became mollified.

"I decided that the best thing, if you agree, is to make Miss Fairchild's house over to you as an outright gift. I was going to sell it but I would like, instead, to give it to you. It is a nice house, a large house, and I think you will be comfortable there. You will be near friends and family, people who will help you over this difficult patch. I would also like to offer you an income, the sum to be determined by your needs, and that we can leave to lawyers. There!"

She stopped and looked expectantly at her sister. If she had anticipated a torrent of gratitude she was, of course, disappointed. Instead of expressing joy or relief, Agnes's eyes grew even more calculating. "Well, that's very nice of you Constance, even generous, but," she pulled a face, "Miss

155

Fairchild's house? Really I don't much care for it. And you know I have never *liked* Wenham." She grew gradually more agitated and moved closer to the edge of her chair. "Now what I would *really* like is the house in Chesterfield Street. That and an adequate income, plus the company of my London friends, is something that really would please me. Now that I really *would* be grateful for."

So happy and expectant did she look that Connie hated to disillusion her; but she had spent the hours since her arrival in Wenham closeted with Eliza and Carson about the plan to help Agnes. It was Carson who had predicted she would want the London house. The fact was that he had already given instructions for its sale. More to the point, he was worried about what Agnes would get up to in London, relentlessly running up debts she would call upon him or Connie to settle. There would be no end to it.

"Much as we would rather she were elsewhere," he had said, "Aunt Agnes *must* remain in Wenham where we can all keep our eyes on her."

His words now echoed in Connie's mind and she shook her head.

"I'm afraid the London house is in the process of being sold, Agnes . . ."

"What, when?" Agnes looked outraged.

"Carson has it in hand."

"He never told me."

"Well, he told me."

"Oh, I see. You have discussed all this, have you?" A look of understanding now dawned. "I see. This is a family plot. I might have known."

The blood began to drum in Connie's head and she wished for a moment she had stayed in Venice and resisted this philanthropic urge to do something for her ungrateful sister.

"It is not a plot. It is my offer." By now Connie was trying hard to maintain her composure. "Take it or leave it, Agnes. I have already had several people interested in Victoria's house.

156

I am not here for very long, and I assure you my offer will not remain open indefinitely and will not be repeated."

"I see you *have* discussed all this with Carson." There was a spiteful note in Agnes's voice. "I suspected as much, but I must warn you, my girl, once again, that if you set your hat at him you will be very badly let down, just as I was let down by Owen Wentworth. If you're foolish enough to marry him Carson will fritter away all of your money and spend his time dallying with common country women. I tell you, the Woodville men never change."

The blood went on drumming in her ears but Connie swallowed hard, saying nothing.

"Very well, I accept," Agnes said with a toss of her head, having failed to goad her sister, with not a trace of gratitude in her voice. "I will accept the house and an income but," she paused and shook her finger at Connie, "it had better be generous. I am a woman used to a certain standard of living, you know, and I expect to be able to sustain this. There will be a car, a butler and a maid. You can't fob me off with any old thing. Don't forget I was married to a Woodville and I have standards to consider, a way of life to which I have become accustomed and which as my sister, my younger sister, it is *your* duty to provide and maintain. Oh and incidentally," she said, almost as an afterthought, "I shall wish to be known in future by my former title of Lady Woodville. It must be for me as though Owen Wentworth, may his soul rot in hell, never existed."

Chapter Ten

Dora was a mystery to all who knew her, including her mother. She had always been a very self-contained person even as a child, fond of her own company, passionately devoted to animals, especially horses. Her parents had been exceptionally happily married and the first great tragedy in her life had been the death of her father, Ryder, when she was eleven. The second had been the suicide of her brother, Laurence, in 1912.

Dora was the middle child, two years younger than Laurence and a year older than Hugh. Surrounded by boys she enjoyed boyish pastimes, liked games and horseriding. Yet she had never shown any romantic interest in the opposite sex and her mother had always been convinced that Dora would never marry.

Dora had joined the VAD nursing service at the outbreak of war. VAD nurses were untrained and unpaid, acting as auxiliaries to the professional medical staff. Dora nursed first in London, then the West Country then, in 1916, she was sent to France and her medical unit was never far from the front line.

After the deaths of her father and brother this was the third most seminal influence of her life. She realised that, up to the time of the war, she had been a very spoilt, aloof, self-indulgent young woman who had never had even to contemplate work due to her mother's second marriage to a wealthy man. She had been free to do as she liked, and that was mainly indulging from morning until night, seven days a week, in anything to do with riding and field sports. She had hunted two or three days a week, competed in gymkhanas and become one of the best known and most prominent of women horse riders in the county.

In France Dora's superior was a woman younger than she was, who had trained as a nurse, called May Carpenter. May was small, almost tiny compared to Dora, with a heart-shaped face and bubbly dark curls. Though a working-class girl from the industrial north, she also had an air of fragility that was belied by the demanding and strenuous nature of her work. She worked in the theatre assisting the front line surgeons in appalling operations, and was never known to falter, flinch or complain however long the hours she was on duty.

Dora fell in love with May, but she did not regard it as sexual love. She was certainly attracted by her but, more importantly, she admired her more than anyone she had ever known, even her father and mother, even Carson, to whom she was close, or her beloved Laurence.

To see tough, doughty little May, only five feet four inches tall, lifting bulky soldiers, going through the most searing operations with calm, serenity and good humour did more to bring Dora through her own hard and, at times, heartbreaking work than anything else.

A strong bond grew between the women which deepened when Dora knew more of May's circumstances. She was illegitimate and had grown up in an orphanage. At the age of fourteen she had been put into domestic service, and it was a tribute to her determination and strength of personality that she had educated herself to a sufficient standard to train at Guy's hospital in London as a nurse.

After the war Dora brought May home to recuperate because they were both in as much need of it as any fighting man. It had been May's intention to return to nursing, but at Dora's behest she gave it up and in the years since the war had ended the two women had become inseparable, even though May did not ride and Dora did not paint or sew as exquisitely as May.

Then May had met Bernard Williams, a local farmer, at a meet, and he had started to court her. Within a very short time they were engaged, and Dora's happy, peaceful world was destroyed.

160

She felt bitter and became estranged from May. Someone with whom she had thought she would happily spend her life, was consigned to outer darkness.

Carson cared a great deal about the cousin who was three years his senior. Dora was an unusual woman, and he not only loved and admired her, in a way he envied her. She was so sure, so single-minded, so unconcerned about what people thought of her relationship with the working-class woman she had brought home as a companion.

Like Dora he was surprised, but perhaps not as shocked, when May was courted by Bernard Williams, and soon afterwards married him. Without understanding much about the relationship, except that it was an unusually close one, he was also very sorry for his cousin. He knew how much it upset Dora to lose someone to whom she was so attached, particularly when she regarded May's much older husband as a rather uncouth, unfeeling man with whom May had little in common besides a desire to be married.

Carson now stood at the top of the steps of the main portico of Pelham's Oak anxiously watching the road below. He kept glancing at his watch and then going back into the house to check the time with the hall clock, coming out again and scanning the narrow road that snaked through fields and past copses, alongside small streams and part of the River Wen, and was usually pretty deserted except on market day. Then it sprouted solitary horsemen, horse-drawn carts and wagons, flocks of cattle or sheep being driven to market and, increasingly these days, automobiles taking farmers and their families to inspect the wares of the market stalls of Wenham or Blandford. There they would meet and gossip with their friends and load up with provisions to take to their sometimes isolated farms and dwellings often miles away from the nearest neighbour. Market day was a great day out.

Suddenly Carson spied a small Ford car being driven at a brisk pace along the road until it turned in through the

161

imposing gates of Pelham's Oak and continued up the drive towards the house. As it came to a stop Carson ran down the steps and stuck his head through the window by the driver's seat to be greeted by Dora.

"Sorry I'm late, Carson."

"I thought you'd forgotten." He continued to peer in through the window, and his face fell. "Where's Connie?"

"Oh, sorry, she couldn't come. She sent her apologies."

Carson opened the door for Dora to alight and stepped back, shaking his head. "She's avoiding me."

Dora said nothing but got out and Carson closed the door behind her. She wore jodhpurs and a hacking jacket, a yellow cravat tucked into an open-necked shirt. She was a tall, striking looking woman, with ash-blonde hair which she wore cut fashionably short at the back and long at the sides. She had a narrow, aristocratic nose, a firm, stubborn mouth and a pair of disconcertingly direct and honest blue eyes.

Not many people were comfortable with Dora, but Carson was. He felt they were two of a kind. He took her arm as they walked round the side of the house towards the stables and looked up at the threatening sky.

"Maybe we should go riding straight away?"

"Suits me," Dora agreed. "I don't want to be too late home because of the dark. Mother still worries about me, even though I'm nearly forty."

"Thirty-seven," Carson corrected her.

"Nearer forty than thirty," Dora persisted.

Carson stopped and looked at her.

"Do you have plans Dora?"

"Plans?" She looked surprised. "What kind of plans?"

"About the future? Now that May, well . . ." his voice trailed off. May was so seldom mentioned these days.

"I'm *perfectly* happy as I am," Dora said coldly. "May has nothing to do with it."

"I thought you were going to buy a house together?"

"Can we change the subject, Carson?" They had reached the

162

stables and Dora looked appraisingly up at her horse which the groom had prepared for her and stood saddled and waiting. She patted the patient mare affectionately. "The future's not something I particularly want to discuss. Mother is quite happy having me at home."

"I'm sure."

"And what is *your* future may I ask?"

"Ah!" Carson sighed and began to mount Pulver who quivered expectantly. "We have all been changed by the war, Dora. We are all, in a way, wounded beings, different from what we were before. In a way we don't belong. Be honest." As Pulver trotted obediently into the yard Carson looked behind at Dora who was following him. "She *is* avoiding me, isn't she? Every time I visit you she is not there, and when I ask you here she doesn't come."

"She is very busy with the house and Aunt Agnes. She's an awful pain, that woman."

"Well, we knew that. But Connie also knew that when she offered her the house."

"She practically wants the place rebuilt. Connie has her job cut out to resist her at every turn. I think maybe she rather regrets offering it to her. The alternative, of course, would have been very difficult for you. Aunt Agnes would have stayed on here, so for that much you can be grateful to Connie."

"I am grateful to Connie."

Dora passed him as if she was anxious to avoid a discussion of personal matters and walked the horse across the paddock next to the house. It was a cold day, the ground hard beneath their feet, and once out by the paddock they set off at a brisk trot, relishing the freedom and companionship as they cantered down the steepish slope that led from the house by way of Crook's farm and across the fields towards the cottage where Dora's father and mother had first declared their love in the year that Carson's parents had married, 1880, forty years before.

Clear of the cottage they began to race, their cheeks red, their hair flying in the wind as the hooves of the horses pounded the earth.

Breathless, they drew up about five miles away from the house which was now but a speck in the distance. Dora was visibly more relaxed, laughing. The pallor that had struck Carson on her arrival gone from her face.

"Oh this is *good*," she cried patting her horse, Molly. "I think I'll have Molly from you."

"Take her as a gift." Carson pointed to the horse with his crop. "She's yours."

"No, no, I'll pay you for her."

"No you won't." Carson drew nearer to Dora and, when the flanks of their horses were almost touching, leaned over to her. "Tell me, don't avoid the question Dora. We have always been so close and honest with each other. Why *does* Connie avoid me?"

Dora averted her eyes and looked out over towards the town. "I don't know."

"You do know. She confides in you. I thought she was attracted to me. I was so excited when she came back so soon, and I've hardly seen her. She avoids me and sends excuses."

Dora gazed down at the horse's neck for a few seconds, as if deep in thought, then she raised her head and met Carson's eyes.

"You're right. We *have* always been open and honest with each other. Well, then I'll tell you. Agnes has warned Connie off you. She said you were a womaniser and also that any overtures would be just for her money, because you are dreadfully hard up and needed money for the house. Agnes said history would be repeating itself all over again."

"*Damn* Agnes," Carson burst out bringing his fist hard down on his saddle. "You *know* it's not true." He turned his horse towards Wenham. "I shall go this very moment and have it out with her."

Dora leaned over and seized Pulver's bridle. "*Don't* be so silly."

164

"But you *know* it's not true. I'll not touch a penny of her damned money . . ."

"I think that doesn't trouble Connie so much, because her money means so little to her. It is the other thing and that *is* true isn't it Carson?"

"No it is not. You *know* it is not Dora."

"I always heard . . ."

"Oh yes you 'always heard', but that was years ago."

"Does a leopard change its spots?"

"Yes it does. In my case it does. You know that, Dora, and you are as close to me as anyone. I have not touched a woman since I came back from the war. I have wanted only Connie and . . . well, another woman, but she wouldn't have me either." He had kept even from Dora the fact that he had loved Roger's wife.

"For all the change in her, her apparent sophistication, Connie is a very simple woman, Carson. She is very vulnerable."

"I know it and that's why I haven't pressed her. I also didn't want her to think I am interested only in her money and, believe me, I am not."

"Mother, for all her love and affection for you, also considers it a little strange . . ."

"*What* is strange?" He looked at her aggressively.

"That you should now take such an interest in Connie."

"I thought Aunt Eliza was my friend?"

"She is."

"But that is not very friendly."

"Mother loves you, but she has a special bond with Connie. She feels protective towards her, *in loco parentis*, if you like."

Carson's tone became petulant. "Then your mother should have spoken to me to find out my intentions. Really, Dora, when I think Connie is on the verge of returning to Venice amid all this misunderstanding I could . . . why, I could weep."

Dora's expression as she looked at him was one of pity mingled with amusement.

"I can't see you actually bursting into tears, whatever the

165

cause." She paused briefly for a moment. "Carson, I think you ought to know there *is* someone else, someone in Venice to whom Connie is very attached. He writes to her a lot. That being the case I think she would not wish to deceive you, so thought it best to stay away. It may be also that she cannot forget the past, when she was so hurt. Anyway in a week or so she will be gone and that might help to put you out of your misery."

"Put me out of my misery!" Carson exclaimed between clenched teeth. "It increases it tenfold." He drew Pulver closer to her. "Dora you must help me to explain myself to Connie before it is too late. I beg of you, because of the love we have for each other, to help me."

Dora glanced anxiously at her watch and then towards the house. "I'll do what I can," she said. "I must get back or it will be dark. Mother worries if it gets dark and I'm in the car."

Carson nodded and they rode in silence back to the house. Just as they reached the stables they saw Jean Parterre talking to one of his workmen. He raised his hat in greeting and, going over to Dora, reached up to shake hands.

"Good day, Miss Yetman," he said politely.

"Good day, Mr Parterre," she replied, smiling at him.

"Had a good ride?"

"Very," She looked down at her horse. "Carson is going to let me keep Molly."

"She's a fine horse," Jean nodded his agreement, then looked across at Carson.

"Carson, your Aunt Agnes is creating about the state of one of the bedrooms. Apparently water is coming in though the roof. I said I'd go over and look at it."

"Please don't mention that woman's name to me," Carson said irritably jumping off his horse and, after unsaddling him, he began energetically to rub him down.

Jean glanced at Dora who shook her head.

"Can I give you a lift to Wenham?" she asked, indicating her car in the drive. "I'll drop you off at Aunt Agnes's."

"Well, that's very kind, but I'm not sure how I'll get back."

"I'll pick you up," Carson said. "I've got to come over later on and see that woman. There's something in particular that I want to say to her."

At first neither Dora nor Jean spoke during the drive back to Wenham. Dora felt rather uncomfortable with this man she scarcely knew sitting beside her, and rather wished she hadn't offered him a lift. To her he was a complete enigma; lean, stern, taciturn, iron grey hair cut *en brosse*, thin unsmiling lips, deep lines creasing the corners of his mouth and eyes. These now stared straight in front of him and, as he clutched his hat on his knees, she noticed his knuckles were white with tension.

"Does my driving worry you, Mr Parterre?" she asked sarcastically.

"Not at all, Miss Yetman." He shifted awkwardly in his seat, but didn't take his eyes off the road.

"You seem rather ill at ease?"

"Oh?" He glanced quickly at her and she saw anxiety in his steady grey eyes.

"Maybe you don't approve of women driving?"

"On the contrary. I think they can do as they please. It is simply that I myself am not used to automobiles. I don't possess one. I can't drive one, so it makes me a bit nervous."

Dora was disarmed by this confession and grinned at him apologetically.

"I'm sorry. I thought that, with the war . . ."

"I was in the cavalry. Now, a horse I can understand."

"Oh, you were in the cavalry?" Dora exclaimed delightedly. "You know I adore horses?"

"I do too." He briefly shifted his gaze from the road. "And I've seen you riding. You've a splendid seat, Miss Yetman, if you don't mind me saying."

"Thank you." She felt herself blushing like a schoolgirl who had received an unexpectedly good report.

They fell silent while she again considered the man beside her, who suddenly seemed to have intruded on her consciousness. She realised she had scarcely ever been greatly aware of him, regarding him as someone who was a cross between a friend and an employee of Carson, someone vaguely there in the background when she visited Pelham's Oak which was, after all, mainly to ride. She wondered why Carson never asked him to join them.

"Do you and Carson ride together often?" she asked after a while.

"Together?" He shook his head vigorously. "I am an employee, you know, Miss Yetman. Carson has been good enough to give me a home and a wage, a job to do."

"And you do it very well." She stopped suddenly thinking that, perhaps, she sounded patronising. He didn't reply which confirmed her suspicion.

"I'm sorry," she said.

"Why should you be sorry, Miss Yetman?" His gaze was amused, quizzical.

"I hope I didn't sound offensive. I mean, about you doing it very well."

"On the contrary, I'm flattered."

Silence again. Then:

"Shall you settle in England do you think?"

"Oh no." He appeared amused by the idea. "I am a Frenchman. But I will stay as long as Carson wants me."

"You seem to do jobs for all the family."

"Quite." His mouth now set in a thin, humorous line. He appeared more at ease and she noticed as they crossed the bridge and drove up the street into Wenham that his hat sat on his knee, and, his hands no longer clenched, rested at ease in his lap. He seemed a very content, self-contained, philosophical man. Now that she knew him a tiny bit better she felt very glad that Carson had saved his life.

The hands of the church clock pointed towards four when Dora stopped outside Agnes's house. It was a dark, lowering January afternoon and the light was fading. Dora was surprised to see that the house was in darkness, so she turned to Jean Parterre, who had put his hat on and was about to get out of the car. "Did Aunt Agnes know you were coming?" she enquired.

"Oh yes. She told me to be here about three." He paused and looked at his watch. "I'm late. Maybe she couldn't wait."

"Funny." Dora shook her head and climbed out joining Jean on the pavement outside the gate.

"Maybe she fell asleep?" Jean suggested opening the gate, allowing Dora to precede him up the path to the front door.

After knocking twice Dora turned the door handle and the door swung inwards. She peered along the hall and saw that everything was in darkness. There was no sign of Grace, the maid – Carson had drawn the line at a butler – and the sense was that the house was deserted.

"Aunt Agnes!" Dora raised her voice. "Grace!"

No reply.

"Well, I'm very sorry." She turned to Jean who had stepped in after her. "Aunt appears to be out. How *very* annoying for you."

Jean removed his hat to scratch his head.

"Never mind, I'll wait for Carson."

"But Carson will be ages." Dora looked at her wristwatch.

"I'll find something to do." He seemed perfectly composed, apparently neither surprised nor annoyed by the vagaries of her aunt. He went back to the door and put on his hat preparing to go back down the garden path.

"Tell you what, I'll run you back," Dora said coming after him and pausing to close the door.

"No, really, it's not necessary. I'll find something to do in Wenham. I'll go and see what my men are doing at the church, they're working on the belfry. Then I have a few errands to do." He removed his hat again and ran his hand over his scalp. "Maybe I'll have a haircut."

"Well, if you're sure." Dora stood at the gate looking dubiously at him.

"Perfectly sure, Miss Yetman, and thank you for the lift. I . . ." They both turned at that moment as Grace, the maid, came running along the path past the church leading from the rectory. Although it was bitterly cold she wore only her uniform, a long grey dress over which there was a white pinafore. On her head was a plain white cap. She was clearly agitated and she gestured theatrically towards Dora who went anxiously up to her. "Grace what is it?"

"Oh, miss . . ." Grace clutched at Dora's arm.

"Something has happened to Aunt Agnes?"

"No, miss." Gulping, Grace shook her head. "It's that they can't find Miss Deborah, miss. She's been gone since this morning and her mother's out of her mind with worry. Mrs Turner came over to find out if she was with her ladyship, but she said she hadn't seen her since yesterday. Mrs Turner was that upset that Lady Woodville went back to the house with her."

"Well, maybe she's with a friend?" Dora took Grace's arm to try and soothe her and began to walk back with her towards the rectory. Glancing round she saw that Jean was following them.

"They've been all over the place, miss. Servants and people have gone in all directions. They fear that something may have happened to Miss Deborah." Grace flung out her arm dramatically. "That she's had an accident, fallen into the river or . . . been kidnapped."

But they didn't kidnap rectors' daughters, quiet respectable young girls who never left home without telling their mothers where they were going. It wasn't reasonable.

Kidnap seemed fanciful, alarmist. An accident, alas, a distinct possibility.

It was Jean Parterre who, once the situation had been summarised for him, took charge. He sent his men who were working on the belfry down to the river with instructions that, despite the cold, they were to wade in and search for the missing girl.

Deborah's absence had first been really noticed at lunch, which the family took together. It was always served at noon and was never missed. The Rector liked his midday meal and it was something of an occasion. Afterwards he went to his study, ostensibly to read or prepare a sermon, but Sophie had good reason to think he also combined these worthy tasks with a nap.

For one who was prone to hysteria at the least opportunity, Agnes had been surprisingly calm, a bulwark of solidarity and good sense. The first to assume a real crisis, she had made practical suggestions as to Deborah's possible whereabouts, and the servants were despatched to explore various possibilities. But by five, darkness having set in, of Deborah Woodville there was no sign.

When Carson arrived Jean Parterre's men had still not returned and there was now an awful feeling that the worst had happened, that, somehow, Deborah had lost her way and fallen into the river. Such a long absence was unique.

She had last been seen at breakfast after which the various members of the household went about their tasks: Hubert on a series of parish visits, Sophie to take a Bible class and attend a meeting of the Ladies' Guild. Deborah was keen on painting, but it was somewhat difficult to find an occupation for her. There were few young women of her age about in term time, and she showed none of her parents' interest in parochial affairs or the life of the church.

Despite her sadness at losing her father at an early age, Deborah Woodville had always been a spirited girl, rather wilful, quick-tempered and with her mother's stubbornness and liking for her own way.

Before her mother's second marriage she and her sister had lived for some time at Pelham's Oak looking after her grandfather and Debbie had never really forgotten that, but for her father's death, it would have been her rightful home now. She had the airs and tastes of a lady, which was perhaps why she got on so well with her step-grandmother, Agnes, with whom she spent a lot of time and who was an influence on her.

Sophie Turner was a devout, deeply religious woman who believed firmly in divine justice and the will of God. In the course of her life she had sinned, but God had been good to her. She had not deserved a second chance, but He gave her one: a good, devoted husband and two more children.

During the last few hours she had had to summon all her energy to avoid a hysterical outburst, to remain stoical and calm. She directed the servants and friends who came to call and offer help, despatching search parties to various parts of the town and to villages in the surrounding countryside. She did her best to calm her husband, who had almost lost control of his own emotions, so fond was he of his stepdaughters, reminding him of the innate goodness of God and His mercy.

But by late afternoon, with the earth blanketed in darkness, and bitterly cold, in her innermost heart she felt the deepest foreboding.

A silence had fallen with an awareness of what might have happened as the company sat round the fire drinking tea and talking in subdued tones. Every now and then they were interrupted by the return of one of the search parties, or a telephone call to report that another blank had been drawn.

Sophie stood by the window looking out at the darkening landscape. Even then the scene, familiar to her since childhood, was etched on her mind. She had been born in this house and lived in it until her marriage. The daughter of the Rector of Wenham, she had never thought she would marry his successor and one day preside as mistress of the house like her mother before her. Below flowed the River Wen which ran past Riversmead, where Sarah-Jane lived with her children, past the Rectory higher up and past the church which stood on the brow of a hill. Opposite was Wen Wood where she'd walked and played as a child, learnt about nature, observed the birds and various forms of animal life.

In the wood and fields surrounding the Rectory her children

played, innocents as she had been, and it would have been natural for Deborah to wander down by the river. But what had happened then?

As the church clock began to strike six she moved restlessly to rejoin the group huddled by the fire when the door opened abruptly and Jean Parterre, grim-faced, appeared with a man they recognised as one of those working on the belfry. He looked dishevelled and his clothes were soaking.

Sophie, fearing the worst, instinctively put her hands over her face and Carson jumped up and put his arm round her. Breathlessly they waited for Jean to speak.

"It is not what you think," he said at once. "We have not found a body." Sophie gave a loud sigh and sank into a chair. Hubert went and sat next to her, taking her hand.

"We may, however, have a clue as to Deborah's whereabouts," Jean continued. "If it is true it is not exactly good news, but I think it is better than thinking she is dead."

"What do you mean?" Sophie clutched at her breast and looked up at him.

"This is Bob Trotman," Jean pointed to the dishevelled workman standing beside him, clearly ill at ease in the exalted company in which he found himself. "He is a stonemason working on the belfry." Jean cleared his throat awkwardly. "Well, Bob tells me that Deborah was in the habit of visiting the belfry site almost every day, sometimes several times a day. She seemed to have a special interest in one of my workmen, Michael Stansgate, and he . . ." Jean looked over at Sophie, "seemed to return that interest. When I went over today to ask for the help of the men I noticed that Michael was not there, but didn't think to enquire. With casual labour you have people coming and going. In the last half hour Bob has told me that it would not surprise him if they had gone off together . . ."

"*Impossible*!" Sophie said sternly. "Deborah would never—"

"*That's* what you might think, my dear," Agnes moved across to sit on the other side of Sophie, "but I *have* noticed recently that dearest Debbie did seem particularly animated,

173

and I jokingly asked her only one day last week if she was in love."

"And . . . ?" Sophie asked raising her head.

"She smiled and said nothing," Agnes replied.

Jean waited politely for Agnes to finish and then continued: "Bob says that yesterday Deborah came over several times and she and Michael went off together and huddled in the churchyard. He had to call him back to work." He paused as if to allow the meaning of his words to sink in.

"Where did this Michael live?" Sophie's voice was flat, unemotional.

Jean turned to Bob Trotman, who scratched his head and mumbled.

"That's the point, Mrs Turner, no one seems to know."

"He is an itinerant worker," Jean explained. "They travel around the country doing odd jobs. He arrived in Wenham about two months ago looking for work and I took him on as a carpenter. He worked first at Pelham's Oak and then I transferred him to the belfry. He was a very capable workman."

"And what age is he?" The Rector finally found his voice.

"About twenty-five, Reverend," Bob muttered.

"And had you any idea where he came from?"

Bob shook his head and shuffled his feet.

"None of us had, sir."

"It seems extraordinary to me," Agnes burst out indignantly, "that you can employ a workman without knowing anything about him."

"Well, you can," Jean replied. "They are taken on, paid and that's it. They have to find their own board and lodging. Some stay for a long time, weeks, months, years. They might settle down in the locality, or they might just decide to move on without notice. They like this kind of life. One day they're there, the next day they've gone."

"In other words," Carson intervened, "it might be impossible to trace him, or know the truth, whether Debbie is with him or not."

Silently Jean nodded, and Agnes turned to Sophie and grasped her hand. "Debbie would *never* do a thing like that! If she has eloped she will get in touch with you. She would *never* make you suffer." Agnes bent towards Sophie and impulsively kissed her cheek. Then she leaned back still holding her hand. "My dear, even if Debbie has run off with this man surely it is better to know she is alive than . . ."

Her voice trailed off. There was a profound silence in the room. It was impossible for those assembled to guess whether Sophie Woodville, a woman of great piety and principle, would prefer her beloved daughter to have suffered death or dishonour.

Sophie raised her head, the expression in her eyes unfathomable.

She gave them no clue.

Chapter Eleven

The little town of Wenham was plunged into gloom by the disappearance of the popular Rector's stepdaughter, its inhabitants for the most part shocked. For the most part because, human nature being what it is, there were some who were more titillated than others when a possible explanation for the disappearance became apparent: the fact that eighteen-year old Deborah may have run off with a man; an itinerant, uneducated workman to boot.

Those with long memories recalled the elopement of Deborah's great aunt, Eliza, with Ryder Yetman, in similar circumstances except that Eliza did not keep her own mother ignorant about her fate. But after the runaways returned and, indeed, were respectably married, it took a long time for her family to forgive her. In fact her mother never did, and the townsfolk never forgot.

Of course these were modern times, a dreadful war had been fought, and views about morality had undergone a profound change. Women, though not all, now had the vote; they were admitted to universities, though not on the same terms as men. Yes, but . . . there was still a definite stigma attached to immoral women – far more than to immoral men – and, doubtless, that would rub off on Deborah and her family, were she ever to return to Wenham.

There were those who thought there was bad blood in the Woodville family and now, as these things do, it had come out again in the apparently innocent, virginal daughter of the saintly George Woodville who had given his life for Christ in the missions in far away Papua, New Guinea.

Wenham was a cheerful, friendly town where people stopped in the streets to pass the time of day and bid each other "good morning" or "good afternoon". It had changed little in the last hundred years, advanced only slowly with the times. The store that Connie's guardian, Victoria Fairchild, had taken over from her parents and run until her retirement still occupied a central position in the High Street between the bank and the solicitor's. Opposite was the Baker's Arms, the local public house and, next to that, the butcher. A little further on, the greengrocer, the saddler, a hardware store and the bakery clustered round the market cross.

One big change that had occurred in the last few years was that the pigs, sheep and cows that used to throng the street on market days had been transferred to a new location on the far side of the town from which, however, their mournful cries could still be heard on market day. The Women's Institute had also taken up a stall in the new market from which it sold freshly baked cakes and bread, cheese, home-cured ham and home-reared chickens, flowers and home-made jam.

A good deal of talk concerning Deborah Woodville naturally went on among the women who ran the stall, and those who purchased goods from it. There was some criticism but much kindness too. Sophie Turner was seen as an irreproachable mother without a stain on her character, but maybe she had been too preoccupied with church affairs to consider what her nubile, attractive daughter's needs were in the modern world. Having been allowed to leave school, maybe some occupation should have been found for her, some form of training, if not for the church like her parents, then maybe as a teacher or a governess. Deborah had been allowed to do as she pleased while her parents got on with their busy lives. Idle bones led to idle thoughts, and with the proximity of some virile young workman, well . . . no wonder.

However these very same people who speculated, sometimes unkindly, also bombarded the rectory with gifts: cakes, pots of jam, chickens, fresh eggs and so on. Some were simply left

178

on the steps or at the gate, some were handed in by those hoping for up-to-date news which they could pass on to their friends, with the cachet that it had come straight from the horse's mouth.

Despite her affliction, Sophie felt surrounded by love, sustained by the power of prayer as the days passed and no news came of Deborah's whereabouts, until she began to wonder if her daughter had first been abducted and then done away with by the man who had made off with her.

The day after the disappearance, Carson and Jean Parterre had set off to look for the couple. They had absolutely no clues and no idea where they should start. Instinctively they chose to go west because the remoteness of Devon and Cornwall might have been thought to offer some protection. Their hunch seemed to have paid off because, while awaiting a train at Yeovil station, they heard by chance that a young couple had been seen there the day after Debbie disappeared and there had been something about them, the girl's obvious youth, a certain furtiveness about the man, that had attracted the attention of the station porter. It was then ascertained that the train they had boarded had been *en route* for Exeter so, with hope in their hearts, Carson and Jean Parterre took a train going in the same direction.

In the circumstances, Connie was as much affected by the tragedy as any member of the family, despite the fact that Debbie was no direct relation. She abandoned her plans to return to Venice to be with Eliza, who was the girl's aunt, and to comfort Agnes who somehow, and erroneously, felt a responsibility for what had happened.

She had been close to Guy's granddaughter who was pretty and entertaining, and the two got on well. In some ways she reminded Agnes of her youthful self; someone who was rather restless, frustrated by the circumscribed life of the parson's daughter. In the painful hours she had had to reflect, the hours that seemed especially long and tormenting at night, Agnes wondered if maybe she had fed the young girl's mind with thoughts of flight by expressing too vigorously her criticism of the provincial nature of the town in which she now felt herself imprisoned? She would entertain Debbie with tales of continental travel, the delights of London, the opportunities offered by the outside world, and contrast it with the dismal prospects one could expect if left forever in Wenham.

Debbie had loved these stories, her eyes had lit up as she egged on her stepgrandmother to tell her more and, delighted to have an audience who appreciated her, on Agnes went, and on and on: stories of the grand hotels she and Owen had stayed in on the continent, the sumptuous restaurants where they had eaten, the sights they had seen: the Forum in Rome, the Colosseum; the Arc de Triomphe and the Eiffel Tower in Paris; the huge palace built by Louis XIV in Versailles; the Bay of Naples; the Matterhorn glimpsed at sunset from the balcony of a Swiss hotel . . . it was endless. It fed not only Debbie's desire for fantasy, but Agnes's too and it also expressed her frustration, her despair at being trapped in a place she disliked so much. Maybe she had unwittingly engendered a similar dissatisfaction in the heart of an impressionable and imaginative young girl?

Oh yes, Agnes felt guilt, terrible guilt, but she didn't tell Connie or the rest of her family the reason for it; she couldn't confess to them how she had fed the young mind with dreams and perhaps, thereby, helped to corrupt it.

Agnes became something of a changed person after Debbie disappeared. She forgot her many grievances and stopped complaining about her lot and thought of someone else instead. She thought particularly of Sophie who she had always regarded as a rather stuck-up, pious prig, considering herself better than other people. She knew that Sophie had very little time for her, considering her spoilt, interfering and demanding. It was Agnes who had been responsible for forcing Sophie and her children to leave Pelham's Oak after her marriage to the children's grandfather. Nor did Sophie approve of all the time Deborah had spent in her stepgrandmother's company but, being such a busy person helping her husband to run the parish and looking after her two little boys, there was little she could do about it.

180

Every day after Debbie disappeared, Agnes would call at Sophie's to see if there was news, ask if there was anything she could do and, generally, try and make herself useful. She would take the boys for a walk, entertain them in her home, being careful not to fill their youthful hearts with the same sort of discontent she suspected she had inspired in Debbie. Instead she read them wholesome tales from Beatrix Potter or other suitable writers of children's stories, and culled her long memory for childish games or educational and instructive things to do.

A week passed, two weeks passed. There was no news of Debbie. The town grew restless, fears deepened. On both Sundays the church congregation swelled to embrace those who scarcely ever passed its portals. It was not only for news or out of curiosity, a nose for notoriety even, although there was some element of each, but also out of a profound and genuine desire to express hope and solidarity with a well-loved parish priest and his family.

Agnes closed the gate leading to her house, having thoroughly briefed Grace and left her more than enough work to keep her out of mischief, and made her way through the churchyard to the Rectory. The crocuses were out, interspersed among the graves, and she always considered this a harbinger of spring, although it was a good way off. Would Debbie be back by the spring? Would they ever see her again? Sometimes in her heart of hearts she felt that the answer would be "no". Debbie was not the sort of girl to inflict such misery on her mother. If she was still alive, ashamed of herself she might have been, but surely, surely, she would not have put her mother through the torment she was enduring now? Surely, in that case, she must be unable to communicate; kept a virtual prisoner or, to think the unthinkable, dead.

Agnes was admitted by the maid, Bessie, who confessed that Mrs Turner was not in the best of health. She was up and dressed, but had cancelled her programme for the day and remained in her small sitting room which was off the main hall. Agnes was asked to wait while Bessie went to see if Mrs Turner felt fit enough to see Lady Woodville, but she returned with a smile and said the Rector's wife would be glad of her company.

When Agnes entered the room Sophie was standing by the window, her face half hidden by the shadow formed by the curtain. When she turned to greet and embrace Agnes it was plain to see that she had been crying.

"No news?" Agnes asked, taking Sophie's hand and leading her to the sofa and the comfort of the warm fire.

"No news." Sophie shook her head and wiped tears from her eyes. "I had a terrible night during which I had visions of Deborah . . . of my darling . . ." momentarily she broke down, "dead. I saw her poor little white face . . ." She then stopped altogether and her shoulders heaved in silent weeping. Agnes put her arm round her and, drawing her head upon her matronly breast, tried to comfort her as she would a small child.

"There, there," she said patting her gently. "There, there." She thought it best not to voice her own strangely similar fears. Maybe they both had a premonition that some harm had, indeed, befallen Debbie?

Bessie popped her head round and asked if Mrs Woodville and her ladyship would like coffee? Sophie wiped her eyes, blew her nose and gave a tremulous smile. Yes, she thought they would, and when Bessie returned a few minutes later with a pot of coffee on a tray together with a plate of little cakes she thanked her for thinking of it.

"I don't think you'd eat or drink at *all*, mum," Bessie said reprovingly. "If the matter was left to you or the Rector you'd starve." She then bobbed, smiled and excused herself.

"So kind." Sophie swept the hair back from her face and began to pour the coffee. "Everyone has been so kind. Our servants have grieved as much as we have. The people of Wenham, oh . . ." she paused and handed Agnes her cup, "it's been unbelievable. It has restored my faith in the goodness of God, and I must say," she paused again to stir her coffee, and sighed deeply, "that has been sadly tried these past two weeks. I think," she bent her head thoughtfully, "I think that God is punishing me for my past sins . . ."

"But you have not committed any sins!" Agnes exclaimed in astonishment. "You have been an exemplary person, a most devoted wife and mother. You were even very nice to me when I was so horrible to you before I married Guy." In her turn Agnes bowed her head in shame. "Do you not think, dear Sophie, how I grieve on account of the way I behaved? This tragedy to Debbie has made me see myself for the single-minded, selfish creature I am, or was. But you . . ."

"No *I* have sinned," Sophie insisted. "And this is the punishment. It is called Divine retribution." She gazed fearfully at Agnes, her eyes puffy, her face streaked with tears. She was an attractive rather than a pretty woman – her character more than her looks had always been considered her strong suit – but now she appeared plain. It also seemed to Agnes that she had aged suddenly, and there were grey streaks in her rich brown hair that had not been there two weeks before.

"My son, Sam, is not Mr Turner's child . . . that was my sin."

Agnes looked at her in amazement.

"But you were married to Hubert when your child was born!"

"But not when he was conceived," Sophie whispered. "I had a liaison of which I am deeply ashamed."

"Does Hubert know?" Agnes stammered having suffered a profound shock, not in the sense of disapproval, someone with a history like hers could hardly feel that, but because it was a situation in which it was almost impossible to imagine the virtuous Sophie.

"The man concerned was unworthy," Sophie continued tremulously. "I became obsessed by him. He promised to marry me and I anticipated the marriage act. He then abandoned me and . . ."

"Does Hubert know all this?" Agnes asked again.

"Oh yes." Sophie gazed at the floor, involuntarily clenching her fists. "He had already proposed to me but, thinking myself in love with this other . . . person, I declined. I was about to leave Wenham so that my parents would not know of my shame, when Hubert asked me to marry him again. I told him everything." She dashed the tears away from her eyes once more. "I can't tell you how much I owe to the goodness of that man. He has become a real father to my two girls, he loves them like one. He is the most considerate and thoughtful of husbands . . . and yet now we find it difficult to reach out to each other, to comfort each other. I think Hubert blames me for not keeping closer control on Debbie. He says I abandoned my parental role. Maybe he also recalls my own sin and thinks too that this is God's punishment. It is also my fear we are becoming estranged, and that he feels, as I do, that God has abandoned me for the sins of my past."

She suddenly threw herself once more into the arms of Agnes, who did her best to comfort her. But it was hard for her to know what to say. For she herself was a woman who had sinned and was only rarely visited by any sense of guilt. When this came it was in the dark hours, depriving her of sleep until dawn. Such guilt as she had was not on account of her past life as a woman of easy virtue, because to her sins of the flesh were venial.

Her real sin, the unforgivable one, was that she had wantonly abandoned her own daughter who now lived not a dozen miles from the mother she would not have recognised. Agnes had tried to put this out of her mind but, with advancing years, it became harder and harder because she realised that she was a woman with few friends, whom no one really liked. Now that Owen had deserted her she so longed for someone she could truly call her own; who would love, protect and look after her.

But she had no one.

Eliza also found it very difficult to know how to occupy her time in those first weeks after Debbie went missing. Although she felt no responsibility for the tragedy – how could she? – she knew that it had awoken memories in people of her own elopement forty years before. Even those who didn't remember it, who were too young or not yet born, were told it by older relatives who did. Some learnt about it for the first time: that Eliza Heering, pillar of society and respectability, had once run away with a man to whom she was not married.

Eliza was aware of the glances she got when she went into the town, knowing sniggers behind raised palms. It revived painful memories of long ago. But now it no longer worried her as it had then; she was far too old, too seasoned, too inured to tragedy and unhappiness to care.

It was, however, extraordinary how vivid the past could be, and how easily she could recall her emotions that time so long ago when she herself was eighteen, and she and Ryder had eloped with only their horses to carry them and trekked all the way up to the Lake District. She recalled the baby she had lost, eight weeks' premature and stillborn, and which Ryder had buried by the light of a hurricane lamp in the hard, snow-covered ground because they could not afford a proper burial. Eliza had watched from their tiny cottage, her heart breaking, her face swollen by tears. They had called the baby Thomas.

She often thought of that small, unmarked grave deep in the Lakeland hills. She knew that even if she wished she would not be able to find it now. Since then another grave had taken another of her sons, Laurence, a loving husband and father of three who had been driven to suicide at the age of thirty. She had buried a husband, a mother and brother, and lost a beloved nephew, George, whose daughter had now added to the family's suffering by her strange disappearance.

It was mid-morning and Julius was pottering in his greenhouses while Connie and Dora were walking the dogs in the woods beyond the house, well wrapped up against the cold. The two, who had not been very close as children, now got on well. Both had changed, but particularly Connie who seemed to Eliza like a butterfly who had finally emerged from its chrysalis. Dora had also matured. She had been deeply affected by her experiences in the war, but she had always had self-confidence, self-assurance and a degree of charm which disarmed those critics who thought she was too aloof, perhaps a touch haughty.

Eliza's relief at May's marriage had been palpable. Though she was too well brought up and well mannered to show it, she hadn't really liked May. She had tolerated her, but not welcomed her as a member of the household. May too was self-centred, but in another person's house this seemed rather out of context. She tended to behave as though she was a daughter of the house, like Dora, and could do what she liked. She seemed particularly to enjoy ordering the servants about and giving them petty errands which she had no right to do. Accordingly she became unpopular with them. If Dora had thought her husband unworthy of May, Eliza felt she was unworthy of Dora. In any event she couldn't understand the nature of this strange relationship between two such different women.

Eliza stood by the window drinking coffee, looking out upon the landscape and the light covering of snow that had fallen overnight and had now frozen hard. She wondered where poor Debbie was at this moment and tried not to think of her sheltering, perhaps, from the elements or even lying somewhere under the white landscape in an unmarked grave like her poor little Thomas.

She went back into the room and threw some logs on the fire. Despite the heat she felt chilled and desolate, and wished she could find something to do, to occupy her mind. In the afternoon they planned to visit Sophie, and these visits gave a focus to days that were largely without meaning. Eliza thought that disappearance was worse than death. Whether alive or not it would be far better if Debbie were to be found.

She heard male voices in the hall outside the drawing room and started up, listening. Carson! She flew to the door and threw it open. The butler was helping him out of his coat and, behind him, beginning to divest himself, was Jean Parterre.

Both men turned as the door opened and momentarily they all gazed at one another, expressions frozen.

"Any . . ." Eliza began but as soon as she opened her mouth she knew the answer.

"No news," Carson shook his head, and went over to kiss his aunt. "We can't find a sign of them. It was a wasted trip." They went into the drawing room, followed by Jean Parterre, who closed the door behind them.

"We scoured the whole of Cornwall," Jean cried, flinging up his arms in despair. "It is such a quiet time of the year that someone should have noticed a young couple without a home, or perhaps seeking lodgings."

"We think we went in the wrong direction." Carson threw himself into a chair in front of the fire, and then leaned forward to warm his hands at the blaze.

"We thought perhaps Michael might have a home and had taken her there." Jean knelt in front of the fire towards which he too stretched his hands. "In that case it could be in any part of the country." He paused shaking his head. "I feel so guilty."

"But there is no need for you to feel guilty." In an effort to reassure him Eliza knelt by his side, just restraining herself from putting an arm round his waist, he looked so desolate. "It is not your fault. No one could possibly blame you."

"I employed the man. I should have found out more about him. It is a lesson to me, one I shall never forget. I shall always, always take names, addresses of next of kin . . ."

"They could always lie to you." Carson extracted a cigarette from a packet in his pocket and lit it with a spool from the hearth.

"True."

"But to feel guilty is absurd." Eliza was anxious to put his mind at rest. "You might as well blame Hubert for having the belfry repaired."

"Or God for putting the church there," Carson added, looking round, "By the way, where are the girls?"

"They're out walking. I thought they might have seen you arrive. How did you come?"

"We took a cab from the station." Carson thoughtfully rubbed his chin which was unshaven. "I must buy a car. I must enter the twentieth century. It is a great handicap not to have one. We travelled everywhere by train and bus."

"Well, you've done all you can . . ."

Eliza paused as the door opened and Dora rushed into the room, followed by Connie. Dora ran straight over to Carson and flung her arms round his neck. "We saw you arrive." She stood back, her eyes closely studying his face.

"No news," he shook his head. "None at all. We drew a blank." Carson looked over to Connie who was shutting the door.

She stood for a moment as if she was not quite sure what to do. Then she came over to him and, rather stiffly, held out her hand. "I'm so sorry," she said as Carson, rising, took her hand and shook it with a formality that seemed strange between people who were so well acquainted. He then leaned forward impulsively and kissed her on the cheek.

Connie shook hands with Jean Parterre and then sat on the arm of the chair Dora occupied, next to her mother. "Tell us about the search."

While the men told their story the butler brought coffee and Eliza ordered the numbers to be extended for lunch.

"Well, you did all you could," Dora said when they had concluded. "What about the police?"

"We have not really been able to interest the police very much." Carson shook his head. "They think it is a case of elopement. They have no reason to think a crime has been committed. If a person disappears voluntarily there isn't much you can do about it."

"But Debbie is under age!" Eliza exclaimed angrily. "She might have been abducted."

"Well they're not doing very much except going through the motions."

"I'm going back anyway," Jean Parterre said firmly.

"But where will you go?"

"I will scour England, if necessary. If it takes years I will find out what happened to Debbie. Whatever you say I feel a responsibility. Michael Stansgate was my man."

"And Carson will you go?" Eliza looked anxiously at him. Carson shook his head.

"If I'm away any longer I'm afraid the management of the estate will become impossible. There is so much to do and without Jean it's hard enough. I understand why Jean is doing what he thinks best, but anyway without a car . . . it's pretty hopeless."

"I'll take you," Dora said suddenly and everyone looked at her.

"But you can't," Eliza began.

"Why not?" Dora stared at her mother, her expression of stubbornness one with which Eliza was familiar.

"Well . . ." Eliza, lost for words, looked at Carson for help. "Can she Carson?"

"I don't see why not."

"No, I would never dream—" Jean Parterre began.

"Look!" Dora said, "Debbie is my cousin. I love her. I want to find her. I have nothing to do and I have a car. Jean can't drive or I'd lend it to him. We can get round the country much more quickly and follow clues. Besides," she smiled easily around at the rather startled group, "I'd like it."

Eliza felt far from happy, but Dora was no child and, knowing her, she would do as she pleased. However, it was like Dora to offer and it was a task she would enjoy and do well.

"When do we start?" Dora's eyes gleamed with excitement as she looked across at Jean, who seemed nonplussed.

"Well, if you're sure . . ."

"You're not *frightened* of me are you?" She smiled wickedly at him.

"Of course not," he said indignantly.

"I mean we don't have to talk to each other if we don't want to. You can regard me simply as the driver, oh and I shall also enjoy the role of playing the detective too."

Jean Parterre suddenly smiled and his tired, worn expression relaxed.

"I think I'd rather enjoy it myself," he said. "At least I know I shan't be bored."

"When do we start?" Dora jumped up excitedly. "Oh I would so *love* to be the one to find Debbie."

"I have to get clean clothes, maybe a night's good sleep," Jean said, rubbing his eyes. "Is tomorrow all right?"

"Tomorrow's absolutely fine," Dora said. "I'll pick you up about nine."

Jean merely smiled, as if bemused.

After luncheon Dora took Jean over to report to Sophie, promising to come back for Carson. Julius went into his study and Eliza upstairs for a nap. She slept so badly at night that she rested in the afternoon.

Somewhat to their consternation Carson and Connie found themselves alone together in the drawing room drinking coffee. Carson lay back on the sofa, a cigarette burning between his fingers, his face pale and his eyes half closed.

"Carson, you look so tired." Connie, sitting opposite him, leaned forward in her chair, hands linked in front of her.

"I am tired. I don't think I've been as tired as this since the war, but then there was a different kind of danger."

"But this wasn't dangerous."

"Yes it was." He looked up at her and flicked ash into the ashtray beside the chair. "You don't understand. I feel desolate about Debbie, about her fate, thinking we may have been near her but not found her. We took off into the dark, and maybe it was rather absurd, but we felt we had to do it. Just as Dora does now."

"Do you think she's alive?" Connie's tone was subdued.

"I don't know. I don't know what has happened to her." He stubbed out his cigarette and closed his eyes. "God, I could sleep for a week. Do you think Jean Parterre and Dora will be okay together?" He opened one eye and looked at her.

"Why shouldn't they be? They're both grown up."

"Quite. Both stubborn people too." Carson closed his eyes again and looked as though he was falling asleep. Surreptitiously Connie studied his face. She felt there was a curious mood of intimacy between them, as pleasant as it was unexpected. She wanted to stretch out her hand and touch him, stroke his brow, but she didn't dare. There, in the silence of the room, a silence broken only by the crackle of logs in the grate, she realised that she loved Carson and always had. She loved him when she was a small, gauche, awkward girl and he was a heroic young Lochinvar character, a daredevil who everyone told stories about, up to no good. She worshipped him and he was kind to her, escorted her home from church, praised her singing. He was so kind to her that she thought, in fact, that he did love her even though it seemed impossible.

For a few short, unbelievably heady months, believe it she did. It was nearly ten years ago, and all that had changed. They had changed. Yet they still knew each other very well. They were at ease with each other.

Carson, eyes still closed, lifted his hand and beckoned to her. Connie remained where she was.

Carson opened his eyes.

"Come here," he said. "Come and sit beside me."

She did as he asked but kept a distance between them on the sofa. She was suddenly that shy, timid little mouse again, almost paralysed with fright.

He moved his hand towards hers and clasped it. She didn't resist.

"I missed you," he said.

Still she didn't speak.

"I thought of you all the time. I have ever since you've been here, and you avoid me."

"I . . ." her mouth was dry. "I don't know what to say."

"You avoid me because Aunt Agnes says I'm after your money"

Connie's face flushed. She felt as though the old Connie had

Nicola Thorne

returned, shy, retiring Connie, and she tried to withdraw her
hand, but Carson hung on to it.

"Also that I am a womaniser."

She tried once more to drag her hand away but he gripped
it even harder.

Suddenly he opened his eyes and sat up, turned towards
her.

"Connie I would never touch a penny of your money. It is
a great disadvantage for a man to marry a wealthy woman. If
such a thing were to come to pass the money that you have I
want you to keep. I want no part of it."

Connie took a deep breath and the vision of that timid little
mouse of yesteryear faded.

"And if such a thing were to come about," she said cautiously,
"it is a great, a very great disadvantage for a woman even to
consider marrying someone to whom she was once engaged, and
to be certain that he loved her."

"But you loved me?"

"Yes. Then."

"I love you now. If I didn't love you then, or maybe I did but
didn't realise it, now I know I do. I used to like the company
of women when I was a gauche youth, but now I only want
the company of one woman. Aunt Agnes is a mischief maker,
and always has been. She is now a bitter, cantankerous old
bitch . . ."

"A very sad person," Connie gently interrupted him. "She has
been completely changed by what has happened to Debbie."

"Aunt Agnes will never change. Once this crisis is over she
will revert. Connie?"

"Yes?"

"Well? What do you say?"

She remembered the last time he'd proposed. She had been
playing the organ in church and he sat at the back waiting for her.
He offered to see her home. Having been propelled by his father
and her guardian his manner was understandably awkward and
his expression unhappy. She asked him if he had a cold coming

192

on. He asked her to marry him. She couldn't believe it, and she couldn't believe it now. She'd told him in those far off days that she could never imagine that he loved her. But now?

She looked into his eyes and saw that they were smiling. They were very blue and beautiful. He was beautiful. He pulled her towards him and she found herself in his arms. He caressed her gently, his lips closing on hers. The first time he proposed his kiss had been so very chaste, a peck on the cheek, nothing more.

This time it was deeply passionate, filled with all his longing to be part of her.

Chapter Twelve

Leaning against the bonnet of the car, Dora carefully studied the map that she'd spread out in front of her. Behind her stood Jean Parterre, coat collar turned up, hands in his pockets, shivering on account of the icy wind that blew through the valley. Behind them rose Bowness and, below them, the clear waters of Lake Ennerdale glistened in the pale spring sunshine. As it had forty years before, a thin layer of snow covered the earth freezing the new-born lambs and stunting the growth of spring flowers.

"Here!" Dora exclaimed, keeping one finger on the map as she turned to beckon to Jean with another. "I'm sure this is the farm where my parents stayed. Come see." She looked up at him with excitement and he took her place, inspecting the position she'd indicated on the map. Raising her binoculars Dora's eyes fastened on a spot about a couple of miles away. This was a large farmhouse with outbuildings tucked into the side of the fell bordering on Lake Ennerdale, one of the most remote in Lakeland.

"I'm *sure* that's it," Dora said over her shoulder, "and there," she pointed at a white speck in the distance, "that, I'm convinced, is the cottage where my parents lived. Mother said it was on the shores of the lake, near the farm."

She handed the glasses to Jean, who peered through them, carefully studying the terrain below him. Finally he turned to her, shaking his head. "It's an incredibly lonely spot. How long were they here for?"

"I think about six months." Dora thoughtfully screwed up

195

her nose. "I'm not sure. The farmer who owned it was a horrible man and they hated him. His name was Frith. My mother had her first baby here. It was a boy. My father buried him at night in the field next to the cottage." She paused and looked gravely at her companion. "It's hard to believe isn't it? How primitive conditions were then. It must have been a terrible time for them both."

"Terrible," Jean Parterre murmured. "What do you want to do now, Dora?"

"Well, seeing that we're here, I'd like to go and have a look at the farm. Tell Mother we've been. Take some snaps. The point is," she looked at the narrow road ahead of them, "how do we get there?"

"There must be a track." Jean studied the Ordnance Map once more. "Yes, see. There must be a gate along the road which turns off down to the left. I hope the farmer won't be as unpleasant with us as he was with your parents. Supposing it's the same family?"

Dora laughed and, folding the map, opened the door of the car by the driver's seat and stuffed it into the glove compartment. Then she slid into the seat and, putting hands to the wheel, looked at Jean. "Hop in."

Once he was seated she started the car, and drove very slowly along the road on the lookout for the gate that she hoped would take them to the farm. "If it is the same family, and it's not unlikely, well they can't do anything to us. Fortunately we are not in the same position as my poor parents. They had no money and my mother was only nineteen. But later on my father returned for the horse they'd had to leave behind and, as well as the horse, he brought home with him Beth, who has been a servant and family friend to us ever since. She stayed at Riversmead with my brother and sister-in-law when my mother remarried. I believe that by way of a 'goodbye' my father also toppled Farmer Frith head-first into a barrel of water, so let's hope he isn't still there!"

"He needn't know who you are," Jean Parterre said laughing.

"If it's Farmer Frith, be sure I'll keep it quiet."

Jean looked fondly at Dora who, intent on the road, was oblivious to his admiring glance. The search for Debbie had proved an impossible task. It literally was like looking for a needle in a haystack, with no clues to go on as to which direction they should take, or where to start.

It was Dora who recalled her parents' epic journey on horseback to Lakeland in that autumn and winter of 1880, a story that she had heard many times from her mother as soon as she and her brothers had been old enough to understand and appreciate what their parents had been through.

It was a hunch of Dora's to go north in case Debbie had heard the same story from her great-aunt and, maybe, had been tempted to go there too. Debbie was a romantic and Dora knew how influenced she was by these tales of the past, how fascinated she had been by Agnes's adventurous life. Dora was not *sure* that Debbie knew the story of the elopement, but it was not beyond the bounds of possibility to imagine that she might have done, and been tempted to flee there with her lover.

"Look there's a gate," Jean Parterre shouted and peered forward to try and see the name on the gatepost. "Hunter's Hill farm," he read out.

"That's it!" Dora cried braking suddenly. And, as the car came to a standstill, Jean opened the door and jumped out, looking over the gate towards the farm at the bottom.

"There's a track," he said on returning "It's very uneven and slippery. Frankly, I think we should leave the car here."

"Right," Dora said and, after manoeuvring the car to the side of the road, jumped out and locked the doors. She wore a leather sheepskin coat over a tweed skirt and jersey and had a stout pair of boots on her feet. She stood beside Jean and gazed towards the farm. It had started to snow again, the sun had gone in, and a thick mist was advancing across the valley, obscuring everything in its path.

Jean opened the gate and closed it carefully after Dora had come through. Then, hands in their pockets, heads lowered against the elements, they trudged along the track, deeply conscious of the significance of the occasion, but having little doubt that, yet again, it would end in disappointment. It didn't seem possible that Debbie and Michael Stansgate could have ended up in this remote spot so far from home, unless they had the same intention as Eliza and Ryder all those years ago: to be married next to the anvil by the blacksmith in Gretna Green. They were now in the sixth week of their quest, criss-crossing the country, and it had been a time of surprises, not the least being how well they got on.

There had been a sense of camaraderie between them almost from the beginning, a friendship based on mutual liking and respect. They were at ease in each other's company and they found they had a lot in common, beginning with the war. They talked about it a great deal, exchanging stories about their adventures, experiences and the many tragic episodes they had witnessed. Jean couldn't speak highly enough of Carson, praised his courage, his strength, his stoicism, his bravery and Dora, who had always loved him, bathed in his reflected glory. Jean found Dora an enchanting companion; interesting, intelligent and a good raconteur. She also liked to eat and drink well, smoke and swap tall stories. In many ways in was like being with a man, a comrade rather than a woman, and he realised that this was because some element was missing: sex. There was no sexual element in his relationship with Dora at all.

Not that he didn't find her attractive, but there was also a curious element of asexuality about her that, he realised, he had found quite often among the nursing staff during the war as if, for professional reasons, they had to distance themselves from men. If this was the case why, then, did she feel she had to distance herself from him?

It was difficult to admit that such a sad, thankless journey should also be an enjoyable one, but it was and now that it was nearly over, because it had to end some time, he knew he would be sorry. He would miss the friendship and companionship of this delightful woman. Without her an important dimension would have gone from his life.

They reached the farm after a few minutes and stood looking about them. There was a water butt in the yard and Dora realised that this must have been the one in which her father had ducked Farmer Frith. The large, comfortable looking farmhouse was in front of them, barns and outbuildings to one side. The cattle were still penned up and gazed mournfully at them, vapour formed by the cold air billowing from their nostrils. There was no sign of anyone about.

Trying to get her bearings Dora indicated a path away from the farm which led towards the lake and, as they followed it, clearing the last of the outlying barns, she saw the whitewashed cottage practically on the very edge of the lake. She clutched Jean's arm.

"That's it. Oh Jean!" She put her hands to her face and he placed a comforting arm round her.

"It's so hard to imagine, isn't it?" she said after a while, lowering her hands. "Mother, just the age Debbie is now . . ." She shook her head and, gazing down at her, Jean saw tears in her eyes.

"I'm afraid that if you think history will repeat itself you're going to be disappointed," he said. "The cottage looks empty."

"Oh, I didn't for a moment think . . ." As he released her, Dora dug her hands into her pockets again and wandered slowly towards the cottage. She peered in through the windows, rubbing the pane with her gloved hand in order to get a better view. Jean, meanwhile, tried the handle of the door but it was locked. Cobwebs hung from the porch, and weeds grew across the threshold. Dora then turned and looked over at the field.

"Somewhere there my little brother is buried," she whispered, a catch in her voice. "They called him Thomas. I wish I'd brought some flowers." She shook her head, "It all seems so sad, so sad."

"What did the baby die of?"

"He was stillborn, eight weeks premature. Mother was undernourished and she had had to work so hard in the house."

"Try and put it out of your mind," Jean said gently and, as they turned their backs on the cottage, over which there hung an unmistakable air of sadness, he put his arm round her shoulders again, and hugged her to him.

"I must take a photo for Mother," Dora said taking her camera out of its box. "I promised I would."

She aimed carefully and took one of the cottage, one of the field next to it, the possible burial place of Thomas, and then, turning, photographed the farm buildings before stowing her camera away.

When they reached the farmyard they saw a man watching them from the doorstep, a scowl on his face. He was quite young so he couldn't be Farmer Frith, who had been much older than her parents forty years before, and was most probably dead. Dora tried to appease the man with a friendly smile but his expression didn't change.

"Mr Frith?" she enquired.

"Frith?" The man's scowl deepened. "You're looking for Farmer Frith?"

"Well . . . yes. We understood this was Frith's Farm."

"Frith has been gone twenty years or more," the man said. "The old man died and he only had a daughter. There was no one to run it."

"I see. Well, thank you. I'm sorry we troubled you."

"You might at least ask before you go snooping round private property." The farmer's tone was aggressive. "Lucky I didn't set my dogs on you!"

"I really *am* sorry." Dora's tone hardened. "But we're looking for somebody, a missing relative and . . . well, my mother and father stayed in the cottage," she pointed the way they had just come, "many years ago, and we thought it a faint, the *faintest* possibility, that the missing relative, a cousin of mine, might have gone there too."

"That cottage hasn't been occupied since I've been here and that is going on ten years." The farmer's tone had softened slightly. "I'm a bachelor and I live here with my dogs, and I would have thought it polite and decent of you to ask my permission before trespassing on my land." He raised an arm and pointed towards the road down which they had come. "Now be off, or I'll put my dogs on to you."

Dora turned and held out a hand to Jean who, from his expression, looked as though he would have liked to do to the present farmer what Dora's father had done to his predecessor, tip him in the water butt. Dora pulled him away and, together, they went as quickly as they could along the uneven track towards the gate, not daring, or caring, to look back.

"Well Farmer Frith has a worthy successor," Jean said grimly as they drove along the road, back the way they had come, towards Buttermere. "Strangers don't seem particularly welcome here."

The mist now almost obscured the whole of the surrounding countryside, obliterating the beautiful views, and as thick flakes of snow began slowly to fall, daylight faded almost entirely and Dora switched on the lights of the car.

"I don't think we're going to make it back to Keswick," she said looking out of the windscreen. "I don't fancy a night in the car, either."

"Wasn't there an inn on the way here?" Jean got the map out of the glove compartment and began to examine it. "It was tucked off the road, if I remember, just on the edge of the forest."

"Keep an eye out," Dora again peered forward. "And pray." She looked at him. "Do you pray? Have you prayed?"

"I've prayed," he nodded reflectively folding his arms across his chest, "but I don't think God heard me. It made me think, after a while, that there was no one there. And you?"

"I've prayed," Dora answered. "Mostly for other people. I've prayed some might die to ease their sufferings. However," she gave him a cheerful grin, "I don't think we can compare these conditions to the ones on the Somme."

201

"Not quite." Jean also smiled then, peering out of the window, put out a hand. "Stop! I think this is our pub."

In the mist Dora couldn't see a thing. It had started to snow so thickly that the windscreen wipers could scarcely do their job. They were getting slower and slower, and soon they would stop completely rendering further passage impossible.

As soon as Jean got out of the car he disappeared, the mist was so thick. Dora wished that the car had some form of heating and thought that, if they really got stuck and could go no further, and there was no inn, they would have to spend the night in it. Suddenly it all seemed rather frightening and the comparison with the war not so strange after all. Even in the most innocent-seeming situations danger lurked. How bizarre to survive the war and die of cold in the snows of Lakeland.

Time passed and she started to worry. Supposing Jean had got stuck in a drift? Supposing? She began to feel cold and got out of the car. It was better to walk about than sit where she was, in danger of freezing.

Suddenly a voice hailed her and her heart leaped. Jean appeared in the gloom flashing a strong torchlight in front of him.

"Jean!" She hurled herself towards him. "You've found it?"

He nodded.

"It's tiny. It's empty, but the landlord appears friendly and cheerful and will give us a meal and a bed. It is also warm. There's a great fire in the bar and plenty of logs stacked by the side of it."

"Oh Jean I do *love* you!" she cried and, raising her head, kissed him on the cheek.

He looked down at her, surprised, and caught her by the hand.

"Do you?"

"What?"

"Love me?"

"Yes, in a way, I do."

Jean went round to the rear of the car and extracted their

suitcases from the boot. Before handing the torch to Dora he pointed it downwards. His footprints were clear in the snow, but were fast being obliterated as it continued to fall thickly. "Now follow that path. Do not deviate for a second, and I'll follow you."

Dora, appreciating his firmness, did as she was told and, within moments, she saw lights ahead and made out the outline of a small pub with a sign proclaiming the name: The Lamb and Flag. Waiting at the door was a burly, bearded man, also with a torch which he shone in their direction. As Dora came up to him he stretched out his hand.

"Welcome. I think you just made it."

"I think we did." Dora shook his hand warmly. "I thought I'd survived the war to be lost in Lakeland."

"You were in the war?" he said, interested, relieving Jean of one of his suitcases as he turned towards the door.

"In the VADS. Jean served all through in the cavalry."

"I was with the Coldstreams," he said over his shoulder. "Got wounded at Ypres. End of war. Bought a pub." As he stomped ahead of them Dora saw that he had a bad limp, maybe a wooden leg. "Ben Reynolds," he said cheerfully, dropping the suitcase on the floor of the bar which was attractively lit with paraffin lamps while, as Jean had said, a great fire roared up the chimney. Dora rubbed her hands with pleasure.

"Oh, this is great!" she cried catching hold of Jean again.

"And what will it be to drink?" The host went behind the bar and looked at them. "And this one's on the house."

"In that case it has to be whisky." Dora went over to the fire, still rubbing her hands. "I think this is one of the happiest days in my life. For a moment I really thought . . . Well," she glanced at Jean, "better not to say what I thought. It all happened so suddenly."

"Well, your husband was most anxious to get back to you, Mrs . . ."

"Dora," she said quickly. "Please call me Dora, and this is Jean."

203

"Parterre's the name," Jean smiled at the man across the bar. "I'll have a whisky too. It's very kind of you."

"I'm glad of the company," Ben said. "My wife went to Keswick to market and phoned an hour ago to say she was staying with her sister. Roads impassable. I thought that I'd close up and have an early night. Lucky you're married," he added with a smile. "We only have two guest bedrooms and one of them is being decorated. I don't really expect many visitors at this time of the year. As soon as you've finished I'll show you your room."

The landlord of The Lamb and Flag was hospitality itself. When they descended from their bedroom he insisted on more drinks and then they dined on a delicious meal which he had cooked himself. With this there were fine wines, held in his cellars since before the war.

They ate in the kitchen in front of the range where there roared another log fire and, as the evening progressed, they got progressively happier and it was possible to forget the icy conditions outside.

Finally at ten o'clock, overcome with a satiety of good food and drink, they said goodnight and went upstairs to bed.

The bedroom was dominated by a large double bed, besides which there was a washstand with a jug and bowl on top, a dressing table and a small wardrobe. The pretty chintz curtains were drawn across a window which, in daytime, looked on to the hills at the back of the pub though whether or not they would see the view the next day they did not as yet know.

It was cold in the room although their kind host had hastily lit a fire when they came downstairs to the bar before dinner. But it made little difference to the temperature. Dora knelt in front of the fire warming her hands while Jean sat on the bed and began to unfasten his shoelaces. He looked up and saw her face, her expression thoughtful in the shadows cast by the flickering flames. Gone was the merriment, the slight inebriation caused by the festivities they'd enjoyed downstairs.

"Penny for them?" Jean asked quietly.

"Why didn't we say we weren't married?" Hands still in front of the fire Dora turned to look at him.

"Well, it would have been very embarrassing wouldn't it? I mean for him. Why do you think we didn't say?"

"The same reason, I suppose." She turned her head again towards the fire. "Cowardice. I don't know what it is."

"Does it matter?" He left the bed and squatted down beside her, uncertain as to whether or not he should take advantage of this unexpected intimacy.

"No, it's childish I suppose." Dora stood up and stretched. Then she looked towards the bed. "I suppose we have no choice but to share this?"

"I suppose not." He smiled and, also standing, attempted to put his arm round her shoulder. He felt very excited and aroused. More romantic conditions could not have been created if he'd tried.

But Dora moved away and sat on the bed, hands clutching the side, gazing at the floorboards. Finally she raised her eyes and gave him that rather direct, startling look to which he was by now accustomed.

"I don't want you to get any ideas, Jean. I mean . . ."

"You mean . . ." he walked over and stood looking down at her, "you're not interested?"

"In sex? No, if that's what you mean."

"I see. Is there any reason . . . I thought you liked me?"

The lowering of his voice expressed his feelings of dejection. Knowing Dora, he knew she wasn't playing hard to get. There was nothing of the flirt, the temptress about her.

"I do like you. I like you enormously, you know that; but I'm not sexually attracted to men."

"So it was quite true what people said about May?" His voice assumed a bitter tone and he slumped on the bed beside her.

"What did they say about May?" He could feel her bristling beside him.

"Well, that you and she . . ."

"We were just very good friends. Extremely close; we'd been through a lot together. People have such dirty minds."

"Yes they do. Well . . ." Jean stood up again and looked round. The pleasant feeling of inebriation, coupled with anticipation once the door had closed, had completely vanished. "Would you like me to sleep on the floor?"

"Don't be silly," Dora said robustly, getting up. "You'll freeze to death. I just wanted you to know, now, so that there is no misunderstanding. You can regard it as a kind of wartime situation. We have to stay together to keep warm. It doesn't mean we have to have sex. Now if you don't mind turning round I'll get undressed."

Jean turned towards the fire conscious of the sounds of Dora preparing for bed. How wonderful *that* could have been, had the situation been different. After a very short time he heard the bedsprings give and she said, "Okay. You can look or, rather, you can get undressed and I'll put my head under the bedclothes. *Not* that I haven't seen a naked man before." She gave a giggle and her head disappeared under the eiderdown. Jean quickly took off his clothes, got out his pyjamas from the suitcase, put them on and went over to the washstand to sluice his face and clean his teeth.

"Golly, I forgot to wash," Dora's head peeped above the bedclothes. "I was just so cold."

Jean finished his teeth and poured the dirty water into a bucket. He then put out the light by the door and climbed gingerly into the bed taking care to keep as near to the edge as he could. It was bitterly cold. Beside him he could hear Dora's teeth chattering.

"I guess Ben thought we'd keep each other warm," Dora said and he felt a hand stretch out towards him.

"I don't know that I can trust myself," Jean replied.

"You mean you might rape me?"

"No I *don't* mean that," he grunted between closed teeth. "But I would find it very hard to keep control of my feelings. I do like you Dora. Very much. I'm attracted to you. I find you strange and fascinating, different. I don't quite know how to put it."

"Strange?" She sounded curious. "How do you mean 'strange'?"

"I can't quite explain it." He began to feel calmer and took the hand that lay on the bed, palm upwards, next to him. It was warm and he clasped it firmly. "I suppose it was the sex thing. I mean I could guess you didn't like sex, didn't welcome it, rather. There was something about you that seemed to say: 'Thus far and no further'." He paused and gazed into the darkness. "Have you never slept with a man?"

"Not until tonight," she said with, again, that explosive, rather untypical girlish giggle.

"I mean . . ."

"I know what you mean. Well, no, I never have."

"You might like it."

"I don't think I would or I'd have tried it. I didn't lack opportunities. I'm just not attracted to men in that way. I know I'm not."

"So you're never going to get married?"

"Probably not." She gave a mirthless laugh. "Anyway I'm nearly forty."

"And children?"

"Too old for them too. I've got a nephew and two nieces, young relations. I get a lot of satisfaction and pleasure from them. I love them very much. That's why I wanted so badly to find Debbie. I adore her." Her voice became sad again and she sighed deeply as if thinking of the missing subject of their quest. "No, please don't misunderstand me. I like men, I enjoy their company. I've enormously enjoyed yours, more than I can say. But I don't want them as fathers, not of my children anyway."

"But you do like women?"

Defensively: "Yes. I do."

"And have you slept with a woman?"

"Oh, hundreds of times. We had to stick together in the war to keep out the men."

"No, seriously Dora, you know what I mean."

"I said people have such dirty minds."

"So you're not going to answer?"

"No I'm not." Her voice suddenly sounded drowsy. "I'm beginning to feel awfully sleepy, Jean. Good night."

"Good night, darling," he murmured, relishing the moment, wondering if this was the closest he was ever going to get to her and, leaning towards her, he kissed her cheek. Dora gave a grunt of pleasure and snuggled up against him like a cat, her body pressing against his. He could feel her warmth seep through him and he put his arms round her tightly and hugged her.

But inside he could have wept.

Chapter Thirteen

The jeweller leaned over the counter, eyepiece in his eye, examining the ring very carefully. He turned it this way and that, held it up to the light, then the shade, and could find no flaw.

"It is a very fine piece of jewellery," he said scrutinising it again with the utmost care. "I would say made in Holland, maybe," he put his head on one side, "eighty, a hundred years ago. It has all the hallmark of Amsterdam." He removed his glass and looked curiously at the woman who had brought it in. Past her prime he would have thought, though maybe younger than she looked; certainly down on her luck with worn shoes and an extremely ill-fitting coat. The anxious expression on her face seemed to betray a nervousness that alarmed him.

"May I ask how you came by this piece of jewellery, madam?"

"Is it any business of yours?" Elizabeth asked brusquely, to which the jeweller replied:

"Well madam, yes, it is. Please don't misunderstand me but . . ."

"It's not stolen if that's what you mean!" Elizabeth exclaimed angrily. "It is an heirloom. I was left it by . . . by a rich uncle."

"I see. I see." The jeweller stuck his glass in his eye and once again revolved the ring between his finger and thumb. "Well, what do you intend to do about it, madam? Do you wish merely to value it for insurance or do you wish to sell it?"

"I want to know how much it's worth. How much I'd get for

it, that is if I wished to sell . . . a hundred pounds?" she added breathlessly.

The jeweller gave an amused smile. "Much more than that." He went on revolving the ring and then he looked across at his customer noting that the degree of her unease seemed to have increased and she kept glancing anxiously at the door. "If you would leave it with me for a day or two I would be in a better position to let you have a more accurate valuation. I might then be able to make you an offer to purchase it."

"Cash?" Elizabeth said quickly.

"If that's what you wish, madam." The jeweller drew up a pad and began to scribble on it. "Might I have your name?" he said looking up.

"Why?" she demanded aggressively.

"So that I can give you a receipt. If I didn't you would have no proof that you had left this valuable ring with me, and might never see it again."

Elizabeth leaned across the counter and rapidly gave him her name and address.

"I'll write to you in a few days." The jeweller carefully put the ring – one of the finest he had seen in many a long year – back in its box. "Good day, Mrs Sprogett. Thank you for coming."

Elizabeth walked down the hill, dragging her feet like an old, or very weary woman. She was not old, but she was indeed very weary. She hated to part with the ring, but to her money was more important than possessions. Money gave one independence, pride, because she so hated acknowledging the fact that her marriage to Frank was a failure; that he was a sick man, rendered useless by the effects of the war. And sickness had made him selfish, boorish. Their life together was hell on earth.

It would be very easy to throw up everything and go back to her mother. Her parents knew something of her difficulties, but she tried to minimise them. She visited them, rather than let them visit her; but her mother came into Blandford every week for market day, and Beth Yewell was no fool. She knew quite well what was going on and longed to be able to help her stubborn, wilful daughter.

Elizabeth Sprogett was an unhappy and discontented woman. She felt she had been born to better things, and life had disappointed her. Consequently she nursed a deep grudge against humanity. She had always been capricious, ambitious too to enjoy the finer things of life, to rise higher than her parents who were servants, her sister Jenny who was the wife of a farmhand, and her brother Jo who worked in the flour mill at Wenham.

Yet Jenny's husband was prosperous as farm workers went. He had a good boss, they had a nice cottage on the farm estate, and two children who were healthy and well cared for. And Jo, also married but as yet with no children, had expectations one day to run the mill. He, too, lived in a neat little cottage not far from his parents in Wenham, and his enterprising wife baked bread from the special, finely ground mill flour and sold it at a good profit to local bread shops.

So Elizabeth, who hoped to outshine the rest of the family had, in fact, drawn the short straw, moved lower down the scale and had been reduced to taking in washing and cutting down the family rations until they existed on a very meagre subsistence indeed. All because she was proud; would not take family charity or help from strangers.

When Elizabeth got home she could hear voices and stood by the door listening. In the background the baby grizzled away. For once she had left the children in her husband's care while she transacted her business with the jeweller, and her only hope now was that no harm had befallen them. She flung open the door and found Frank, face chalkier than usual, looking angrily at a man who stood with his back to the door, and who turned round when it opened.

"Ah, Mrs Sprogett," the man said, with relief in his voice.

"I'm very glad to see you." Producing a handkerchief he mopped his brow.

"Oh?" Elizabeth closed the door examining him suspiciously. "And who might you be?"

"I'm from the brewery, Mrs Sprogett." The man's expression was cheerful, but his faltering voice betrayed his unease. "I've been trying to explain to your husband . . ."

"We're to be flung out," Frank cried. "Flung out into the street."

"It's not that at all, Mrs Sprogett," the man protested. "I was merely telling your husband that the brewery has, in fact, been very good. It is three years since the war ended and we have allowed you to live in this house which in fact belongs to us, and which we need, despite the fact that your husband is an invalid and cannot work."

"Very good!" Elizabeth exclaimed, removing her hat and tossing it into a chair. "Huh!"

"Betsy's wet, Ma," Mary informed her, finger in her mouth.

"Then she'll have to stay wet," Elizabeth retorted, turning her attention to the man from the brewery, whose name she did not know.

"You consider you're very good, do you Mr . . . ?"

"Kemp, Mrs Sprogett, Roylston Kemp."

"What a very fine name, Mr Kemp. Roylston, indeed."

"Thank you, Mrs Sprogett." Mr Kemp, even more ill at ease, shuffled his feet.

"And do you have a nice house, a family perhaps?"

"I have a house owned by the brewery like you, madam. Only I still work for the brewery, and Mr Sprogett unfortunately, through no fault of his own, does not."

"Exactly!" Elizabeth took off her coat and threw it on the same chair as the hat, only with a little more force. The baby, obviously in discomfort, bawled even more loudly, and a disagreeable odour emanating from her pram slowly permeated the small front room. Elizabeth ignored it, metaphorically rolling up her sleeves for a fight as she looked at Mr Kemp.

212

"And were *you* in the war Mr Kemp?"

"Ah, mmm . . ." Mr Kemp cleared his throat and pushed his spectacles up his nose. "Unfortunately I was not fit."

"Oh, not fit!" Elizabeth mocked, hands on her hips and, tossing back her head, uttered a raucous laugh.

Mr Kemp looked aggrieved. "I have a weak heart and poor eyesight. I would *like* to have served my country . . ."

"Well, my husband *did* serve his country," Elizabeth bawled, leaning forward, "and he lost his health and his wits doing it. He's good for nothing, unemployable, and not a penny does he get for it save what the army welfare lets him have. These men were called to give their lives, they did it willingly – Frank was one of the first in these parts to volunteer – and now the country doesn't want to know and I, Mr Kemp," she emphasised her point by stabbing her finger at her breast, "I have to keep this household fed and take in washing and . . . oh my God, you people make me sick. You and others like you!" She swept over to the door, flung it open and shook her hand at him. "Now get out and stay out, and you can tell your masters that if they want to get me and my family out of here they'll have to call the *undertaker*. Feet first it will be. Feet first."

Mr Kemp's attitude was now reduced to that of a small rabbit on whom a large, ferocious domestic cat was about to spring. He looked right and left but there was no escape. He hastily made his way towards the door. Then he paused:

"I must tell you, Mrs Sprogett that my superiors will not take kindly to this. I have been asked to give you notice, and I now hand you this." He thrust a set of papers he had produced from his pocket at her, keeping at arm's length. "My superiors have been generous, having in mind the circumstances and the service provided by Mr Sprogett in the past. Three months, Mrs Sprogett, three months they are prepared to grant you, after which—"

"GET OUT!" Elizabeth screamed, moving menacingly towards him as, panic on his face, he turned and rushed out into the street, hotly pursued by his tormentor. "Don't come back," she cried

213

after him as lace curtains were hastily drawn aside and curious faces appeared at the windows of neighbouring houses, "or if you come back don't forget the hearse. I say: don't forget the BLOODY HEARSE."

But by this time Mr Kemp was well out of earshot.

Face flushed, trembling from her efforts, but well pleased with their effect, Elizabeth returned triumphantly to the house. "There, I told him, the bugger," she said. "He won't dare come here again in a hurry."

"It's pointless," Frank looked at her sullenly. "You'll only get his back up. I was trying to speak to him reasonably, plead with him, appeal to his better nature, and then you burst in and start behaving like a fishwife."

"Then I *am* a fishwife," Elizabeth snarled, "and get that stinking baby out of here, Mary, and change her nappy, do you hear me?"

"Yes, Mother." Mary, who was only four, yet older than her years, pushed the pram out of the room, kicking the door shut behind her.

"No need to shout," Frank grumbled, pausing to roll a cigarette which he lit with trembling fingers. "We'll have to go, Elizabeth. I reckon you'll have to go and see your mother."

"And what do you expect my mother to do?"

"Maybe they can help. Mrs Yetman—"

"Mrs Yetman has got enough to do; besides I don't want to ask my parents for help. I've told you that before, Frank. I've got too much pride, which is more than anyone can say of *you*."

"Then it's the workhouse for us," Frank moaned. "We'll be split up and separated. The children taken from us. Will that make you happy?"

"*Yes*," Elizabeth said sitting down and wiping her hair away from her face with an air of complete exhaustion. "Yes it will. Very happy. I'll have no more responsibilities. I'm sick of battling with the world, Frank Sprogett, without any help. Now the world can do what it likes. See if I care."

*   *   *

But Elizabeth did care. She was stubborn and she was proud. She was not a woman to give in; it was against her nature. When she was small she used to imagine herself as a fine lady, like Lady Woodville or Mrs Heering, people who had money, class, power. Even Sarah-Jane Yetman was someone to emulate, despite the fact that she was a farmer's daughter and her husband had been a builder; not what you'd call quality, not what you'd call class, but better than her. She fantasised all the time about what might be.

Once when she'd worked on a farm, Carson Woodville had tried to proposition her, made advances, until her father found out and banished her to Blandford where she had become a maid at the Crown Hotel. But for that she might have become Lady Woodville, mistress of a fine house ... well, fanciful the idea might be, but stranger things had happened. While a maid at the Crown she had waited on Mrs Agnes Gregg, who later married Sir Guy ... which brought her back to thinking why he had left her a hundred pounds and the ring she was trying to sell.

During the days that passed after the visit of Mr Kemp, Elizabeth waited anxiously to hear from the jeweller while plotting in her mind what she might do with a large sum of money. Maybe it would be enough for her to take off and begin a new life, somewhere overseas, as Mrs Gregg had told her she had, entertaining her with glamorous stories about far distant places.

Would she leave her children? Well, she'd miss Jack. He was an engaging little fellow, as good as gold. Mary was always whingeing, her nose was always running, the baby always screaming. She knew that she was a conscientious but impatient mother, and an indifferent wife. She lost her temper with the children and she despised her husband. She had married Frank for better or worse and she was not true to her marriage vows. But she felt that life had dealt her a bad hand of cards and she deserved better, or she deserved at least to do as well as Jenny or Jo, who lived in nice houses, were properly fed and clothed, and had money to spend.

So Elizabeth began to plan what she might do with the money she got from the ring, and the daring idea gradually formed in her mind that, perhaps, she would abandon her family altogether and set off for pastures new, just as Agnes Gregg had, returning a rich woman.

Several days passed and Elizabeth heard nothing more from the jeweller, so she resolved to go and see him. She got through the morning's washing, changed the baby, wiped Mary's nose for about the twelfth time and was standing in front of the mirror pinning on her hat when there was a knock at the door. With an exclamation of irritation she hurried over and threw it open thinking it might be Mr Kemp and preparing, with some relish it must be said, to give him another piece of her mind.

However, in front of her stood a broad-shouldered policeman, and his expression was not friendly.

"Mrs Sprogett?" he enquired, consulting a notebook in his hand.

"Yes, what is it?" she asked sharply, having as little respect for the law as anyone else who crossed her path.

"Could I come in and have a few words, madam?" Without ceremony he pushed past her and stepped inside looking round.

"Is this your property, Mrs Sprogett? Is Mr Sprogett about?"

Elizabeth closed the door and came slowly towards him.

"Who sent you?" she asked.

"I am not at liberty to say that at the moment, madam."

"The brewery was it? Being thrown out, are we?"

"Oh!" The policeman who, with a tall helmet on his head, nearly touched the ceiling, consulted his note book again. "This house belongs to the brewery does it?"

"Yes it does, as you probably know, and so do all the other houses in the row."

"Thank you, Mrs Sprogett, I am obliged to you for that information."

"Well now you can get out." Elizabeth pointed towards the door.

"Now just a minute, madam, just a minute. Not so fast, if you please. I am here on another matter." The policeman cleared his throat and fixed her with a still unfriendly eye. "It concerns a valuable diamond and sapphire ring which you gave to Harris the jeweller for valuation. Can you tell me how you came by that ring madam?"

"I certainly can," Elizabeth retorted angrily. "I was left it."

"Oh! May one ask by whom?"

"No you may not. It was part of a bequest, and it's none of your flaming business."

"I see." The policeman put his notepad in the pocket of his tunic and fastened the button. "In that case I must ask you to accompany me to the police station, madam, and if you refuse you will be taken there by force."

"But you have *no* right . . ."

"I have every right," the officer of the law put his hand firmly on her arm. "Is your husband at work madam?"

"No he's upstairs. He's an invalid."

"Then may I go up and advise him?"

For the first time Elizabeth's aggression disappeared and an expression of fear came into her eyes, her attitude changing from defiance to supplication. She laid a hand on the policeman's arm. "No!" she said sharply. "I don't want him to know about this. I'll go and tell him to look after the children. I'll come with you. It can all be explained. I came by the ring quite legally, but I don't want my husband to know about it. That's all."

Mr Temple of Parson, Wilde and Brickell looked apologetically at Elizabeth. It was afternoon and she had been in the police station, virtually in detention as a thief, since morning. She had been served lunch in a cell and although she hated the location she was grateful for the food, and ate up every scrap. The solicitor had been unavailable, attending a client in another part of the town, but when he returned to his office and was given the message he hurried over and almost at once cleared Elizabeth of the charge of theft.

She had left the police station accompanied by Mr Temple without a stain on her name, but she felt humiliated and angry. Mr Temple had taken her to his office, which was quite near the station, and given her a cup of tea. He then went and recovered the ring from the jeweller and they now sat with it in its box on the table between them.

"I'm terribly sorry you went through this ordeal, Mrs Sprogett. It was very wrong of Mr Harris."

"He took advantage of me, he misjudged me because I am poor and the ring is so lovely." Elizabeth gave a pathetic sniff and her eyes filled with tears. Her defences were very very low, her self-esteem almost nil. "Things haven't been easy, Mr Temple. My husband has not had work since the war. He gets a very small pension and we are hard pressed for money. We are about to be evicted from our house and have nowhere to go. I . . ." Elizabeth looked at the kind expression on the face of the solicitor and her defences suddenly crumbled. She burst into tears and, rushing over to him, leaned her head on his chest, clinging to him.

To his credit Mr Temple rallied to the occasion. He put his arm round her waist, led her back to her chair, and sat next to her trying to comfort her.

"Mrs Sprogett, Mrs Sprogett. There is no need for tears. My dear lady I am so sorry to hear of your predicament."

He stopped, knowing it was useless to go on while she was in such a state. He proffered her a clean white handkerchief and looked on sympathetically while she wiped her eyes, gave her nose a good blow and then sat very still, the handkerchief clutched in her hand.

"I'm ever so sorry," she said at last. "I don't know what's happening to me, really I don't." She sniffed again and struggled to brush her straggly hair out of her eyes. "I've had ever such a hard time. My husband is no good at all, good for nothing.

We have no money, little food and nowhere to go, three small children who get on my nerves. To tell you the truth I was thinking of running away; selling the ring, taking the money and running."

"There now." She looked up at him, eyes wet, nose shining, mouth turned down. He thought that, even in this state, she was a very attractive, even noble woman, and his heart went out to her. He was a bachelor who lived with his parents and it occurred to him that he was very fortunate. Compared to the plight of this poor woman very fortunate indeed.

"Have you no one you can turn to, Mrs Sprogett? No family? I can't imagine a woman as young and as attractive as you without friends."

"Yes, I have a mother and father, a sister and brother. Or at least, they're not my real parents. They adopted me after my mother died giving birth to me. She was the sister of my adoptive mother, Beth; but I always think of them as my real family, never having known another."

"You knew nothing of your real mother's family?" Mr Temple put his head on one side as he continued to look at her. Elizabeth shook her head.

"They came from the north of England, the Lake District. They were very poor. I don't think my mother was married but my adoptive mother never talks about it. She was brought south by the Woodville family. The wealthy Mrs Heering, Sir Guy Woodville's sister, was my mother's employee and friend for many years." She raised her head, her chin trembling. "I am proud Mr Temple. It may seem a weakness, but I don't like to beg, to admit defeat . . ."

"My dear woman," Mr Temple resisted an impulse to put his arm around her again, "I assure you there would be no shame, none at all, in going to your family for help. By all means sell the ring – and I will make certain you get a fair price if it is what you wish – but I am not sure that even that would be enough to keep you in comfortable circumstances for very long. Now, why don't you do the sensible thing?

219

Go and see your mother? Does she know about the bequest, incidentally?"

"Oh, she knows."

"And did she say anything?"

"No, not at the time. Just that I was lucky."

"And she didn't say, or know, why Sir Guy had left you this bequest?"

"No. She was very thoughtful though."

"Did he leave her anything?"

"No."

"Well if I were you I'd go and see your mother and seek a solution to this mystery."

"But why should I?" She looked at him curiously.

Mr Temple shook his head as if pondering something. "Well, that there *is* a mystery there seems certain to me. By further enquiry you may find out something to your advantage, Mrs Sprogett. Something of which you were unaware. Perhaps someone has been hiding something. That's what it looks like to me. Maybe some help is at hand. I do urge you to consult your parents. That's all that I can say." He looked at her and gently pressed her hand. "But do please regard me as your very good friend, ready with help, whenever you need it. Now may I escort you home, Mrs Sprogett?"

Elizabeth thrust the box containing the ring towards him. "Keep it," she said. "Look after it for me. I don't want my husband to find out about this. He'll force me to sell it and spend the money on him and the kids. It's my little nest egg. I want it for myself. Do you understand?"

"I understand." Mr Temple took the box and smiled down at her. "I will keep it *very* safe and when you want it I'll deliver it to you, and not a word shall be said about it until then."

Eliza sat on the bench in the garden at Riversmead looking at the photographs Dora had taken in the Lake District. Next to her was Beth, and both women had tears in their eyes, handkerchiefs clasped tightly in their hands.

"I can't get over the way it looks just the same!" Eliza exclaimed. "It was *exactly* like that forty years ago. Even the snow."

"Yes'm," Beth snivelled into her hanky. Of the two she had cried the longest, perhaps because she had gained most from the move south. It had changed her life. "It's like time stopped still."

Eliza put an arm round Beth. Forty years before Beth had been a servant girl at Farmer Frith's farm, an orphan whom he treated as badly as he treated everyone else. When Eliza and Ryder left to go home Beth had begged to be taken too; but then they were not able to. When Ryder later returned for Eliza's horse he took Beth with him too and there began a new life for her as a friend and servant, first of Ryder and Eliza and then of their son Laurence and his wife Sarah-Jane. After Laurence's death it was Beth and her husband Ted who became the mainstay of the bereaved family, and they all loved them as though they were part of the family which, by this time, they were.

Sarah-Jane was a robust Dorset woman, a farmer's daughter, but she had been terribly affected by the death of her husband and the circumstances surrounding it: his bankruptcy, the threatened seizure of the house by the bank which precipitated his suicide.

However, she put her woes behind her and continued to bring up her three children in an exemplary manner: Abel, now seventeen, Martha fifteen and Felicity, twelve. All went to local schools and were a credit to their mother who had sacrificed much of her own personal happiness for them. She had rejected the advances of a prosperous farmer who wished to marry her because the children did not like him.

Eliza had bought Riversmead from the trustees in bankruptcy of Laurence's estate, and had settled a small sum of money on her daughter-in-law which enabled her to take care of the house and the children without having to work.

Sarah-Jane stayed tactfully out of the way while Eliza and

Nicola Thorne

Beth examined the photos and shed tears over them, recalling the hardships of long ago.

Now, thinking that they had had enough time for a good chat and a good weep, she came over to them, a tea tray in her hands, which she put down on the table to exclamations of pleasure and surprise.

"And I have another surprise for you," she said looking towards the house. "We have a visitor."

"Elizabeth!" Eliza gasped rising to her feet as Elizabeth emerged from the house and stood looking at the pair on the lawn. "Why, *Elizabeth!*" Eliza kissed her on the cheek and then gazed at her with concern. "You don't look very well. Is anything the matter?"

"Here, have some tea, dear." Beth got up to make room for her daughter and sat her down next to Eliza. "A cup of tea will do you good."

Elizabeth sat down, still suspiciously quiet. Her face was indeed very pale and her fair hair scraped back into a rather unattractive bun at the nape of her neck. She wore a cotton dress, no stockings and a pair of off-white shoes which had seen better days. Eliza also thought she had lost weight.

"You're not pregnant again are you?" she asked anxiously, leaning forward, but Elizabeth shook her head vigorously.

"I nearly went to gaol!" she burst out and it was obvious that she was in an overwrought state, close to tears.

"Gaol!" Beth looked appalled and her hands flew to her face. "Whatever for?"

"I've got things to do in the house," Sarah-Jane said hurriedly.

"No, do stay," Eliza pleaded.

"Seriously. I've got the children's tea to get."

"I'll come." Beth rose to go too, but Elizabeth put out a hand.

"I want you to stay, Mother. There are things I want to know, about my past. About who my mother and father were."

A shadow flitted across Eliza's face and, involuntarily, she

222

shuddered. She had a feeling that fate was now going to catch up with them.

"I also want to know, though it may have nothing to do with this other question, why Sir Guy left me money and a ring." Elizabeth swallowed. "The solicitor said I should ask. In his opinion someone is hiding something."

Elizabeth, hands resting on her lap, looked calmly, first at Beth and then at Eliza. Her gaze was now level and controlled. "Sir Guy left me a hundred pounds and a ring which is very valuable. I went to have it valued because I needed the money and wanted to sell it. The jeweller thought that, as I looked so poor, I must have stolen it and told the police . . ."

"Oh my *dear*!" Eliza clasped her arm. "Oh Elizabeth, you should have come to me . . ."

"But I didn't *want* to come to you, Mrs Heering, don't you see? You have been very good to me and my family. I chose to marry Frank Sprogett, and the fact that the war came and things didn't turn out as we hoped, well . . ." She fumbled with her skirt, her long thin fingers notable for their delicacy, even though the palms of her hands were calloused with work. "Anyway the solicitor, who was very nice, rescued me from the police station, restored the ring to me and said he would do all he could to help me. He was a real gentleman."

"He sounds *very* nice," Eliza said approvingly.

"He said it was a very strange bequest, made to no other member of my family, and he implied there were things I should know." Elizabeth looked straight at Beth. "*Is* there anything I should know, Mother?"

"Well . . ." Beth's own fingers, not nearly as fine as Elizabeth's, plucked anxiously at her skirt and she looked across at Eliza, who straightened her back and clasped her hands in her lap, resigned, now, to the inevitable.

"Yes, Elizabeth, there is something you should know, and now that it has come out like this, and you have endured such humiliation, I feel guilty that you were not told before. It is only . . ."

223

Suddenly overcome by a feeling of inadequacy, she looked over to Beth for help, but Beth shook her head, her face flushed, and she avoided looking either at Elizabeth or Eliza.

Eliza appeared to make an effort to compose herself and put an arm lightly around Elizabeth's waist.

"It is time you knew the truth, but, well, it was very difficult. Extraordinarily difficult. Perhaps, when you hear the circumstances, you will realise why."

And there and then, keeping her voice as unemotional and as steady as she could, she told Elizabeth how Guy Woodville had had an affair with Agnes Yetman thirty years before. Guy was married and Agnes an unmarried woman working as a governess for Lady Mount who, when she discovered her pregnancy, dismissed her.

She, Eliza, arranged for Agnes to go to Weymouth in the care of Beth; but soon after the baby was born Agnes disappeared and was not seen or heard of for another twenty years. Those were the days, Eliza said, when illegitimacy was such a stigma, indeed in many ways it still was, but then it was considered a disgrace. Beth agreed to pass the child off as her sister's and brought her home and, under Eliza's supervision, was willing to bring her up.

Once Guy found out she was his daughter he wanted to recognise her but, of course, his wife Margaret was still alive and, well, being a man, he lacked the courage.

When, however, Margaret died and Agnes returned and subsequently became his wife he wished to acknowledge their child openly, but Agnes would not hear of it.

All in all it was a very difficult situation, was it not, and one that poor Guy tried to redress by leaving her a small sum of money – he was not a wealthy man – and a ring that had belonged to his mother.

In a way, Eliza concluded, it was a shameful tale and one that was bound to cause Elizabeth much anguish. No one, other than Beth and Elizabeth herself, came out of it very well, even she, but also in many ways it was understandable, and at the

time everyone had acted in the way they thought best. It was
so easy to be wise after the event.

When she stopped no one spoke for some moments. Beth
realised that none of them had touched their tea which was stone
cold. The singing of the birds in the garden seemed particularly
loud, not sweet but strident and accusatory.

Looking at Elizabeth it was not difficult to believe that this
was one of the most momentous, if not the most momentous,
day in her life. Momentous, and shocking too.

Eliza put out a hand and clasped Elizabeth's, which seemed
to lie lifelessly in her lap, and did not respond to the woman
she now knew was her aunt.

"I understand how difficult it is for you to take all this in.
In telling it I can hardly believe it myself, or that we were so
foolish as to keep it from you all these years; but you must
believe how strong and determined Agnes was."

"She was ashamed of me." Elizabeth's tone, when she spoke
for the first time, was hard and bitter.

"I think she was ashamed of herself."

"I worked as her maid at the Crown Hotel. My own mother!
I was not married then. She could have spared me Frank and
all the misery that I've had since."

"Well . . ." Eliza gesticulated hopelessly, "she didn't."

"It's because I was a servant, a maid."

"My dear, do not torment yourself as to the reason. Now
you know and now we must try and make up to you for the
mistakes of the past, which we as a family truly regret."

"And what does my 'mother' think now?" Elizabeth demanded,
in the kind of haughty tone Agnes might have used. Eliza realised,
not for the first time, how like her mother Elizabeth was, in looks
as well as temperament.

"I think Agnes might not be averse to seeing you. We will
have to break it to her gently, that you know. She has been
very damaged emotionally recently and is not in the best of
health. However she is a lonely woman; you are her flesh and
blood and, who knows?"

Eliza tentatively reached out to stroke her hair. "My darling Elizabeth, in order to find happiness, which you both desire, you must try and be generous with each other. You need each other, and must help each other and, in the process, which might be painful, you might at the end form a bond of deep affection."

Chapter Fourteen

She had not seen her since 1912 when she had returned to Blandford after years in exile with the purpose of claiming her inheritance, that which she believed to be rightfully hers: Pelham's Oak and the title of Lady Woodville. Then it was as a serving maid, waiting on her in a hotel, neither realising that they were mother and daughter, though Agnes, deducing it after a matter of time, kept the knowledge to herself. After she became Lady Woodville she never saw her daughter Elizabeth again and resisted all Guy's attempts to claim her openly.

But here she was: her closest living relative, flesh of her flesh. Yet a stranger who now had a look of such uncompromising hostility on her proud face that it reminded Agnes even more vividly, if that were possible, of her own rebellious youth and young womanhood.

At first Elizabeth had not wanted to meet her real mother. The shock of discovering that she was a Woodville, that Sir Guy had been her father, Carson was her half-brother and that she had been left to survive in near poverty since her marriage, at first made her very angry and resentful. She determined to sell her ring and continue with her plan to disappear; but then reality set in and with it came a sense of proportion, an idea for taking advantage of missed opportunities as she took stock of the situation.

Well she *was* a Woodville; there was no question of it. It was no dream. Everyone admitted it. She had a baronet for a father and a 'lady' for a mother. However disreputable their behaviour, so much was fact. She had blue blood in her veins.

Instinctively she'd known all along that she was different. But people – the children at school, her adoptive brother and sister, Jo and Jenny – had all laughed at her for giving herself airs and graces.

But she was right. She *had* a stack of posh titled relations with money. The lawyer had said the money from the ring wouldn't last long, even if she kept it all for herself. She felt now that it was time to cash in on her new-found fortune, however bitter she was about the past. Let them pay.

It had been decided that mother and daughter should meet alone, at Agnes's house. Eliza took her there, left her at the door and said she would be close by with Sophie at the Rectory if needed. She would then drive Elizabeth home again.

Grace, the maid, admitted Elizabeth and led her to the drawing room where Agnes, feeling far from comfortable herself, awaited her.

Elizabeth wore a new dress, printed cotton, simple but charming. She had on silk stockings and white calf shoes with a high heel. Her pretty hair had been set professionally and was coiled about her head, giving her a rather old-fashioned appearance. Dressed like this she looked more like her mother in her youth than ever. It almost took Agnes's breath away.

For a long time Elizabeth stood by the door and looked at her. Agnes had changed in the nine years since she'd seen her. Her beauty had faded and so, seemingly, had her arrogance. She realised it was almost impossible to think of her as her mother.

Agnes took a step towards Elizabeth and held out her hand. Instead of embracing her, Elizabeth took her hand and shook it. She had no inclination to fling her arms round her, on the contrary.

Agnes invited her rather formally to sit down. Tea was brought in immediately by Grace and served in silence. Agnes, pouring tea, observed that she thought it was going to be a very fine summer. Elizabeth thought so too. As if struggling to find words they both looked out of the open French windows into

228

the garden. The lupins were a splash of bright variegated colour and the equally tall delphiniums with their gentler shades of blue and purple were in bloom. Agnes handed her her tea and they looked at each other over the cup before Elizabeth took it and set it on a table by her side.

"This is very awkward," Agnes said at last. "There is a lot to talk about. I am almost entirely in the wrong."

" 'Almost'?" Elizabeth smiled for the first time since she'd entered the room. "Isn't that an understatement, Mrs Wentworth?"

Agnes bristled at the title but maybe no one had told her that, as she had wished, she was now known as Lady Woodville. Or was Elizabeth being deliberately malicious? Agnes studied her daughter carefully. She was basically very attractive, with a potentially good complexion, but a lot more could be made of her. She looked tired and run down. She was certainly not as Agnes remembered her when she first set eyes on her after the passage of many years in 1912. Then she had been a fresh-faced young beauty.

Now she was thirty-one and her best years were behind her. She had been brought up by servants and her manner was slightly common; she had a strong regional accent.

Yet, for all this, Elizabeth was her daughter; her flesh and blood. Would that something about Elizabeth might encourage her to take her in her arms, but there was nothing, no hint of warmth. Elizabeth's expression was cold and unforgiving, and Agnes began to feel that, whatever Eliza had said, and she had talked to her for many hours, the meeting was a mistake. Elizabeth began to think so too. She put down her cup, having finished her tea, declined a cake and looked hard and long at Agnes. When she spoke it was almost as though she had read her thoughts.

"I am thirty-one, Mrs Wentworth. I was brought up as a servant by servants. Yet my father, who was a baronet, lived but ten miles away, and my aunt, his sister, who lived next door to me, knew it. Everyone deceived me for all those years. I married a man of very low rank who drove a brewer's dray, and no one tried to stop it. It was all right for me because at the time I expected nothing better. But you would have thought that those who knew, and they all knew – Mrs Heering, you, Mrs Turner, Mrs Yetman, my adoptive parents – might have thought it an unsuitable match for the daughter of a baronet. Yet I was an outcast, born on the wrong side of the sheets, so what did it matter?

"I married Frank, a man I thought of my own station, and had we continued like that I might have lived quite happily for the rest of my days, knowing no better.

"But now not only do I know better, I have had five extremely hard years. My fine, healthy young husband who went eagerly off to the war returned a nervous and physical wreck. He could not earn a living. I had to take in dirty washing belonging to other people—"

"You could have asked," Agnes burst out unable to endure any longer this string of accusations. "Eliza told me that you always refused offers of help."

"That was you in me, wasn't it, Mrs Wentworth? Stubborn, hard. I didn't want pity. I don't want it now."

"Then what do you want, Elizabeth?" Agnes's tone of voice was so low that the woman next to her hardly heard it.

"I want justice, Mrs Wentworth. I deserve it and so do my children, your grandchildren, and those of Sir Guy. I want them brought up as I was not. Sent to good schools. I want a house of my own with a garden, maybe a servant or two. It is no less than I deserve. I think the Woodville family owes me this, Mrs Wentworth, for what it did to me, and as for you . . ." she paused and gazed scornfully at the woman who had borne her thirty-one years before, "I suppose you expect *me* to be grateful? You, who rejected me all those years ago, I suppose you now feel I should love you, as though nothing had ever happened? Do you?"

Agnes, who had been looking straight ahead into the garden, her ears buffeted by the justified reproach and recriminations of her daughter, didn't reply for a long time. Somehow, now that the past had caught up with her, it all seemed so cruel, so undeserved, so very unfair, because she too had had a hard life, even if much of it was her own making.

Now just when she needed the love of a daughter she would find hatred, resentment and revenge instead. She wished now that the truth had never come out. She had been right all along. Elizabeth, knowing no better, should have been left to her hovel, her stupid working class pride. If only Guy had not left her that legacy. It was his way of getting his own back. And yet . . . Elizabeth was her daughter; her children too were her flesh and blood, the only grandchildren she would ever have. What joy Eliza got from hers! It was lovely to make them clothes and give them gifts, take them out for treats. Two girls and a boy. She had never seen them. Maybe, if their mother didn't love her, they would?

Perhaps it was time to woo Elizabeth, to try and make amends?

"I do not expect you to love me, Elizabeth," she said, "though I would like nothing better, and I would return that love a hundredfold, believe me. I only beg you to try and understand, and forgive me."

She then lowered her head and uttered a deep, heartfelt, sigh which, as it happened, left her daughter completely unmoved.

Carson looked round at the small, rather dark room. At one end there was a range, the fire now out. The window, looking on to the street, was grimy as though it was a long time since it had been cleaned. There was a strong smell of washing and, through the door leading into the kitchen and washroom, he could see rows of clothes lines in the back yard where she'd once hung out all the sheets, shirts and goodness knows what else belonging to people who were better off than she was. The damp, soapy smell still permeated the house.

Elizabeth stood dressed in her best hat and coat, her cases at her feet, the children also neatly dressed, at her side. Carson had never even met them. He had greeted the little girl, kissed the baby and gravely shaken hands with Jack who, with a well-scrubbed face, gazed hopefully up at him.

"I feel ashamed," Carson said continuing to look round.

"I don't blame *you*, Carson." Elizabeth placed one hand protectively on Jack's head. "You're as much a victim as me. You didn't know. It was kept from you too. Remember when we worked at Sadler's Farm?" She gave him rather a flirtatious, decidedly unsisterly smirk.

"I remember," he said. "I fancied you."

"And I fancied you. No wonder they separated us."

"We should have been told then. It was wrong. What my father did was wrong. I can't defend him, but my mother was alive and he didn't want to hurt her." Carson looked earnestly across at Elizabeth. "But he loved you, Elizabeth. Aunt Eliza said he knew who you were and he left you something, which maybe was his way of hoping that, in the end, all would come right."

"You think it's come right, Carson?" She put her head on one side and he saw how coarse her skin was. In her teens she had been stunning. But now fine lines were etched down each side of her eyes and mouth. She didn't look her age. She looked much older and they, the Woodvilles, shared a collective burden for this grave injustice that had been committed against her.

Aunt Eliza said that she was very bitter. The meeting with Aunt Agnes had not gone well. There were no more plans to meet.

Aunt Agnes had wept the rest of the day, and the day after that. In the end the doctor was sent for and gave her a sedative. Instead of being a happy, joyful time at the reunion with a sister, he could see it would be fraught.

Carson looked towards the door.

"Connie's waiting for us in the car," he said. "You know we've become engaged?"

"Again?" Elizabeth smiled. "No I didn't know. I hear she's quite a beauty. It's amazing what money can do, isn't it, Carson?"

"It's not just money. It's self-confidence. She was held back, kind as Miss Fairchild was to her. Like you, Elizabeth, Connie suffered but in a different way." He stood aside to let her pass, saying gravely: "We were all changed completely by the war."

Carson opened the door and the little procession trooped out on to the street. This time there was a scattering of onlookers who had ventured from their homes to watch the departure of a woman who had become both notorious and a celebrity. No one had ever liked her very much with her sharp tongue, the manners of a fishwife yet, at the same time, the airs and graces of a woman of quality. Quite a contradiction. Now everyone knew why. She was a Woodville, a bastard, but a Woodville nevertheless; a name to be reckoned with in the neighbourhood, second only, perhaps, to the Portmans.

Connie jumped out of the car when she saw the procession exit from the house. She felt rather shy, a little awkward, and held out a hand as Elizabeth came up to the car.

"Hello Elizabeth," she said. "I suppose you can say that it's been a long time."

"It has, Connie." Elizabeth looked at her and then, impulsively, leaned towards her and kissed her, "I hear you're to be congratulated. Second time around?"

"Exactly!" Connie blushed, self-consciously. "This time for keeps, I hope."

Mary and Jack stood by their mother's side looking awkward and Carson held Betsy in his arms. She was a very beautiful, contented looking toddler with golden curls and bright blue eyes. Connie leaned towards the two youngsters and said "Hello". They looked at her but said nothing. Elizabeth gave Jack a cuff on the back of his head, and he said "hello" very quickly, Mary rapidly following suit to avoid similar chastisement.

"Where's your husband?" Connie looked towards the house, the door now shut.

"He's gone to stay with his brother while we get sorted out. I wish he'd stay there for good. Too much to hope for, I expect."

Connie glanced rather helplessly at Carson, who opened the back door of the car and said to the two children standing on the pavement, "Hop in."

They gazed with awe at the big car. "You ride in front, Elizabeth," Carson said. "I'll keep the children in order in the back." He then put the children into the back seat and put Betsy between them while he went back for Elizabeth's cases which he stowed in the boot.

He then saw Elizabeth to her seat next to the driver and, shutting the door, got into the back with the children.

"Next stop Pelham's Oak," he said.

As Connie pulled away from the house and drove up the street a few people waved, but Elizabeth ignored them, eyes straight in front.

This time there was to be no turning back.

The air about them was quiet. Most of the family had left and Elizabeth was upstairs, her children in bed. It had been a day of great excitement, and everyone was tired. There had been much emotion, a few tears. All the family except Agnes had been gathered to greet the new member, even though they had all known her since she was a baby. It was different getting to know her as a Woodville, someone who had been shamefully treated for many years. There was a lot to atone for, much to be done.

Yet, unlike her meeting with her mother, Elizabeth charmed the family with her graciousness, her pleasure at being among them. She seemed to harbour no ill-will towards them at all. That she reserved entirely for her mother.

Everyone had been there: Eliza, Dora, Julius, Lally and Alexander, Sarah-Jane and her three children, Sophie with Ruth, Ted and Beth but not Jo or Jenny. It was six months since Debbie had disappeared and Sophie had aged visibly, her lustrous brown hair generously streaked with white. She was reconciled to the fact that she might never know the fate of her daughter. Reconciled, but she would never be the same again.

Hubert was not at the lunch either. A normally cheerful, extrovert man, he had been driven into himself by the tragedy, unable to share his grief with his wife. Even though Debbie was her daughter, not his, he had loved her dearly. Except for their duties in the parish Sophie and Hubert led almost separate lives; Debbie's loss had created a complete chasm between them.

After the main party had left, Dora and Jean had gone for a long ride together. For them there was sadness too. Jean had recently told her that his work at Pelham's Oak was done for the time being and he was to return home.

Dora had become so used to him as a companion that the news was shattering. No more rides, no more long talks over cigarettes late at night. A friendship which had begun in Cumbria had turned into a platonic love affair, rewarding and fulfilling in itself. Now they sat on the terrace, smoking, waiting for the others to join them for supper.

"What an extraordinary day," Dora said, tossing back her hair. "I must say I thought Elizabeth was splendid. It must have been an ordeal for her."

"But didn't you always treat her as a member of the family?" Jean, who was in love with Dora, stole a glance at her splendid profile, in the shadows as twilight fell.

"Well yes, in a way. I mean she lived next to us and we played together. Mother always took a great interest in her. Now we know why."

"And your mother never told anybody?"

"Never."

"Do you think it was wrong of her?"

"I wouldn't condemn my mother." Dora, still in her jodhpurs, stretched out her legs before her. "She did what she thought was right. She protected Uncle Guy, and we didn't know where Aunt Agnes was anyway. I think she thought she was protecting Elizabeth too. I must say I think Elizabeth has taken it all very well, except for her attitude to Aunt Agnes, but that will take time. Understandable."

"Quite." Jean paused. "I shall miss you a great deal, Dora."

"And I'll miss you." She held out a hand and he clasped it. "We've become great pals. But you'll come back?" She looked anxiously at him. "Won't you?"

He wrinkled his nose. "I'm not sure. I could get to like being here too much."

"Then why go back?"

"Because I must. Dora . . ." he paused.

"Yes?"

"Come with me?"

She looked at him, amusement rather than surprise showing on her face. She let his hand drop. "Are you serious?"

"Perfectly. Come as my wife."

"Your *wife*?" She sat up abruptly and the happy, amused expression on her face turned to bewilderment.

"Yes. I'm asking you to marry me."

"But I told you . . ."

"I know. I'm prepared to go along with you."

"A marriage without sex?"

"If you like, if it's what you want. You see I love you, Dora, and it's not just physical love. I want to be with you and have you near me. You never know, you might change your mind . . ." As she tried to interrupt him he held up a hand. "Please don't speak, just yet. I shan't pester you; but I can't live without you. I can't bear the thought of being separated from you. We're such good friends."

"The best," she said softly.

"We are happy together."

"We are."

"It's terrible to think I might never see you again."

"Then stay here."

"I can't. I have business interests in France, an estate."

"An estate? You never said."

"I put everything behind me to try and forget: the break-up of my marriage, the war. Now I've recovered, but I've fallen in love."

"We *can* stay best friends," she protested.

"It will look better if we're married. Your mother would like it," he added slyly.

"Oh, my mother would like it *very* much."

"Then let's do it."

"I'll have to think about it," she said reflectively. "I want to make sure that you've thought about it too, *and* the consequences."

"Oh, I have. I have never been more sure of anything in my life."

"No babies?"

"No babies. I've got two anyway. I just want you."

They linked hands again, just as Carson and Connie wandered on to the terrace, also hand in hand. They too looked very happy. The engagement had been a low key affair only known to the family, although it had slowly got round the town. Connie didn't wear a ring. At the time it had seemed wrong to celebrate so close to Debbie's disappearance; but now, as the weeks passed and there was no news, they were tentatively planning a quiet autumn wedding.

Jean rose to greet them and gave his chair to Connie.

"Did we interrupt anything?" Carson asked.

"No, we were merely saying what an extraordinary day it's been." Dora, feeling very happy, leaned back in her chair clasping her hands behind her head.

"It *has* been extraordinary." Carson flopped down next to Connie.

"How long is Elizabeth staying?" Jean asked curiously.

"As long as she likes. There's plenty of room . . . that is until the wedding." Carson looked hastily over at Connie. "I don't think Connie wants to share the house with Elizabeth."

Connie didn't reply but sat looking across the countryside she loved so much, towards Wenham where the lights were just beginning to appear as pin-pricks at windows and on the streets of the town.

Sometimes she thought of Venice, but not in the way she'd thought of Wenham when Venice was her home. Her roots were here, as much as Carson's, and it was here she wanted to be. However, she wished he'd let her do more to help, but he wouldn't. Pelham's Oak still needed a lot doing to it, but

237

there was no more money to pay Jean, who now felt the call anyway to return to his home.

But that was not the only complication. She could live anywhere with Carson, but with Elizabeth too?

It would be nice to say that she was drawn to Elizabeth. She wasn't. She never had been. They were very different people. When they were very young she knew Elizabeth, only three years younger, looked down on her, considered her bookish and frumpish. Elizabeth had been a little madam, always trying to draw attention to herself.

Both had had hard lives, but in different ways. Certainly Elizabeth's had been the harder, at least in the last few years.

She knew that she and Elizabeth would not get on; they would soon clash, and yet Carson felt so guilty about his half-sister that she risked his displeasure if she agreed with him now, that is if she said that it *would* indeed be difficult to have Elizabeth at Pelham's Oak after their marriage.

The long silence convinced Carson that he was right. Connie did *not* want to share her home with his half-sister, and then there would be her husband and children. He sighed.

"Well, that's a problem we can face when we come to it. In the meantime I want her to feel welcome in a home that, rightly, should have been hers."

" 'Rightly'?" Dora looked sharply at him. "How do you mean 'rightly'?"

"Well, if her father and mother had acknowledged her, as they should, she would have had a home here, and as long as she wanted it. Subject now to Connie's agreement, she has a home with me."

Suddenly it was as though a little breeze had blown through the valley and on to the terrace, and no one spoke.

Deborah Woodville stirred restlessly in bed. She opened her eyes and saw that daylight was streaming into the room. She had only gone to sleep at dawn and the dreams were fearful.

She lay awake hugging her bedclothes to her. If only she could go to sleep again and not wake up.

It was a week since Michael had gone. He had not come home one night from work and she had not seen him since. She had toiled up the hill to the big house where he was working, asking for him, but no one knew where he was, or where he had gone. Michael once again had done a flit, only this time leaving her behind.

How she wished he'd done that when he'd left Wenham, instead of persuading her to come with him.

At first it had seemed a lark, a joke, a bit naughty, certainly, unfair to her mother, but different. Debbie, the daughter of a man of the cloth – even though her father had not been an ordained clergyman – was also the stepdaughter of a full blown priest of the Church of England. Her mother was very religious. She had always been taught to say her prayers night and morning, church twice on Sundays, sometimes three times if you included Sunday school.

Debbie had been a good girl, not much chance to be anything else, but inside she had disliked her role and secretly rebelled. She started to hang around the men working on the church, and then Michael Stansgate had introduced her to the delights of forbidden love . . . once even committed in church after the rest of the workmen had gone. Maybe that act of sacrilege was why she was in the condition in which she now found herself: pregnant and abandoned by the man who had seduced her.

Michael had had very few belongings, he seemed to prefer travelling light, but he had taken one or two things she only noticed after he left. His shaving kit, spare trousers and a jacket, extra pair of boots. He must have stowed it all away while she slept, knowing that he would not return.

They'd reached the small Yorkshire village high up in the Pennines about a month after they disappeared from Wenham. Michael said it was near his home, Hull, and they were working their way towards it. She longed to ring her mother and tell her she was all right, but Michael forbade it. He'd even said

239

he would kill her if she told her parents, and she believed him. This was not a very nice man, after all, that she'd cast in her lot with. He was a seducer, a thief, and she knew not what besides. As long as she was with him she felt herself a prisoner.

She thought he was rather like Heathcliff, who had seduced poor Catherine Earnshaw, and she felt, sometimes, especially here on the edge of the wild Yorkshire moors, that Catherine's fate would be hers also.

Finally Debbie dragged herself out of bed, trembling. She was hungry, she was exhausted, her belly was beginning to show. She was sure that's why Michael had left her. He had tried to get her to have an abortion, but she refused. She not only thought it was against the laws of God, she was too frightened. She feared what would happen to her more than she feared what Michael might do.

And now he had gone.

Debbie sluiced her face, brushed her teeth and rapidly dressed. It was very hot in the little cottage and the milk in the kitchen had gone sour overnight. She knew she had to go home. She had somehow to make her peace with her mother. But she was frightened. Really she was terribly afraid, much as she loved her mother, of her wrath.

She drew water from the tap in the yard and, making a scoop of her hands, drank it. There was a little bread left and she ate it all. She put a coat over her dress and she started up the hill towards the big house which was owned by a lady called Mrs Middleton whom she had never met.

Her hopes now were pinned on the kindness of this stranger whose employment Michael had so abruptly left. Supposing Mrs Middleton was a dragon? What would she do then?

The house stood on a side of the hill overlooking the village. Mrs Middleton was building an extension and Michael had been taken in as casual labour to work on it. It was a lovely house with landscaped gardens and a waterfall. Debbie stood on the road outside looking at it, at the high cliffs behind it, and the blue sky above.

It was not like Pelham's Oak, but in her mind's eye she could see Pelham's Oak, the home of her father's family for generations. She hoped Mrs Middleton would be understanding, and she trudged up the drive towards the back door. There was a beautiful black Labrador lying outside sunning itself, and as she approached he rose and, wagging his tail, came over to greet her. For a while she stood stroking it, not quite knowing what to do.

"Can I help you?" a voice said and she looked up to see a thin, decidedly unfriendly face looking suspiciously at her.

"Mrs Middleton?" Debbie asked. The woman continued to look at her, as though not quite being able to make her out. She had the air of a lady, and a refined accent to go with it, but she looked unkempt and her clothes were those of a gypsy. She was about to shoo her off, but something in Debbie's expression stopped her.

"Who shall I say wants her?" she asked.

"Deborah Woodville."

"Just a minute." The woman turned her back and disappeared through the kitchen door. Debbie went on stroking the dog, her heart in her mouth, her teeth chattering with fear.

"What can I do for you?" This time the voice was more kindly, the tone cultured, and she looked up to see the lady of the house, who was not as old as Michael had suggested, maybe late forties, early fifties, about the age of her own mother. She had softly waved brown hair and wore a striped cotton dress with a white cardigan. She looked a friendly, cosy body who could be somebody's mother, perhaps a grandmother too.

"I wonder if I could speak to you?" Debbie asked, looking past Mrs Middleton at the sharp-eyed woman who was probably her housekeeper, "in private, if you please."

Mrs Middleton pointed towards the garden and Debbie followed her into an arbour on the far side of the lawn.

"Gertrude will bring us coffee, presently," she said looking curiously at her guest. "Now, in what way can I assist you?"

"I very much need help," Debbie said. "I've been abandoned . . ."

"Oh my dear!" Mrs Middleton exclaimed, putting a hand to her face.

"I was here with Michael Stansgate, one of your workmen. He's left me."

"The foreman was saying that one of the men had gone without notice." Mrs Middleton glanced in the direction of the new extension. "Unfortunately they do that all the time." She looked closely at Deborah again. "You're not married, you poor little thing, are you? And you're pregnant?"

"Yes." Debbie hung her head shamefully.

"Not more than eighteen, or nineteen either I'd say."

"Eighteen."

"But, my dear child, you must have a family, parents . . ."

"I ran away with Michael. My stepfather is the Rector of Wenham."

"And have you no mother?"

"Oh yes," Debbie plucked at her dress: "I just dare not tell my mother."

"And has she any idea where you are?"

"No."

"But that's awful." Mrs Middleton looked appalled. "How long is it since you left home?"

"January."

"January! And you have not been in touch?"

"No." Debbie's spirits sank lower and lower. She began now to regret that she had ever approached nice Mrs Middleton. She made her feel worse, more ashamed, if that were possible, than she'd been before.

"She must be out of her mind with worry. Are you afraid of your mother?" Again she looked closely at the girl.

"A little. She's very religious. My father was a missionary who died of fever in New Guinea where he was trying to convert the savages. My father was a saint and a hero, and I feel I've let the family down." Deborah kept her eyes on the ground.

"Didn't you think it was a little selfish of you, Deborah?" Mrs Middleton's tone was still kindly, but more censorious.

"Michael threatened to kill me. I believed him. He has been gone a week. I don't think he'll come back. I have no money, nothing to eat."

"You must let me call your poor mother at once." Mrs Middleton got to her feet. "Where is Wenham?"

"Dorset, but please," Debbie also hurriedly rose, "*please* call my uncle, that's my father's brother. I would rather you called him. He's a very kind person and he ... well, he can tell my mother."

Then Debbie sat down on the bench again and gazed abjectly at the ground, feeling utterly wretched and helpless. But, strangely, she was no longer afraid.

"A call for you, Sir Carson!"

Carson was standing outside the west wing of the house going over plans with Jean, who was due to leave quite soon. He was saying "I shall miss you Jean," when Arthur interrupted.

"Who is it Arthur? Would they call back?"

"It is a lady, sir. A Mrs Middleton, calling from Yorkshire. She sounds rather agitated. She says it is about your missing niece."

Carson shoved the plans he was examining into Jean's arms and rushed into the house, seizing the phone once he was in his study.

"Sir Carson Woodville." The woman's voice sounded mildly astonished. "Is that Deborah's uncle?"

"Yes, yes ..."

"It is about your niece."

"Yes, is she all right?"

"I have her here to speak to you, Sir Carson ... Deborah."

When Carson heard her voice he nearly sank to the floor in gratitude to a God in whom he had thought he no longer believed.

Carson, Connie behind him, crept into the church. The light was shining through the stained glass window that had been dedicated

243

to his brother, George, and his cousin Laurence. Sophie would often go into the church and sit by the window:

Sacred to the memory of George Pelham
Woodville . . . also in loving memory of
his cousin Laurence Thomas Yetman.

They had been told at the Rectory that she was probably there, these days she went a lot. And, indeed, she was, her head bowed in the beam of sunlight that shone through the window directly on to her.

Carson, his heart full of joy, his hand in Connie's, went up to her and sat beside her. He touched her arm and, startled, she looked up at him and he could see she'd been crying.

He looked at her tenderly and, reaching for his handkerchief, dabbed at her eyes.

"She's found. She's all right. I spoke to her," he said, and he held Sophie very close to his chest. "Connie and I are going straight up to Yorkshire to get her. We've packed and the car's outside. In a couple of days we'll all be together."

Connie drove swiftly through the narrow lanes of Dorset and Wiltshire until she struck the main road to the north. Carson sat beside her, arms folded, head slumped on his chest.

"Penny for them?" Connie said after a while.

"Just thinking." He raised his head and smiled rather wearily at her.

"Why didn't you tell Sophie that Debbie was going to have a baby?"

"You can read my mind," Carson replied. "That's exactly what I was thinking about."

"So?" Now that they were on the open road she put her foot hard down on the accelerator. If they were to get to North Yorkshire by the next day she had no time to lose.

"I thought it would take the joy out of the news. It would be too much of a shock for her. You know how religious she is."

"But she has to know some time. Possibly the day after tomorrow, if we can make it. Don't you think it might have been better to prepare her?"

"Maybe we'll go back to Pelham's Oak, first."

"Sophie already wonders why Debbie phoned you and not her."

"I think I convinced her that Debbie was too scared. Maybe, by spending a few days with me . . ."

Connie briefly took her hand off the wheel and put it on his knee.

"Carson darling, you are too nice, too sweet. You give succour all the time to the needy and the hopeless. You will have Debbie taking up cause with Elizabeth."

Carson remained silent.

"You'll turn Pelham's Oak into a home for needy people." Connie's voice had an edge to it, and Carson looked anxiously across at her.

"Maybe I should. A home for lost causes?"

"I wish you'd let me help you with it."

"Connie we've been over all this a thousand times. I don't want your help."

"But if it is to be my home too? If I am to be your wife?"

"It is perfectly all right as it is. Jean has done a very good job. We can all be comfortable there. There's stacks of room."

Connie's heart fell at the word "all". Carson was going to turn it into some kind of community home.

"You realise," his tone changed to one of wheedling excitement, "that now we'll be able to get married as we wished, with all the family, the town band . . ." He reached out and put his arm lightly around her waist.

"You're trying to change the subject, Carson."

"No I'm not; but as soon as we get back with Debbie we can start preparations for the wedding."

Silence.

"Connie?"

"I heard you."

"You still want to, don't you?"

"Of course. I'm just concerned that our home should also be a home for waifs and strays. Elizabeth is the main problem."

"*Why* is she the problem?" Carson set his mouth in a firm line, prepared for an argument.

"Because Debbie will go back to Sophie, no question of that. What will Elizabeth do? She has nowhere to go. She's homeless. You know she likes Pelham's Oak. She kept on saying at lunch how she loved it."

"Well, that's not unnatural. We all love it. It's a lovely place. Look, darling, I think Elizabeth has had a bad deal. I feel as head of the family that I owe her protection."

"Maybe one of the houses on the estate could be given to her? Eliza has also offered. Darling I *would* prefer to start our married life alone, together. Don't you understand that?"

"I understand," Carson said, "but as much as I love you I don't want to hurt Elizabeth. She's suffered so much."

Connie looked ruefully at him again. "We'll work something out. We haven't got this far not to be able to find some solution."

"We'll find a solution," Carson said, reassured by her tone. "Be sure I never want to lose you again."

After Carson and Connie had set out on their journey to Yorkshire – they had packed within an hour of the phone call, pausing on the way to bring the news to Sophie – and there had been tears as well as rejoicing, Sophie crept back to the church and took up her seat in front of the window. It had been dedicated almost eight years to the day, in August 1913, to George and Laurence. She recalled how the family had gathered for the ceremony: herself, Hubert who officiated. It was also the occasion of his installation as rector in place of her father. Debbie and Ruth were there, naturally; Eliza, but not Guy, who was too ill. Dora, Hugh, Prosper, Lally, Carson, Sarah-Jane and the children, Roger and Emma.

All lives had been changed, hers perhaps least of all but,

fter the war, no one could say their lives were the same. How
ften in these past, agonising months had she looked at the
indow and tearfully imagined that one day Debbie's name
iight appear near to that of her husband?

Eliza had come over to rejoice at the news about Debbie, and
ad just left with Dora. There seemed to be talk of marriage
i the air between her and Jean Parterre, and Eliza was very
xcited.

Suddenly everything seemed to have changed for the better.
Iow Carson and Connie would be able to celebrate their nuptials
i fitting style. Maybe Elizabeth would extend forgiveness to her
1other?

Sophie devoutly hoped that she and Hubert would resume
neir loving relationship, all tensions gone now that Debbie
as to be returned to them, safe and unharmed.

Tearfully, Sophie bent her head in thanksgiving to a God
/ho had sometimes treated her and her family harshly, who had
ppeared on occasions not to listen, whose very existence she,
daughter and wife of the rector, had occasionally doubted.
t one time she had thought she'd lost her faith altogether.

But now the long ordeal was over, and all the family, their
riends and the parishioners of the little town of Wenham, would
ejoice.

Sophie Turner raised her eyes to the window and, as
communicating with George, paraphrased those beautiful,
omforting words from the Bible, saying softly to herself, over
nd over again:

". . . this my daughter is come to life again, was lost and is
ound."